THE BEST AMERICAN

NONREQUIRED

READING

2019

D0448817

THE BEST AMERICAN

NONREQUIRED
READING™

2019

■

EDITED BY

EDAN LEPUCKI

AND THE STUDENTS OF

826 NATIONAL

MANAGING EDITOR
BEATRICE KILAT

NO LONGER PROPERTY
OF ANYTHINK
RANGEVIEW LIBRARY
DISTRICT

MARINER BOOKS
HOUGHTON MIFFLIN HARCOURT
BOSTON ■ NEW YORK
2019

Copyright © 2019 by Houghton Mifflin Harcourt Publishing Company
Introduction copyright © 2019 by Edan Lepucki
Editors' Note copyright © 2019 by Beatrice Kilat

ALL RIGHTS RESERVED

The Best American Series® is a registered trademark of Houghton Mifflin Harcourt Publishing Company. *The Best American Nonrequired Reading*™ is a trademark of Houghton Mifflin Harcourt Publishing Company.

No part of this work may be reproduced or transmitted in any form or by any means, electronic or mechanical, including photocopying and recording, or by any information storage or retrieval system without the prior written permission of the copyright owner unless such copying is expressly permitted by federal copyright law. With the exception of nonprofit transcription in Braille, Houghton Mifflin Harcourt is not authorized to grant permission for further uses of copyrighted selections reprinted in this book without the permission of their owners. Permission must be obtained from the individual copyright owners as identified herein. Address requests for permission to make copies of Houghton Mifflin Harcourt material to Permissions, Houghton Mifflin Harcourt Publishing Company, 215 Park Avenue South, New York, New York 10003

ISSN 1539-376X (PRINT) | ISSN 2573-3923 (E-BOOK) |
ISBN 978-0-358-09316-9 (PRINT) | ISBN 978-0-358-09303-9 (E-BOOK)

Printed in the United States of America
DOC 10 9 8 7 6 5 4 3 2 1

"Arabic Lesson" by Latifa Ayad. First published by the *Indiana Review*. Copyright © 2018 by Latifa Ayad. Reprinted by permission of the author.

"As the Sparks Fly Upward" by Renée Branum. First published by *Alaska Quarterly Review*. Copyright © 2018 by Renée Branum. Reprinted by permission of the author.

"Naked and Vulnerable, the Rest Is Circumstance" by Sylvia Chan. First published by *Prairie Schooner*. Copyright © 2018 by Sylvia Chan. Reprinted by permission of the author.

"I Worked with Avital Ronell. I Believe Her Accuser." by Andrea Long Chu. First published by the *Chronicle of Higher Education*. Copyright © 2018 by Andrea Long Chu. Reprinted by permission of the author.

"The Gettysburg Address (Sound Translations 1 and 2)" by Keith Donnell Jr. First published online by *Puerto del Sol* at www.puertodelsol.org. Copyright © 2018 by Keith Donnell Jr. Reprinted by permission of the author.

"The Lake and the Onion" by David Drury. First published by *Zyzzyva*. Copyright © 2018 by David Drury. Reprinted by permission of the author.

"The BabyLand Diaries" by Angela Garbes. First published by *Topic*. Copyright © 2018 by Angela Garbes. Reprinted by permission of the author.

"Diagnosis in Reverse" by Kate Gaskin. First published by *32 Poems*. Copyright © 2018 by Kate Gaskin. Reprinted by permission of the author.

"The Brothers Aguayo" by Devin Gordon. First published online by *Victory Journal* at VictoryJournal.com. Copyright © 2018 by Devin Gordon. Reprinted by permission of the author.

"The Frog King" from *Cleanness: Stories* by Garth Greenwell. Forthcoming from Farrar, Straus and Giroux in January 2020. Reprinted by permission of Farrar, Straus and Giroux. Originally published by *The New Yorker* on November 19, 2018.

"Spring" by Mikko Harvey. First published in *Indiana Review*. Copyright © 2018 by Mikko Harvey. Reprinted by permission of the author.

"To the United States Congress" by the Holton Arms Class of 1984. First published online at StandWithBlaseyFord.com. Copyright © 2018 by Holton Arms Class of 1984. Reprinted by permission of the author.

"Barbearians at the Gate" by Matthew Hongoltz-Hetling. First published online by *The Atavist* at www.atavist.com. Copyright © 2018 by Matthew Hongoltz-Hetling. Reprinted by permission of the author.

"Follow the Drinking Gourd" from *Night Hawks: Stories* by Charles Johnson. From Scribner in May 2018. Reprinted by permission of Simon & Schuster, Inc. First published by *The Kenyon Review* in July/August 2018.

"black queer hoe" and "open letter to the mothers who shield their daughters from looking at me" by Britteney Black Rose Kapri. First published by Haymarket Books. Copyright © 2018 by Britteney Black Rose Kapri. Reprinted by permission of the author.

"Self-Care" by Robin Coste Lewis. First published by *The Paris Review*. Copyright © 2018 by Robin Coste Lewis. Reprinted by permission of the Wylie Agency.

"On True War Stories" by Viet Thanh Nguyen and Matt Huynh. First published by *The Massachusetts Review*. Copyright © 2018 by Matt Huynh. Reprinted by permission of the author.

"Our Belgian Wife" by Uche Okonkwo. First published by *One Story*. Copyright © 2018 by Uche Okonkwo. Reprinted by permission of the author.

"Barbara from Florida" by Maddy Raskulinecz. First published by *Zyzzyva*. Copyright © 2018 Maddy Raskulinecz. Reprinted by permission of the author.

"Child A" by Emily Rinkema. First published by *Sixfold Fiction*. Copyright © 2018 by Emily Rinkema. Reprinted by permission of the author.

"Macho" by Margaret Ross. First published by *The Paris Review*. Copyright © 2018 by Margaret Ross. Reprinted by permission of the author.

"it's natural" by Nathaniel Russell. First published by *The Smudge*. Copyright © 2018 by Nathaniel Russell. Reprinted by permission of the author.

"Hill Country" by Patricia Sammon. First published by *december*. Copyright © 2018 by Patricia Sammon. Reprinted by permission of the author.

"Almost Human" by Deborah Taffa. First published by *A Public Space*. Copyright © 2018 by Deborah Taffa. Reprinted by permission of the author.

"Curse for the American Dream" by Jane Wong. First published by *The Asian American Literary Review*. Copyright © 2018 by Jane Wong. Reprinted by permission of the author.

CONTENTS

Editors' Note

A FEW YEARS AGO, I was visiting friends on the East Coast when I found myself with a full day alone. I made up a plan for the day that included walking and hoping to happen upon something great, which is what can happen when you take the time to do things with intention. I visited gardens, boarded trains, and eventually ended up at a modern art museum.

I went inside and proceeded to go straight to the top floor—I always like to start at the top and work my way down. In fact, this is how I like to work through everything: Begin one hundred feet in the air and then move closer and closer until you've seen everything up close and far away.

On the top floor of this particular museum, there was a new exhibit featuring the rarely seen work of an integral modern artist of the twentieth century. Please excuse me if it seems I'm being vague, but the point isn't the artist, exactly, it's . . . well, the work is the point.

And, oh, the work.

At times large and graphically bold, other times small and black and white, the exhibition was a lesson in contrasts and cohesion.

But I didn't immediately understand that. When I first laid eyes on these paintings and sculptures, I didn't know how to interpret them. I couldn't figure out what I was seeing.

So, I looked and I looked and I kept looking.

I noticed that the painted lines didn't just form trapezoids and squares, they were parts of something bigger, possibly the edge of something else. The lines led to a sort of horizon, acting as indicators that there was more out there, more to see, more to come.

In my mind, it seemed like somewhere past those painted horizons there could be a different version of me, standing in another museum, contemplating sightlines and endings and what lies on the other side of where you are.

By witnessing the lines and arrows pointing to the unknown, I was participating in the sort of endless, collaborative timeline that art can create. I was witnessing and becoming a part of a new history.

For the past year, a group of teenagers in the San Francisco Bay Area have been congregating in a basement classroom under McSweeney's Publishing to discuss storytelling and stories of all stripes, as well as what's happening around the world and at home. What you're holding is the product of those meetings.

A lot has happened this year, and you can see change happening in these pages, in unexpected, at times painful and startlingly beautiful ways.

I think the committee was working toward a horizon, toward some meeting point where they could pass or pick up a baton that could carry them to the other side of somewhere else.

It's a big ask—asking people just barely out of their adolescence to consider more and more of themselves and of others, but, believe me, these teens were more than up to the task. I think most people are. If you're reading this book, I bet you are, too.

Every week, the BANR committee showed up ready to work and ready to create something special for you, a monument to the year in America and where we were.

In our last meeting, Dasha Bulatova, our wonderful helper from San Francisco State University, transcribed our last conversation as a group. Our overlapping ideas crisscrossed into this paragraph:

It's less of a drought. The bees got better. We found ten bumble-bees in our house by the window just in the last week. It seems like the earth is repairing itself. In California they have new commissions for solar energy requirements for new buildings. Shrooms are now legal in Denver. "I grew as a person. That's all I'll say."

Time passes and things change for the better, sometimes for the best. Even a little bit of time can reveal great changes.

Flip to the end of the book to read more about the committee and the work that 826 National enables us to do. It's great work, and I'm so grateful we were able to look and look and look at our world and make something out of it. I'm so grateful you're curious about what we found.

Anyway, I guess that's all I'll say, too.

Thanks for reading along with us. We hope you'll enjoy the collection.

BEATRICE KILAT and the *BANR* Committee
June 2019

INTRODUCTION

WHEN I WAS ASKED to guest edit this year's *Best American Nonrequired Reading*, I didn't hesitate to accept. The job was a dream. Each week, I would get to submit a couple pieces of fiction, nonfiction, poetry, or a comic for a committee of high school students to read for possible inclusion in the anthology. Twice, I would travel to San Francisco to meet with these teenagers (and their fearless leader Beatrice Kilat) to join in their discussions. Then I would be expected to write this introduction.

Yes, please, I said.

The thing is, I love to read. Also, I love teenagers. Teenagers! Not only the tender clichés of them—how they travel in packs, dressed alike, bags of Cheetos or those tall cans of Arizona Iced Tea in their fists—but what they symbolize: beautiful and/or awkward creatures at the precipice of adulthood. They're focused on the wide world beyond, but they're also, for the first time, assessing their own families and histories. I imagine a teen alone, lying across her bedroom floor, reading Anne Sexton or writing her own bad poetry, listening to Weezer or Bikini Kill, her faux fur coat and vintage Partridge Family lunch box flung across the bed behind her.

Oh wait. That was me as a teenager. Way back in, like, 1997. Was it that long ago?

Now I'm thirty-eight and I have two children and—lord help me—a third on the way. I never get to hang out with high school students, and, most likely, my next opportunity will be when I myself am a mother of some. And that will be a different role altogether.

Editing this book, I figured, would give me the chance to meet some young people in 2019, and find out what matters to them. Now.

When I first started, I sought out work that I thought a group of teens would connect with—a fool's errand, obviously; it felt like I was skulking through a Forever 21, dropping some cringe-worthy slang as the beautiful babies glided past (in my mind they're vaping . . .). Thankfully, I abandoned this plan quickly, and began to send pieces I simply loved, or found intriguing, or because I thought they would be fun to discuss with a group of smart readers. I reminded myself of *Nonrequired Reading*'s unique set-up: although the anthology is curated by readers between the ages of fifteen and eighteen, the series is meant for every reader, regardless of age.

Since I would only be present for two meetings, I began a weekly ritual of reading the Google Doc session notes (which were impeccably taken by poet, and series intern, Dasha Bulatova). The no-nonsense script of what went down cracked me up every time. Allow me to fictionalize a characteristic interaction:

COCO: This piece was just . . . whatever. I didn't care.

ALTHEA: I loved it! I totally loved it.

What a revelation, to see how one person could feel so cold about an essay, while another person gnashed their teeth at the thought of not having said essay included in the collection! It reminded me of what the late poet Marvin Bell instructed in his "32 Statements About Writing Poetry": "Try to write poems at least one person in the room will hate." As an author, reading the session notes was a sobering but welcome reminder that it's not possible, or even preferable, for everyone to love and connect with your writing all the time. The spectrum of opinions is, actually, quite beautiful: as readers, we bring our own needs, biases, experiences, and pleasure points to a text. It's the sheer diversity of readers that allows for all kinds of writing to exist, persist, and develop, decade by decade. It's what makes a connection to a text, that heart-clutching love for a piece, seem so personal, why it feels as if this was written for me.

By the time I was due to visit the group in person, I was excited and a bit nervous. These were spirited meetings, as far as I could tell from the transcripts. I was right. Around that conference table, the students ate tangerines, peeling their skins into ribbons. They popped doughnuts into their mouths. Checked their phones. Bea starts every meeting by asking what's happened in the news since last week, from the local to the international, from Donald Trump to

Khloé Kardashian, and so there was a lot of joking around and saddened murmurs and disgusted eye rolls.

I tried to play it cool, but, honestly, I was enthralled. Teenagers!

When we got to talking about the reading, the opinions began to fly. As in any class, some students hung back, waiting to be called on, while the more outgoing personalities dived right in. Regardless, everyone got a chance to speak. I was struck by how respectful everyone was, even when they disagreed. At that first visit, a young woman revealed that the story we were discussing was the only submitted piece that she'd truly loved — but oh, how she loved it.

On my second visit, a student suggested a story felt more believable to her than it did to me because she herself was from a mixed-race family like the one in the piece; hearing her point of view didn't change my opinion of the story, but it did give me a new perspective on my own reading experience. I easily could have discussed the topic for another hour.

Sitting with the committee reminded me of being in a good college seminar, or in a graduate writing workshop, where talking is a productive exercise, a way to see a text—and, thus, the world—anew, from myriad angles. To stop and admire a turn of phrase or a final paragraph. To question a shift in tense. To have someone toss a set of photocopied pages on the table and say, "No. Just, no."

One question persisted at both meetings: "Does this need to be in the book?" The committee's mission, as they explained it to me, was to showcase new ideas, styles, and writers to a wider audience. They wanted to choose work that hadn't already been read and shared a thousand times on the internet. It also wasn't enough to like a piece; it had to make sense among the other selections. Sure, this is "nonrequired" reading, but the potential breadth of the book's audience meant the students shouldered a certain level of responsibility. What would it mean to say yes to this poem or that story? What were they trying to express through this particular curation of disparate voices?

In the end, nothing within these pages was uniformly beloved by the entire committee. Also, only two of the pieces I myself submitted for consideration made the cut. Knowing this, I was, of course, eager to get my claws on the twenty-odd pieces that finally got the nod from this group of passionate, discerning readers.

I was not disappointed. This book is by turns wise, brutal, funny, elegiac, informative, beguiling, and beautiful.

As varied as the pieces in this anthology are, there's connective tissue. The foremost motif is the way in which personal experience is not detached from larger political or socioeconomic forces, or from historical context, but inextricable. I tend to hate how words like "intersectionality" and "patriarchy" get tossed around like empty catchphrases, as if using them absolves the speaker of complicity in damaging power structures. Overuse of these words prevents us from expressing or understanding the specificity and messiness of human lives, or from figuring out how to fix real problems. Reading many of these pieces was an antidote to my language-fatigue, for they manage to vividly capture an individual experience, while also showing how that experience is always webbed to something larger. Pain and joy and love and grief don't exist in a vacuum.

For instance, in her essay "Almost Human," Deborah Taffa investigates how familial dysfunction, particularly for a mixed-tribe Native American family, can't be excised from larger societal and historical oppression. She is writing about her childhood and her father, but she's also grappling with government policies that shaped her family's past, present, and future. She writes, "Injustice is when someone privileged like me, someone who has reaped the benefits of electricity and national security, turns around and vilifies a poor indigenous man for taking the only job he had available to him."

In her poem "Curse for the American Dream," Jane Wong depicts her father's gambling addiction not as an isolated problem that only affects her family, but one that hurts the community at large. She writes, "Casino buses roll into Chinatowns across the country like ice cream trucks for a reason." Just because the speaker's wish, "May the casino turn into a window, a seat at the dinner table," is shot through with intimate longing doesn't mean it isn't also the wish of many, many other people.

I was reminded of this with "I Worked with Avital Ronell. I Believe Her Accuser," when Andrea Long Chu writes, "Structural problems are problems because real people hurt real people."

Let us not forget that. We aren't merely labels, or victims of larger forces we barely understand. We are human, and we suffer.

There's also terrific, off-kilter humor in this collection. For instance, the comic "It's Natural" features, to my great delight, drawings of various butt shapes. Butt shapes!

In "The BabyLand Diaries," which chronicles "the birth" of a Cabbage Patch Doll, writer Angela Garbes asks, "Does Mother Cabbage have a mucus plug?" Reader, I laughed out loud.

In David Drury's short story "The Lake and the Onion," there were amusing lines like, "When we ran the numbers through spellcheck and presented them to our finest sketch artist, he snapped all his pencils and took his estranged daughter to lunch."

The poetry of Britteney Black Rose Kapri is urgent and serious, but the surprising comedy of everyday life persists as well. In her poem "Black Queer Hoe," I loved the image of the speaker recently home, drunk after a night at the club, making sure her lesson plans for the next day are ready. She even checks her email "before the room starts spinning." It's an accurate, and thus comic, portrayal of life, and it's what makes the speaker, the eponymous "Black Queer Hoe," a multifaceted human being, despite the world's attempts to flatten and stifle her.

This year's *Best American Nonrequired Reading* also values formal daring. In my first meeting, student Huckleberry said part of the committee's mission was to find unusual pieces that weren't "within the general accepted literary sphere." They've succeeded. Before reading this anthology, for instance, I'd never read, let alone heard of, "sound translation" poetry, which is Keith Donnell's project with "The Gettysburg Address." Donnell's two poems echo the sounds and rhythms of Lincoln's original speech, but without an attachment to content. After reading them, I revisited the president's words. Then I circled back to the poems. This feedback loop had me ruminating on the ghost of hope that our country "shall have a new birth of freedom," which made Donnell's question, "Who'll weed our graves?" all the more haunting.

On this question of what might belong in "the literary sphere," I was surprised by the committee's inclusion of a letter to Congress.

This letter, signed by members of the Holton Arms Class of 1984, calls for support of their classmate, Dr. Christine Blasey Ford, attesting that "her decision to provide information pertaining to a sexual assault is not a partisan act." At first, I was puzzled to see this letter among the other accepted pieces. Then again, the Brett Kavanaugh hearings bled into all aspects of my own life, from my marriage to my friendships to my parenting to my work—and, yes, to my reading. Why shouldn't a historical document be read alongside poetry and comics? I loved the choice to include it here.

Last, I will say that so many sentences in this collection knocked me out; they were poetic, unexpected, and true. In the story "Barbara from Florida," about a female pizza delivery boy, Maddy Raskulinecz writes that the pizzeria's "small square television nestled into the ceiling corner like a hornet's nest." In Patricia Sammon's "Hill Country," gas station convenience store worker Lynelle listens to the "fisted shape of traffic on the highway." Margaret Ross, in her poem "Macho," describes "cigarette butts gone tender, floating" in coffee cans of water. In "The Brothers Aguayo," Devin Gordon writes of Tallahassee's humidity, "so thick you can write your name in it." Gordon's essay is about two football-playing brothers (they're placekickers, actually), a subject I did not care about whatsoever—until his sentences made me realize that, in fact, I did.

Again and again, I was dazzled by this collection. I experienced a little zing imagining the teenagers—Althea, Annette, Coco, Hannah, Hayden, Huckleberry, Juliana, Liv, Max, Mimoh, and Xuan—being dazzled, too.

Or, well, at least some of them were, some of the time. Remember: they're opinionated.

If there's a piece in this collection that leaves you underwhelmed or confused to even downright annoyed, take comfort: there was probably someone in that basement conference room who felt similarly.

And when you discover among these pages—and you will—that story, or that poem, or that essay, or that comic, that raises your pulse, gives you that tingly feeling in your arms, that makes you want to read faster and slower at once, know that there was another person on the committee who felt that love and connection too, that need to share what they've read with another human being.

To share it with you, it turns out. That piece is for you.

Teenagers! Aren't they great?

EDAN LEPUCKI

THE BEST AMERICAN

NONREQUIRED

READING

2019

PATRICIA SAMMON

■

Hill Country

FROM *december*

THE CONVENIENCE STORE WAS IN TENNESSEE, but only just. Customers, pumping gas, often seemed transfixed by the sameness of the
clover beneath the WELCOME TO ALABAMA sign. Travelers who
paid at the pump and who had no reason to go inside the store never
discovered that the store's metal door scraped hard against its doorframe. But store regulars knew to clench their teeth when pulling
open the door, and again when leaving, clutching their paper sacks
filled with predictable secrets: a can of Coke, a roll of Life Savers, a
pepperoni Hot Pocket, hot from the store's microwave. Some of the
regulars were long-distance truckers traveling the New Orleans/Chi-
cago route. They didn't know the cashier's name but they called her
Darlin', or Sugar, or Ma'am.

Lynelle thought her name was the prettiest thing about her and
she had once suggested to her boss that he should require her to
wear a name tag. But her boss told her that name tags were the kind
of foolishness that national chains like Stop n' Shop or 7-Eleven required of their franchisees.

His own name appeared in large neon letters on a sign by the side
of the highway: HENRY'S STATE LINE EXPRESS. In order to claim
the attention of drivers, he had lined the store windows with strands
of purple Christmas lights that flashed night and day. He had set
a timer so that they sometimes blinked in unison, and sometimes
raced up and over and down and across, never tiring.

Most of the regulars whom Lynelle saw were locals: plumbers and electricians stopping by the store before their first appointment of the day; landscaping crews who worked for the highway department or for the wealthy family that kept Tennessee Walkers; shift workers on their way to the chicken processing plant up the road. Hispanic, black, white—the narrow aisles of the store made a family of them.

At 7:15 every weekday morning a green station wagon pulled up to the store. And in would come Deshaundra, who had a singing way of speaking, and Tammy, who never spoke and had long, straight hair and the build of a teenage boy. Tammy always had exact change for two packs of Pall Mall Orange. And because Mr. Henry had no rule about smoking, Tammy would light a cigarette and listen while Deshaundra sipped a blue Ice Slurpee and told Lynelle about the places they'd be cleaning that day: that house in New Bethel where the lawyer and his wife had a bay window with glass shelves for all their violets; or the senior center whose activity rooms would have glitter in between the linoleum tiles no matter how often they were mopped. Deshaundra knew Lynelle's name but she called her *Baby* because she called everyone Baby. To the electrician who dropped his dollar bill—"Here you go, Baby." To Lynelle: "Baby, tell that Mr. Henry to get you one of them high-up, swivel stools to sit on. Good-sized woman like you, standin' all day, you gonna blow out your knees." And at the mention of them, Lynelle's knees, as if touched by the bluish lips, briefly ached. More recently Deshaundra had told her, "Baby, don't you worry 'bout your hair. It'll even out in a week or two." Lynelle had smiled, but ahead of her smile, she had lifted her hand to cover her smile. Deshaundra had never said, "Baby, don't worry 'bout your teeth." Because no customer, not even regular ones, had ever glimpsed the gaps where the decayed ones had been pulled.

Lynelle's boyfriend Cory had taken a trucking job four years earlier, when little Brandi was born. By the time Brandi was learning to crawl, his routes no longer included middle Tennessee, but he still sent money orders from time to time. Each morning, in the predawn darkness, Lynelle carried Brandi across the parking lot joining the apartment complex and the convenience store, Brandi's heavy head riding the rise and fall of her shoulder as she walked.

Every morning, at the squawk of the door to the doorframe, the night cashier would get up to leave. His report, and the words of his report, had become smoothed into oneness: "Same like always." Then Lynelle would settle Brandi on the fold-out cot behind the counter and let her sleep till Cory's mother came to bring her to the daycare center she ran. Cory's mother had several times curdled her lips and complained, "Church says she's not my real granddaughter." But she never charged for the daycare.

Over the years Lynelle had gotten to know the preferences of her regulars. The traveling home healthcare aides liked Diet Pepsi and Lorna Doone cookies and pocket-size bottles of *Kleen!* hand sanitizer. High-schoolers skipping class favored Doritos and Salem menthols. The very thin guy who worked with the landscaping crew stole a Milky Way every time he came by the store. Lynelle had gotten to recognize the flow of his gestures as he slipped the candy into his pocket while dropping a knee to the floor, pretending to tie a shoelace. When he stood up again he would always pick out a few other items to buy. At the cash register Lynelle simply added, without ever mentioning it, the cost of the Milky Way. And he had never pretended shock at the total or asked for a receipt. Lynelle decided he was probably no better at math than she would be if she didn't have the cash register to calculate change.

The previous week a group of middle-aged women had come to the store announcing that they would become regulars. They had just discovered how easy it was to drive across the state line and buy a ticket for that month's lottery. Before the women made their shared purchase, they performed a little ceremony that involved a jump, a clap and a hug and a wish: "The Ritz in Cancun!" Lynelle longed to ask them if *Cancun* was another kind of saltine, like a Ritz. And why would such a snack mean so much to them. But she just wished the women luck. She had learned not to ask questions. One time Lynelle had phoned Cory's mother to tell her that Brandi didn't feel well enough for daycare. "Well, did you give her 7 Up and saltines?" and Lynelle, who knew exactly where in the store to find 7 Up and saltines, asked how those things would help. "Well, you knew enough to get yourself pregnant. What did you do for morning sickness?" And at that remark Lynelle had just stared at the phone in her hand, unable to say anything because she was abruptly back in the tenth grade, gripping the edges of the desktop and not knowing why she was thinking of a ship at sea when she had never been on a ship.

After the lottery women left, a long-haul trucker who'd been help-ing himself to a bowl of chili from the Crock-Pot shook his head with gentlemanly decorum and said, "I hate to see people throwing away their money like that." Lynelle asked the trucker what kind of things he was hauling that day. But in order to make sure he wouldn't mis-take her question for flirting, she added, "My husband drives a semi." She not only made up the part about Cory being her husband, but she also gave him a place to be, somewhere not so very far away—Kansas. And she gave him a bill of lading—logs. The trucker teased her, *Well, Sugar, there can't be too many of those in Kansas.* In a smiling instant, the correction came to her. "No. I said, *hogs.*" Because right there by the Crock-Pot was an advertisement for pork rinds that fea-tured a cheerful little pig wearing an apron and a chef's hat.

Cory's most recent money order had been sent from a 7-Eleven in Bend, Oregon. After Lynelle cashed it, she studied the receipt. The amount was for $72.63. She closed her eyes and tried to see Cory. But he'd always been quick in his bashfulness, turning away from a kiss or her whispered words. She wished she could ask the 7-Eleven cashier if he had seemed tired as he was paying for the money or-der. Or if maybe he had looked proud to have so much cash. Maybe he had been uncharacteristically talkative, saying, "I have a wife and baby in Tennessee." She studied the receipt another moment longer and then the whole transaction made itself known to her: he had set down four twenty-dollar bills and a five, and he'd bought a pouch of chewing tobacco—Red Man Select—and he had used the balance for the money order. And he had not lingered. And he had not called the cashier *Sugar.*

Lynelle put the receipt and the cash in her purse and then walked over to the store shelf that was stacked with travel aids. She picked up the spiral-bound State-by-State Atlas. After a lot of looking she found Oregon and then she finger-found the city of Bend. It was next to a big forest named Willamette. Maybe he really was hauling logs. She returned the atlas to the rack. Outside, just beyond the gas pumps, a work crew was positioning a historical marker beside the black walnut tree. She carried out a tray loaded with paper cups filled with chili. She wanted to ask the men why they were putting up the marker. Weren't all good-sized walnut trees anywhere in the state at least a hundred and fifty or two hundred years old? But she didn't have to ask the men why this particular tree was being identified as special because the men, thanking her for the chili, joked that the only reason they were there was because Mr. Henry had pestered the Tennessee Historical Society about having a very old tree.

The person who knew well the motion of a ship at sea was named Mvemba. With every ocean swell, the people, bolted to one another below-decks, slid and slammed into the screaming darkness.

The solitary Tennessee farmer who bought Mvemba at auction gave him the name Cicero. The farmer taught him some English words: Walnut tree. Garden. Hogs. In April when everything was in blossom, the farmer joined the militia to bash the Yanks.

At the end of the lane, as he climbed up onto the militia wagon, he had yelled over his shoulder that he'd be back in a month. "See to things, Cicero."

Lynelle gathered up the pleated, empty paper cups, dumped them in the garbage can, and walked around to the back of the store to clean the bathroom. She held up her can of Lysol as Deshaundra had taught her, as if writing on air. But just as she was about to press the nozzle on the aerosol can, she noticed that someone had scrawled an angry remark on the comment sheet taped to the back of the bathroom door. **Filthy.** And above it, **A stinking disgrace.** Lynelle stared in confusion. *Was **grace** really inside that word? Whenever Cory's mother pronounced it, she said dis-crace. Who would have written such criticism? The women with their lottery ticket? The long-haul trucker? Perhaps it had been some traveler who had paid at the pumps but had not gone into the store to buy anything?* Lynelle strode back inside the store, grabbed one of the Sharpie markers from the display rack, went back out to the bathroom, and joined the comments together so their angry meaning drained away to politeness. *I seen some places along this hi way that was a* **stinking disgrace.** *Thank U that this place is kleen! and not* **Filthy.**

*The day that a bandaged man with a crutch came stabbing along
the road, Mvemba happened to be seated beneath the young tree, smashing open walnuts with a flat rock. When the man called out "Cicero!"
Mvemba guided him up the lane, into the farmhouse, and positioned him
on a pallet of straw, spooned him some bone broth, and sat with him as
he died that evening.*

*Mvemba dug him a grave against the hogs, then marked the location
by placing the smashing rock upright. Then he took up a sharp stone and
joined the blotches of walnut stains to secure the image of a hippo:*

*It had been a hippo at the mouth of the Congo River that had shrieked
its outrage that Mvemba was being led in chains up the gangplank. Those
wide-hinged jaws, that roaring fury—the last that Mvemba ever saw of
home.*

Lynelle leaned against the open door. Still undone by the angry comment, she closed her eyes and listened to the fisted shape of traffic on
the highway. Then she opened her eyes and considered her familiar
surroundings: the steepness of the hills, the dusty weeds along the
roadside, the walnut tree. And beyond the tree, at the far end of the
parking lot—the row of efficiency apartments—their repeated series
of doors and windows looking like one of Brandi's clapping games.

There was one place within sight that Lynelle tried to avoid looking at. It was the sandy lane leading from the highway, straight up
the side of a steep hill. The lane could be mistaken for a driveway
leading to a quaint log cabin just out of view. But she knew that the
lane had no destination. It led only *up*—because it was a lane for runaway trucks. Lynelle stood in the cold breeze and dared herself to
look directly at the sandy lane, the deceptive quiet of its readiness.
Then she imagined that just a few miles to the north, there was a
highway trucker in trouble. His brakes had failed and he'd lost control of the rig, which was making spastic jumps. There were sparks.
And bucking and thrashing. Now he was no longer a man in a truck
on a highway. He was deep inside the tunnel of a different world—a
world made only of speed. And at that very moment Lynelle sent her
thoughts to him as he was gripping the steering wheel with one hand

and yanking the cord of the truck horn with the other. She told him with all the concentration of her mind, *Don't worry. In just a couple of miles, there's a runaway lane. You know the one. You've seen the sign for it. Just before the state line. Right near that convenience store with the purple lights.* Then she looked over at the lane and thought of the trucker being able to swerve from the highway and plunge upwards, up its brief distance. She sighed with him and felt the relief at being slowed and then stopped by the deep sand, —of being held, —of being able to look through the windshield into a perfectly ordinary-looking sky, —of knowing that for just that moment he was completely alone in the world, and completely safe.

Lynelle turned away from the view of the lane and thought, almost out loud, "To have a job where you need to know that such a thing exists."

Mvemba abandoned the drafty quiet of the farmhouse and the shed with its many sand-trays packed with turnips and squash and potatoes. He left behind the winter field. He climbed far up into the hills, into their cave-riddled summits, and partook, for some unknown amount of time, of the freedom of having disappeared, unmissed.

Each year, the dirt in the winter field bulged with a harvest of icy stems and branches.

Until the winter that Mr. Henry, ever certain of his own mind, refused to delay construction of his store until spring—so the concrete slab that was poured did not achieve a perfect float. It tilted slightly at one corner.

Meaning the door and doorframe would always cry out.

Back inside, Lynelle spent a few minutes trying to make some more space on the counter. It was so crowded with displays that she often didn't notice quickly enough that someone had left an object behind—a pair of sunglasses, a garage door opener, a pink plastic barrette with glued sparkles, a driver's license. She placed any forgotten item in the shoe box that she kept under the counter. She knew she didn't save these items because she was Sunday-school honest, but because she was afraid. What if one of the truck drivers who called her *Sugar* came back looking for the sunglasses and she didn't have them? People could be unpredictable. The photo of the man on the driver's license looked far meaner than a simple "no smiling" instruction would have required of him.

A trucker in a flannel shirt and baseball cap interrupted her organizing efforts. He asked for a pack of Marlboros and then said, "What the hell" and pointed to the "instant winner" scratch-off cards beside the cigarettes. She handed him one and he leaned forward and said, "Warm it up for me, Darlin'." So she held it in a pretend kind of prayer. Then the man scraped away the metallic surface and discovered he hadn't won. So she apologized to him as he was leaving, telling him, "I guess I'm just not lucky."

But she knew well that she was lucky. She had Brandi. And free daycare. And Cory hadn't forgotten her. She wished someone would walk into the store and say, "Hey there, Ma'am, I was wondering what you would do if you won the jackpot?" Because she knew exactly what she'd do. *First, I'd get my brother a better lawyer. And next, I'd go by Buell's "Buy and Sell" lot and I'd get a car.* And before anyone could say, "Do you even have a license?" she'd say, *And I'd pay somebody cash money for a booster seat that their kid doesn't need anymore.* She knew she'd have to begin talking more quickly because the customer would be losing interest. *Then when I let Mr. Henry know I'm quitting, I'd tell him to just give me that State-by-State Atlas over there 'cause nobody needs maps anymore, not with all their fancy phones telling them what they need to know. Then I'd tell my boyfriend's mother that her days of puke and pee at the daycare are done. Then my little girl and me and Cory's mom, we'd set off across the country and whenever we got tired we'd stop at any motel that suited us and when we got hungry we'd stop at any store that advertised good coffee and snacks and then we'd catch up with Cory and I'd tell him he doesn't have to send money orders no more. Then we'd buy a cabin way up in the mountains where it's too snowy to ever have to work or go to school. And the cabin would have a master bedroom and a bedroom for Grannie and one that's just for Brandi. And in the front room there'd be a couch that nobody has to sleep on, except if they wanted a nap.*

* * *

At the sound of the metallic yelp, Lynelle looked up to see a lady who looked like she might actually have won a jackpot. Her sparkling dress was tight and black, cinched with a wide, red belt. She had red high heels. As she tilted her head in the direction of the door, her pearl drop earrings twirled about. "That scraping sound must make your teeth hurt." Lynelle covered her mouth and said, "I hardly notice it anymore." The lady picked out a celebrity magazine, two diet sodas, a bottle of cold water, and a package of peanut butter crackers. She asked for a pack of Newport regulars.

The lady indicated Lynelle's hair by tugging at her own. "Let me guess. One of those damned awful home perms. I tried one of them kits a while back. My hair fell out in handfuls. Don't worry, honey. It grows back."

Lynelle said, "I got distracted and left the chemicals in too long." She rang up the items and handed the full bag to the lady, who cradled it in her arm.

"That'll be $25.72, please, Ma'am." A damp spot was already forming on the paper sack from the cold of the sodas and Lynelle was about to offer a plastic bag. The lady gave her a hundred-dollar bill, then turned, calling over her shoulder, "Anyway, a pixie cut is *in* right now."

"Wait. You forgot your—" Lynelle called out.

The lady shoved open the door while saying, "If I bring him back change, he thinks I'm telling him he's cheap."

In the sudden quiet of the store, Lynelle looked down at her already moving hands. They were thick and slow, like a menacing of bees, and they knew what they were doing. She watched herself reaching for her purse. She was taking out some of the money that Cory had just sent her. She was putting a twenty-dollar bill and a five-dollar bill in the cash register. She was making plans for the future. *I'm gonna get a ride to the Dollar Store and I'll get Brandi a bath towel with the Little Mermaid on it, and some bubble bath, and No Tears shampoo.* She was placing the $100 bill inside the zippered dark of a purse pocket. But her thoughts would not stay put. Maybe instead of the towel, she would buy that big Children's Encyclopedia that Brandi loved to hold whenever they went to Walmart. It was a book that seemed to be a block of gold but when the book was opened, the gold-trimmed pages showed everything there was to know—the parts of a ship, the names of trees, a list of countries, pictures of animals from jungles and deserts. *I'm gonna buy her that book and not even wait for Christmas.*

She began to have second thoughts about the beautiful gold book. It would be more sensible to buy Brandi a raincoat and rubber boots. Something practical. That's what Cory's mom would do. She didn't have to decide right away. Her hands nestled the purse back in its place between the plastic milk crate and the folded cot. What she knew for sure was that she was not going to do what Mr. Henry told her she had to do if a customer overpaid: put the money in the cash register to help cover the cost of the next drive-off out at the pumps.

A customer walked in. She knew him, though not by name. He worked at the feed store and he liked salt-and-vinegar potato chips. She smiled at him as he approached the cash register, but the fact of the $100 bill in her purse made her so giddy she hardly remembered how to ring up a sale. What a strange thing it was—she had to grip the narrow counter, thinking of it—to be a store cashier. To see people day after day and hand them pennies and paper sacks across such a brief distance and yet not know them. The man from the feed store held up his bag of potato chips and handed her a dollar bill. As she handed him the change she watched the soft thorns of water traveling the locks of his hair. It was raining outside and she hadn't even known.

Anyways, she told herself, as the feed store employee left with his snack, Mr. Henry had no right to the $100. With the installation of the credit card machines, it wasn't possible to pump gas without paying beforehand. And, not counting the Milky Ways (because the landscaping guy was paying for them without knowing that he was), the only real stealing occurred when teens dashed outside, laughing, clutching some ice cream sandwiches and a few bags of chips, and then speeding from the parking lot. On those occasions she'd tell Mr. Henry about the cash register being short by $6 or $7 and then he'd fume and say, *Why didn't you get a license plate?* She never explained to him that a few weeks later, when the kids would finally dare come back to the store, she would call out, I've missed you! And contrition would make their faces shine. She never explained to Mr. Henry that calling the police and filing charges would change those kids from being foolish teens into being angry teens. And angry teens ended up in jail. So Lynelle explained to Mr. Henry that the kids had simply run out to the car to show their friends everything they could choose from, and then they'd gotten distracted and climbed into the car, forgetting to come back in to pay.

If an actual robber ever burst in, shouting above the scraping sound, *Hands up!* and demanding all the cash, she would give over all the stacked bills in the register drawer, and if he had forgotten to bring a bag to hold all the money, she would empty the shoe box of its lost items and give it to him, and then she would turn away so she would be sure not to see the moment when he was briefly aligned with the yardstick glued to the doorframe. She didn't want to be able to make any kind of report. Because everyone was 5'7" or 6'1" and everyone had a flannel shirt or a heavy metal band T-shirt, or a denim jacket, and everyone was thin or heavy-set and dark or pale or telling jokes in Spanish.

Beyond the glass door, the rain clouds had cleared. She could see the first pinks of sunset. Soon she would be unbuckling Brandi's seat belt and marveling at the gold sticker on her worksheet. Soon she would be getting Brandi inside the store and helping her to step up onto the milk crate so she could show customers her coloring. Then the night shift cashier would arrive and she would be able to leave the store and have Brandi all to herself. They'd make their macaroni and they'd play a guessing game and then they would curl up together to get some sleep because 4 a.m. would be coming soon enough.

He drove northward through the darkness of very early morning, well ahead of schedule yet unable to keep from speeding. He knew from other, day-lit trips, that he was entering a region of hills. The black air around him was probably already crowded with their hunched forms.

Silently, but somewhat formally, he addressed himself: *You need to stop and get some fresh air.* He slowed as he crossed the state line and he drove up to a particular gas station that he had noticed on previous trips. The one with the purple, pulsing lights. He got out, stretched, and very consciously inhaled the cool of the night air. He took his time topping off the fuel tank, grateful for a task that could

be conducted outside and that did not require him to speak to anyone. To guard the calm of the moment, he looked away from the race
of the purple lights. And as he did so, he detected, just within the pal-
est reach of the floodlights, a moving shape that became a woman
holding a long-limbed, sleeping child. He dashed from the side of
the car and opened the store's door for her, startled by the quick metallic scrape. He went back to his car, replaced the fuel cap, and then,
to his own annoyance, he reached into the car to get his wallet so he
could go inside. *You don't have the energy to talk to anybody. The last
thing you need is more coffee.* As he walked inside he held the door for
an old man leaving.

Again the scrape. He told the cashier, "You could probably get that
fixed. All you'd have to do is get someone to shave down the side
of the door." The cashier looked up and smiled but didn't answer.
His mind raced through the procedure by which the repair could be
accomplished. He would need a circular saw, a metal file, a magic
marker, and also a ruler to note the exact width to be removed. Take
off too much and there would be a constant draft. His frustration
with himself—for coming inside, for speaking, for wasting time
thinking up solutions to problems that had nothing to do with him—
joined the shrill complaint of the electric can opener she was using to
open cans of beans for the Crock-Pot.

He walked over to the coffee maker. Watched his hands trembling
as he worked to hold the too-hot paper cup and to press the lid in
place. Then he had to pry off the lid again to add a packet of milk
powder. He looked around at the overcrowded shelves. The *too bright*
and the *too much* of it. He thought he might be about to run back outside and he reminded himself that if he did flee, he'd have to be sure
to set down the coffee first so she would know he wasn't stealing.

To steady himself he grabbed hold of the shelf below the coffee
maker. He studied the little numbers ascending on the carafe. He
refused to cry. And if someone—this cashier for instance—were to
come up to him and say, "Hey there, Sir, do you happen to have a little daughter about the same age as mine? How is she?" he would say,
*She's doing much better. The Vanderbilt leukemia folks told me to be there
at 7 a.m. to see some very promising lab results.* And if this cashier were
suddenly to look sad at the mention of leukemia and perhaps touch

his arm out of concern for him, he would speak reassuringly. *No, no, it's all good. The doctors are very upbeat.*

His daughter really was looking better. She was still bald, still thin. But the bruises, formed from no injury, were disappearing.

He listened as the cashier tapped the spoon against the side of the Crock-Pot and set the glass lid in place. He stared down at the dirty linoleum tiles. They were somehow so inviting. He longed to drop to the floor, to stretch out along its length. To weep and never have to cease weeping. What a relief that would be—to fall to his knees and be a penitent, a supplicant, an accuser—to crawl across the floor, a dumb beast, silently screaming at a God he didn't believe in, and very much did—who had reduced him to begging, and then who had answered those prayers, singling him out among all those other parents sitting in that large waiting room, giving him good news that could be withdrawn at any moment during all of his daughter's growing-up years, or during her adult years, or during her old age when he was no longer alive to help her.

He sipped the dreadful coffee. He reached into his pocket for his phone and checked for messages, knowing there wouldn't be any. The Oncology Offices wouldn't be open for another two and a half hours, and he'd be there by then, learning, in person, the good news.

The cashier came up beside him and said, "Let me make you a fresh pot." He cupped his hand to his mouth but failed to stop a sobbing cry. He coughed to disguise the sound. But there were tears making a swimming confusion of the whole store. In his embarrassment and panic he held out the phone still in his hand and blurted out a news item he had learned the day before. "Do you know that children in West Africa—I'm talking kids just seven and eight years olds—they spend their days digging for the cobalt that goes into our cell phones. Can you imagine? Children digging children-sized tunnels. With their bare hands. Gathering the ore in a bag. It's too sad."

Her quick blinks, her tears, they surprised him. She mumbled, "I had no idea. Those poor, poor babies. I didn't know."

"But as you see," he said, shrugging, "I own a phone. I have to have it. Still . . . little children. Scraping for metal . . . "

He saw her glance quickly over at the door. Maybe she was desperately hoping for another customer to walk in. He was probably making her uncomfortable, talking about horrors on the other side of the world.

But no, she was smiling and reassuring him. Her fingers were pressed to her lips, as if she were telling him a secret: "But don't you just know those kids, smart as they are, they gonna grow up and figure out a better way to do everything and teach us all."

He nodded and managed a real smile. He told her that he didn't need fresh coffee. He followed her over to the counter and opened his wallet.

She said, "That'll be $1.53."

He pointed at the cot behind her and asked her if that was her little girl, sleeping. The cashier smiled again behind her fingers, and added—"Yes, indeedee. And she's super smart. She can tell you all kinds of things. The capital of Tennessee, the names of some oceans. She can count all the way up to a hundred."

"Well," he said, feeling himself beaming as he talked to her, "if she can get to a hundred, there's really no reason not to just keep going. Hundred and one, a hundred and two . . ."

She was saying something cheerful in reply. He looked down again at the grimy floor. In the smudges he could make out stains shaped like kneecaps and the toe-tips of shoes, the heels of hands. Had he actually dropped to the floor? Had he already gotten up?

He looked again at the cashier. The word *beautiful* had nowhere in particular to land on her— but she was beautiful. Her hair was oddly short, but not chemotherapy short. Perhaps it was a style. He picked up the coffee and before he turned to go he saw into a possible future and without hesitating, he chose that future for his daughter: *This lady at the cash register is my little girl, years from now. She is happy and plump. She is a mother. She understands the world. She always knows just what to say.*

The cashier was still telling him about things her daughter knew.

"And see this, here." The woman was pointing at the side of the cash register. It was engraved with the words Atlas Machines. And it had an insignia — a figure of Atlas holding up the world.

"She even knows the name of this giant. And she knows he ain't real. But, see right here, my little girl scratched a line underneath him so he wasn't kneeling on nothing."

CHARLES JOHNSON

■

Follow the Drinking Gourd

FROM *The Kenyon Review*

Think I heard the angels say,
Follow the drinkin' gourd.
Stars in the heaven gonna show you the way,
Follow the drinkin' gourd.

—Black American folk song

AFTER ESCAPING FROM SLAVERY IN ALABAMA, he went back willingly into the bleak, macabre world of slaves once again. Five years ago, in 1850, he'd fled the nightmare of bondage, with his wife, Adele, traveling by night from Mobile to Kentucky. It had been a hellish journey marked by weeks of hiding, disguises, last-minute escapes, and name changes. But after reaching Paducah, Kentucky, he kept moving and established himself in southern Illinois as a versatile craftsman based on the skills he'd learned as a bondsman. His name was Christian Fowler and, as Thoreau had written five years earlier about living in Walden, Fowler had developed during his thirty-five years as many "skills as fingers on the hand." He was a saddlemaker and carpenter, a barber and a cook. Of course, he was still a wanted man in Alabama, a fugitive with a $200 bounty on his head. There were padderolls and soulcatchers eager to collect that money if he showed himself anywhere near his old master's place. But why in the world would he do that? He had slipped away from bondage—the whippings, the sound of the daylight horn calling him to work—and built a decent life for himself from scratch. It was funny to him sometimes how slave owners could never understand why black people ran away. Their doctors even concocted a disease to explain this behavior—*drapetomania,* a sickness that supposedly made slaves flee their shackles and chains. Others just saw runaways as criminals—as people who had stolen *themselves* from their masters. At any rate, he was safe from all that in Illinois, and now Adele had given him two fine sons. Just the same, he *had* to go back to his borning ground, because never a night passed, as he and his family enjoyed the relative freedom of their new home, that he didn't have survivor's guilt and screamed himself awake when he saw in his dreams the faces of those family and friends he'd left behind when he cut dirt from the plantation of Captain William Boswell.

This would be his last trip. That was what he promised Adele. No more placing himself in danger after he guided to freedom her cousin Ida, a young woman around eighteen—perhaps two or three years younger—with chestnut-brown eyes, a mole beneath her ear like a grain of pepper, her hair arranged at the back in broad basket plaits, and her one-year-old baby, Sara. They'd been traveling light for weeks through backcountry that smelled mucilaginous and faintly sweet, through villages and tobacco fields, bringing only a little food, and Fowler carried his double-barreled shotgun, his bowie knife, and a canteen filled with old orchard to steady his nerves. As always, he followed that reliable beacon in the night—the Big Dipper stars that were shaped, if you looked at them carefully, like a wooden gourd pointing to the pole star. "I've always been lucky," he'd told Adele when he left to rescue her cousin. "The North Star ain't ever let me down. And God takes care of me."

But maybe not this time.

When they reached Mississippi, they'd covered a little more than half the distance to their destination, and he realized something was stalking them. Two men, soulcatchers, were a half mile away, taking their time so as not to startle their prey, giving the runaways a little breathing room to relax and let down their guard before taking them by surprise. And he knew these two bounty hunters. Oh, yes, he even knew them by name. They were brothers, Caleb and Joshua Weems. He could smell them on the wind the way a rabbit did a hound. Now and then he could see their campfires. And they were good, those two, cagey and ruthless. The best manhunters in Alabama, who knew how runaways thought—it was rumored they had a little Negro blood, had at one time themselves been slaves—and they, with their savage tempers, had littered this landscape with slaves that resisted capture, wasting their lives like water. They'd done this ancient pas de deux together before. The eternal dance of death between the hunter and the hunted. They were in his dreams or—more precisely—in his exhausting, emotionally draining nightmares since he escaped from Captain Boswell.

Not far away, Fowler saw, off to his left, a lichened, twelve-stanchion barn, large, dark, and imposing, floating in the mist. He waisted Ida's short body with his free arm and guided her and the baby there over stumps and mudholes, miry places in thigh-high weeds, and brush-whipping tree branches. The entrance to the abandoned barn was boarded over. Fowler tore away the planks of plywood, pulling so hard the muscles in his neck bulged, and cutting his right hand on a rusty, square nail. Inside, the air felt tight, dead. Old farm equipment covered in gossamer-thin cobwebs was everywhere, as was an odor of musty hay and straw and old oats gone bad in their bins. The place was quiet as a temple, its silence floating hither and yon over old horse collars, sawhorses, scrap metal, and lumber. He could hear Ida moan from a corner where she'd sat down in her heavy, homemade buckram skirt and was rocking the baby back and forth. She asked him if the men following them were going to take Sara and her back to Captain Boswell.

"No, honey." His voice was waxy, unused in hours, hoarse. "I won't let them take you back there."

Her eyes searched his face. "What about you?"

"We're going to wait here until them men are gone. But you have to keep that baby quiet. If she starts crying, they'll know right where we are."

"I think she's hungry," said Ida. "I can try to feed her."

She undid her blouse and turned her back to him. He was touched by her modesty and decided to step away as she breast-fed the baby, moving cautiously, his arms stretched wide. Night pressed against the window, but the hazy mist had distilled, and he had a good view of the direction death or anything nocturnal might come in the darkness. Pieces of that same darkness were clinging to his congested mind. He could feel how tired he was of running, how light-headed from hunger. The gash where he'd cut his bloody hand throbbed. He needed rest. The temptation to just lie down in darkness, close his eyes, and let his mind sleep forever was overwhelming. But he remembered that new life, the home he'd made in Illinois, the caring woman whom he loved more than his own life. And their beautiful children, William and Zachary, whom he loved beyond measure and prayed they would grow up free, knowing nothing of slavery in a place where you could go-as-you-pleased, a world so much better than the one he and Adele had somehow survived every day—even though, like a soldier, he still felt the trauma of once being enslaved. The damage, the fear of being recaptured, was still there like scar tissue. And a feeling that he didn't deserve freedom if everyone wasn't free, or maybe that being free was temporary, an illusion, and might be snatched away from him at any time. These thoughts, he knew, were mad. No one should suffer them. That was why he came back for Ida and baby Sara. But they would never know freedom and an end to the madness if a crying Sara gave away their location. For an instant—and it was an instant that made him hate himself—he remembered in the hindmost corner of his mind how Captain Boswell was oftentimes fond of quoting a poet named William Blake, whose words now trumpeted through his thoughts: *Sooner murder an infant in its cradle than nurse unacted desires.* That thought made his scalp crawl. If it came down to that, did he have the grit for silencing the baby—forever—to save Adele's cousin and himself? From the satchel slung over his shoulder, Fowler removed the canteen, then took a long pull, shuddering as the whiskey plunged down his throat pipe into his belly like a burning wire. Strong drink erased the image of infanticide in William Blake's poem from his mind. Drink dulled the pain in his hand and made veins stand out on his temples. He, the hunted, lumbered back toward Ida, feeling the darkness like a blind man, fighting his terrible exhaustion, found with a painful crack the edge of a mule's harness with his shin, suppressed the urge to swear, and kept his eyes to the left of her, because she was still trying to nurse a mewling baby who might at any moment let fly with a cry that would condemn them both again to beatings and chattel bondage.

"You gotta keep her quiet, okay?"

"I'm tryin'." Her voice was shaky. "But she's teething, and I think she caught her death 'a cold. You know, from all the nights we had to sleep on the ground when the weather was wet. Here, feel her forehead."

She lifted the baby toward him. Sara was burning up beneath his fingers. He took the canteen from his satchel and handed it to Ida. "Spread some of this on her gums. That might he'p to quiet her some." Then he said, looking into her eyes, "There's something else—something really important—I need for you to do for me. You remember that song I taught you? I want you to sing it for me. Real soft. Just whisper the words to me."

"Why?"

"Don't question me." He drew his mouth down, and looked hard at her. "I have my reasons." Then he cut the sudden harshness in his voice by half when he saw how Ida's face, like those of everyone who lived enslaved, always relaxed into a beautiful yet fragile mask of sadness. "That song will save your life," he said. "Please, just sing it."

And so she did, her voice soft-breathing, gently singsong, so beautiful a contralto, controlled and clear, that it lifted him out of himself, reminding him of how his wife often sang as she worked, and he almost forgot the life-or-death urgency behind his need to make sure she got every word right. "Sing that last part again for me, all right?"

"All right." She lifted her head. "The river bank will make a mighty good road / The dead trees show you the way / The river ends between two hills / There's another on the other side / Follow the drinkin' gourd where the great river meets the little river."

"Good. Very good."

Just as he took a little heart at this, as something in him relaxed, as he started to think with a smile of getting back home, there came from baby Sara a cascade of chest-shattering screams that filled the barn, filled the night outside, and filled Fowler's ears like explosions. It felt to him as if she cried for an eternity, and he stared—just stared—helplessly at the child as Ida tried to quiet her, unbuttoning her blouse again, revealing her small, pear-shaped, brown-nippled breasts—this time Fowler didn't look away. But he was coiled up inside, his teeth grating, silently trying to will the child into silence, thinking, *Be quiet, be still,* noticing only now that his right hand had picked up a clump of wood from the floor to silence her squall. Was he about to kill the child? He couldn't tell. But Ida finally got the baby to suck. The wide-ribbed barn was quiet again. He let the wood slip from his hand.

He stepped back to the window, his knees feathery, and sat there like a statue with his head tipped and shoulders crushed down for a long, long time, emptied of hope. Emptied of all thoughts of himself. Everything was simple now. Had the hunters heard those high-pitched, earsplitting screams? He was certain-sure they had. There was no way to repair what the baby had done, no more than he could unring a bell. Like as not, the slave catchers were on their way. He was dead already. And he knew what he had to do. What any righteous, right-thinking person in this situation would do. It was time to dance again with devils. After gathering himself together, he opened his satchel. Silently, he removed two shells. Silently, he carefully examined his shotgun, snapping both triggers and checking the firing pin before loading both barrels and closing the breech. And silently, he waited, there at the window, where the moon was an hour higher since he'd last looked at the sky, feeling peace, a kind of gallows serenity he could not describe, as if suddenly he could accept and welcome whatever came, that he had no fear and was equal to any task, no matter how difficult or distasteful it might be. He grasped the shotgun by its carved pistol grip, the stock placed under his arm against his body, the butt pushed into his armpit. As he pressed the barrels more firmly against his left leg, his thoughts lapsed to a line from John 15: *Greater love hath no man . . .* but the words broke off when he heard away in the night the breathing of horses. He could feel his face stretch at the sound, then sure enough, he caught a glimpse of two travel-stained, spectral shapes materializing out of the mist. Fowler shot a glance toward Ida, one finger pressed to his lips. When the men dismounted from horses with rags tied to their hooves—a gray Medley and the other an Appaloosa—he could see, in a splash of silver moonlight, Caleb Weems, husky, hairy-necked, ponderous but quick as a trout, his head rammed forward, craning his neck to cock a look toward the barn door, and right behind Caleb was his toad-like, bandy-legged, jug-eared older brother, Joshua, with hair like moldy hay, carrying an owlhead pistol, half of him covered by a horseman's cloak white from road dust, both of them advancing toward the barn like wolves. Ida was standing now, holding her daughter on her hip. Over his shoulder, he flung a whisper to her, *No matter what comes of me, no matter what you see next, follow the North Star.*

Then he waited, his teeth set, bone against bone, as Joshua noisily blew his nose in his hand and in a roosterish voice told Caleb to check the barn. Waited, being now the trapper and the trapped, as the barn door creaked on its hinges. Now it opened, and Fowler made a hissing intake of breath. It opened, he saw Joshua step inside, and the hunted blew the hunter to kingdom come. He bolted outside, clambered over Joshua's shattered body, and, his chest pounding, rammed the stock of his shotgun against the side of Caleb's head. He ran south, swift as a deer. Ran so hard he felt he was nothing but legs and burning lungs.

After a moment, his running slowed to a few steps and he stopped, facing round, pausing to make sure an enraged Caleb, bent on revenge for his brother's death and not thinking clearly, was pursuing him. When he saw the hunter closing the distance, he—the hunted—smiled bleakly. If something happened to him, if he could not outrun or outwit Caleb, then his argument was that he had known happiness and freedom before—let that do—and Ida and her baby would know it now, because "Follow the Drinkin' Gourd" was much more than a song. It was a black American charm with back-and-hidden instructions in every stanza. A coded message only Negroes on the run could know. A detailed map for someone to follow to freedom. The first river was the Tombigbee, which would take them to Mobile Bay. The two hills were Woodall Mountain and a smaller one at the highest point in Mississippi. Earlier, he'd marked the dead trees with charcoal as a sign. The ribbon of river on the other side was the Tennessee. Its left-hand side would take them to the Ohio River and to Paducah, Kentucky, where his wife, Adele, would be waiting. Yes, he thought, as he started to run again, so fast his feet seemed scarcely to touch the ground, yes, they would be fine. And that meant, one way or another, he would be fine, too.

JANE WONG

■

Curse for the American Dream

FROM *The Asian American Literary Review*

MY FATHER PLAYED blackjack all night in Atlantic City. He did not stop to eat or go to the bathroom or ask where his family was. My father owned a Chinese American take-out restaurant on the Jersey Shore and he will lose this one asset from gambling. He did not dither in that red velvet world of his. When we drove home from Atlantic City together, my father glowed over his winnings. He flailed an arm back in that poorly won BMW and tossed a couple of $20 bills at us. "Liar," my mother said, staring out the window. "You lost. You always lose." The new leather burned our thighs as we watched the Parkway smokestacks grow exponentially. This story is not about small enterprises. This story expands like an oil spill; it touches the fins of every faraway shore. This is a story poor immigrants share, like those packed bunk beds shared with false uncles and aunts. Just to be clear: We are targeted. This is no mistake. This can't be boiled down to "cultural proclivity for luck." Casino buses roll into Chinatowns across the country like ice cream trucks for a reason.

Hex the executives who can't see beyond their golden watches, hex the cigarette smoke that swarms around each gleaming video poker machine. May the casino turn into a window, a seat at the dinner table, a swing set where a daughter and father can laugh endlessly toward the sky.

■

Barbearians at the Gate

FROM *The Atavist*

IN THE SUMMER OF 2017, the survivalists began to worry—*really* worry—about the bears.

The problem wasn't the animals' nighttime behavior; that was just a nuisance. The survivalists were used to catching sight of the hulking intruders emerging from the darkened woods of rural New Hampshire to damage property, steal food, and deposit huge piles of excrement. Recently, though, the bears had started showing up in broad daylight, and not just at the survivalists' encampment. Throughout Grafton, the tiny town on the outskirts of which the camp sat, residents told stories of furry forest dwellers pushing through porch windows, chasing house pets, getting drunk on fermented apples, and capering on rooftops. One bear had cleaned out a chicken coop by lying on its belly, reaching inside the structure's tunneled entrance, and scrabbling around with an extended paw. The bleakest anecdotes told of bears swiping their claws through human skin as if it were tissue paper.

The survivalists agreed that something had to be done to defend their makeshift home. But no one suggested calling law enforcement. This was Tent City, a place people came to avoid government. The messy jumble of cabins, trailers, and tarps, anchored by an old carport that served as a communal lounge, was a crucible of self-reliance. Residents believed in untethering themselves from institutions, foraging for food, and hunting game with guns, arrows, and knives. When society inevitably collapsed under the weight of bureaucracy and corruption, they would be ready. Their lodestar was freedom.

Tent City, where the population swelled to 30 or more on any given night, was an extreme manifestation of cherished local norms. Reachable by one paved road and policed by one full-time cop, Grafton has no stoplights, zoning laws, or building codes. Personal freedom springs eternal, so much so that don't-tread-on-me types from across America have moved there in search of a laissez-faire utopia. People live where and how they please: in ramshackle homes, solitary yurts, old cars, or shared camps.

The survivalists sketched out a multifaceted plan to protect themselves from the bears. Adam Franz, a bearded, restless man in his late thirties, managed the land that Tent City sat on. In his younger days, Franz had studied economics, designed computer programs, become an ordained minister, and played professional poker. Now he was the closest thing Tent City had to a mayor—which is to say that when he talked, people listened. This included both cohorts of the unregulated idyll: left and right. When I remarked on a Confederate flag slung across the front of a cabin, Franz directed my attention to a Bernie Sanders sign attached to another. "If you're an anarchist of any stripe," said Franz, who tends toward the left end of the spectrum, "this is a good place to be."

Franz's anti-bear arsenal included firecrackers. "I also think we should get bottle rockets," he said one day, talking loudly to be heard over the constant buzz of a generator. Guns were a given; they were as much a staple in Grafton as picket fences are in the suburbs. Franz had recently traded his .357 Magnum for a Taurus Judge .410. The Magnum was more accurate, the owner of his favorite gun store had told him, but if a bear got too close for comfort, the Judge would do more damage. Though it looked like a six-shooter, its bullets were so big that it held only five.

The residents of Tent City decided they needed a barrier of some sort. One man scrounged several cheap metal posts and scrap rolls of chain-link netting from local suppliers, and a small crew of volunteers got to work. They inched along Tent City's winding perimeter, methodically erecting sections of a fence. They adorned it with bells, beer cans, and bottles filled with BB-gun pellets. This would be the alarm system.

One day the workers were hammering posts into the rocky earth when they heard a woman who lived in the camp call out. Urgently. Scanning the area around them, they saw why: A black bear was swaggering along a finished portion of the fence, not 30 feet away. It was as if the bear had appointed itself foreman and was inspecting the men's progress.

What a goddamned insult, thought Franz, who was working on the fence that day. He shouted at the bear like someone trying to get a kid off his lawn: "Go away!"

The creature paused, as if calculating risk versus reward. Then, on heavy paws that doubled as lethal weapons, it lumbered toward the men. Still shouting, Franz held a lighter to a pack of firecrackers he'd stashed in his pocket. *Flick, flick, flick*—the fuse caught. He hurled the explosives toward the incoming enemy.

Popping and sizzling, the firecrackers hit the ground between the foes. Startled, the bear reversed course and galloped clumsily away from the men. When the clamor ceased, however, the animal stopped short of the forest. "He started watching us," Franz recalled.

Several tense seconds dragged by. Finally, the creature slunk into the undergrowth and disappeared from sight. The humans took a gulp of air. They'd won the latest skirmish in Grafton's escalating bear war.

"In my opinion, there is nothing out of the ordinary going on in Grafton." So said Andrew Timmins, a wildlife biologist employed by the state of New Hampshire. Timmins is tall and muscled, with grizzled hair that he often wears tucked beneath his Fish and Game Department cap. He showed me a spreadsheet that documented the annual intake of "bear complaints," his department's name for reports of human encounters with the 6,000 or so black bears that roam New Hampshire. There was Grafton, a community of about 1,000 people in the state's central region, with 50 complaints over the previous decade. It ranked 29 out of 227 towns, which placed it in the top 13 percent of bear-afflicted places. But was that really so surprising, given its forested location? Timmins insisted it was not.

He diagnosed a kind of xenophobia: People are often frightened of black bears for no good reason. Sure, the creatures are big—they can grow to 500 pounds or more—and they've got sharp teeth and claws. But according to Fish and Game's public-education campaign, "Something's Bruin in New Hampshire," which is intended to "enhance public tolerance towards bears," the animals "do not typically exhibit aggressive behavior."

That was the opposite of what I'd been told in Grafton. I'd first visited the town for an assignment that had nothing to do with bears. It was bears, though, that kept me coming back. I was lured by tales told over kitchen tables, in gardens, and on front stoops about an unprecedented conflict between man and beast.

People in Grafton said that, year after year, the bears were getting bolder. The same anti-authority ethos that gave rise to Tent City convinced locals that the threat needed to be dealt with, no matter what any government data said. It's illegal to kill a bear in New Hampshire without a special hunting license, yet I heard whispers that a vigilante posse had embarked on a clandestine hunt. Meanwhile, here was Adam Franz, flinging firecrackers and pledging to use his new Judge on a moment's notice. "This is my baby," he said when he let me hold the firearm, placing the weight of his trust in my palm. "I fuckin' love that thing."

I visited Grafton several times over two years to determine if, to poach Timmins's words, "anything out of the ordinary" was happening there. When it came to bears, where did truth end and myth begin? What I found was more revealing than I expected: a parable of liberty, disinformation, and fear. A parable, really, of America.

Grafton's unruliness and disdain for authority dates back centuries. Fittingly, when the town incorporated in the late 1700s, it took its name from the third Duke of Grafton, who'd served as England's prime minister and scandalized his constituents by divorcing his wife because she was pregnant with the child of a lover, no doubt taken while her husband engaged in a very public affair with a courtesan. By then colonists in Grafton had long ignored the native Abenaki people's respect for nature, divvying up and then clear-cutting vast tracts of forest. Eventually the settlers decided that royal laws were also impediments to their freedom and joined the revolutionary fight against colonial oppression. At every stage of this history, they turned their muskets against black bears, a species they'd decided was better off dead. They delivered the carcasses for bounties.

Over the century following the American Revolution, Grafton residents demonstrated mastery of their domain by transforming it into New Hampshire's most intensively farmed region. They denuded hills and covered them with sweeping grasslands, hordes of sheep, and miles of stone walls. In 1868, they banded together to protect their livestock from a bushy-tailed black wolf described in the local newspaper as four feet tall and seven feet long. People built homes, mills, two churches, 12 schoolhouses, and several mines, including one that, in 1887, produced a 2,900-pound aquamarine crystal, the biggest ever found in the nation at that point. Three years later, about 15 miles from town, a wealthy, eccentric land speculator named Austin Corbin built a game reserve for species imported from out of state, including bighorn sheep, Russian boar, bison, and elk.

Then came a seismic change. As the U.S. economy shifted toward industry, farmers abandoned their livelihoods in droves. Over the course of the 20th century, Grafton lost nearly all its agricultural land. Neatly cultivated fields reverted to impenetrable thickets, stagnant bogs, and tangles of young trees. Clearings shrank until they were tiny islands, adrift in an inexorable sylvan tide.

The new forest had a strange, ominous flavor. In 1938, a hurricane breached the fences of Corbin's reserve, releasing hundreds of animals into the wild, and Grafton residents described frequent encounters with the creatures' startling descendants. Packs of coyote-wolf hybrids, once unheard of in the area, trailed people who were out walking their dogs. There were taller tales, too, of a Bigfoot-like creature, dragonflies as big as hawks, and birds with claw prints larger than a human hand.

For a long time, *Ursus americanus* didn't rank on locals' list of worrisome fauna. Though the black bears' habitat included some 90 percent of New Hampshire, they gave humans a wide berth. Attacks were exceedingly rare; the most recent was in the mid-20th century, and the last fatal one in 1784. Statistically speaking, and not only in

New Hampshire, a person was (and still is) much more likely to suffocate in a giant vat of corn than be killed by a bear.

All was well until 1999. That's when the cat massacre happened.

I heard about it when I first visited Grafton, in the fall of 2016. I was there to interview 62-year-old veteran Jessica Soule about her difficulties accessing support from the Department of Veterans Affairs. As I drove into town on Route 4, I observed that the town had no medical services or grocery store; one of its two gas stations had shut down.

Soule lived in an area of Grafton known as Bungtown, which received that name after an incident in the mid-1800s when bungs—a type of cork—came loose from barrels while they were in transit, allowing the liquid inside to spill out. Soule's house had white siding and a creaky metal wheelchair ramp leading to the front entrance. When she answered the door, she wore a button-up shirt under two sweaters. A long, neat braid hanging over one shoulder softened her face.

Inside her house, the smell of cats hung in the stale air, trapped by tightly sealed windows. Several felines jockeyed for Soule's attention. I sat on a lumpy couch with a quilt spread over it and was startled when one of the mounds beneath me began to move. "He's hiding," Soule said.

As we meandered through the usual small talk that precedes an interview, I noticed that Soule used a striking phrase: *before the bears came*. As in, "I used to let my cats outdoors, but that was before the bears came." I asked her to explain.

One fine July night in 1999, Soule sat down at the picnic table in her backyard to enjoy the cool air. The moon had already risen. It looked like liquid silver—what the Abenaki called *temaskikos*, or the grass-cutter moon. Soule's only companions that night were three cats, all less than a year old, wrestling near her feet.

As Soule relaxed, she heard footfalls behind her, quick and heavy. Before she could react, the bear was within a few feet of the picnic table. But instead of snatching her, it scooped up another feast: two of her kittens, whose mewling Soule could hear as the bear blew past her and disappeared into the woods.

It reemerged just beyond the tree line behind Soule's house, near a small creek. The animal cut a bulky silhouette in the moonlight. Smaller shadows joined it: hungry bear cubs. All Soule could do was watch, horrified, as the creatures finished off their dinner and sauntered away.

Soule hunted desperately for her third cat, named Amber, in the woods. It wasn't until morning, when the sun was up, that she found the tiny feline, huddled beneath a carpet of leaves. The cat was terrified but alive.

I asked what happened to Amber after that. "She's right here," Soule said, pointing to a cat nestled in the center of her lap like pet royalty. The milky-eyed feline, now 17 years old, was so rough coated that she looked taxidermic, and so decrepit that she could no longer retract her claws. Like her owner she was a veteran, a survivor.

"That," Soule said, "was the beginning."

In Soule's telling, the bears that ate her kittens developed a keen taste for felines. When other cats in Bungtown went missing, locals knew why. Soule said that a bear approached her front door one day. Perhaps it was the same mama bear, she thought, back for more. By then she'd gotten wise; she kept her cats inside, no longer left food scraps in the backyard for birds, and opened doors and windows only when she absolutely had to.

Andrew Timmins told me that he'd never received a bear complaint involving a cat, from Grafton or anywhere else. Plus, the idea that wild bears could acquire a taste for felines seemed dubious to him. When a Grafton resident told me about a bear that drained his biodiesel supply—a five-gallon container of two-year-old French-fry grease—I was reminded that bears will devour even the most loathsome fare, so long as it adds to their winter stores of fat. They're after calories, not cuisine. Despite local perception, the cats of Bungtown probably weren't the bears' *preferred* target; they were just there.

Perception, though, matters a great deal when people craft stories about how they overcome obstacles and cope with conflict. Once the seed of the purported bear hazard was planted, stories nourished it. Often the light of reality was refracted such that it transformed an animal into a totemic version of itself: bandit or strongman, noble savage or mythic monster, bumbling idiot or cunning predator.

Alongside the stories, a few key ingredients influenced people's assessment of the bears in their midst. First was a quantifiable increase in New Hampshire's ursine population. In 1990, the state had some 3,000 bears. Steady annual growth, which peaked at 10 percent around the time that a bear got clawsy with Soule's kittens, nearly doubled the population in the next quarter-century. During that same period, New Hampshire got serious about bear monitoring. Based on what wildlife experts deemed prudent preservation goals, the state designated population targets and bear-management strategies: how many annual hunting licenses to grant, how long hunting season should last, and even what hunters could use as bait. Chocolate, for example, was banned, because it could be toxic to bears. If a human wanted to kill a bear, they'd have to shoot it, not feed it a brownie. Fair's fair.

The edicts and regulations didn't sit well in Grafton, particularly with the town's newest colonists, who started showing up in 2004. It sounds like the start of a bad joke: A lawyer, a firearms instructor, and the owner of a mail-order-bride business walk into a fire station. The three men were Tim Condon, Tony Lekas, and Larry Pendarvis, respectively, and they were avowed libertarians with the Free Town Project, a splinter group of a national initiative founded in 2001 to convince some 20,000 liberty-loving Americans to move to a chosen place, where they could concentrate their voting power and rid the political landscape of pesky rules. On the anything-goes frontier that Free Towners envisioned, people would be able to keep as many junk cars on their property as they wished, buy and sell sex without shame, gamble at will, consume drugs of all kinds, and educate their kids however they liked. Hell, they could even debate the merits of incest and cannibalism if they wanted.

Condon, Lekas, and Pendarvis were scouts, tasked with looking for the right spot to pioneer the project. They focused on low-population states, including New Hampshire. An added bonus of the "Live Free or Die" state was that it didn't impose income and sales taxes. The trio drove from town to town; some places were too far north—excessively cold and isolated—while others had strict zoning laws or a tight real estate market. Finally, the men came to Grafton, situated on a rugged stretch of 42 square miles. They met up with local volunteer firefighter John Babiarz, who had recently run for governor on the Libertarian ticket and won 3 percent of the vote. Now he and his wife, Rosalie, welcomed the three men around a folding table in Grafton's firehouse, because there were no coffee shops or restaurants in town. They discussed their shared pet peeves, namely busybody bureaucrats and onerous laws.

Grafton was the mecca the scouts had been looking for. The town had more land than people and virtually no statutes governing property. There were fewer than 800 registered voters, most of whom didn't bother showing up at the polls, and because Babiarz already had a base of support, he could help tip the political scales in the project's favor. What's more, natives loved their guns as much as they despised meddling government. The scouts stopped their search and sent word to their fellow Free Towners, along with the phone number and email address of a local Realtor.

How many people answered the call to move to Grafton is hard to say. Libertarians aren't exactly known for keeping records. According to the federal census, between 2000 and 2010, the town's population swelled by more than 200 residents. Soon after the project was launched, Free Towners began purchasing hundreds of acres of land, which they made available, at their discretion, to like-minded people who wanted to establish permanent homesteads or temporary encampments. Tent City, then in its early days as a home base for Grafton's most extreme natives, served as a model of the type of loosely organized community that might work for the newcomers.

Grafton's newest denizens infused its relaxed culture with impudence. At the annual apple festival, they encouraged children to dip homemade United Nations flags into a bonfire. At town meetings, which were usually sleepy affairs, they emphatically insisted that Grafton withdraw from the regional school district, condemn *The Communist Manifesto*, and eliminate funding for the local library. None of those proposals gained any traction; for all the ideological DNA they shared with the new arrivals, longtime Grafton residents thought some of the Free Towners' ideas crossed the line of common sense. Still, the settlers managed to pass measures to slash the town's budget by 30 percent (later rescinded on a procedural technicality) and to deny funding to the county's senior-citizens council.

Babiarz, who went on to become Grafton's fire chief, gradually distanced himself from the project's purists, deciding that he preferred a less evangelical brand of liberty. Yet he maintained common ground with Free Towners on plenty of things, including the threat of bears.

The same year the Free Town scouts came to Grafton, a bear stole onto Babiarz's farm on Slab City Road, where he and Rosalie live in a converted 19th-century schoolhouse, and eviscerated one of his rams. By the time I visited Babiarz in 2017, bears had infiltrated his property numerous times, making off with chickens sleeping in their coop, sheep locked in their paddock, and apples swinging from tree branches. Babiarz, a tall, lean 60-year-old who has now run unsuccessfully for governor four times, became convinced that one bear in particular watched him from somewhere in the forest. It waited for him to run an errand or visit the fire station, and then it struck. This damn bear was a seasoned criminal, Babiarz told me in his small kitchen, where amid potted plants and household clutter an old sign urged me to elect Libertarian Harry Browne president in 1996.

Babiarz and the bear had a fundamental disagreement over how many of the farm's livestock were there for the taking. His starting position was zero. The bear's was all of them. "It had no fear," Babiarz said. "Which is a problem." He decided that pain-based deterrence was called for. He loaded an electric fence with strips of bacon, hoping to zap any hungry bears in the mouth. On the ground outside his chicken coops, he laid down boards with nails or screws sticking skyward to puncture the soles of bear paws. One board I saw had claw marks on it and a screw was missing. "Yep, it went right through," Babiarz said, referring to the unlucky bear that had stepped on the board. "There was blood pouring. There was nice red all over."

One September morning, he came home from town to find a bear—*the* bear, Babiarz claimed—sitting on its rump and feasting on a chicken. "Like a human at a campfire, munching," Babiarz recalled with dismay. How had it gotten past every line of defense? Babiarz sprinted into his house and grabbed a Ruger .44 Magnum from his closet, but by the time he got back outside, the bear was galumphing toward the refuge of the forest. Panting, Babiarz took aim and pulled the trigger. The Magnum bucked in his hand, exploding with sound.

"Apparently, I missed him," Babiarz said. A concerned look crept over his face as he told this part of the story. He gestured toward the woods, adding, "He was a moving target against a black background."

I realized that Babiarz felt he had to defend his marksmanship. Competition was everywhere, after all. In 2012, New Hampshire had attained America's highest per capita rate of machine-gun ownership; federal data showed nearly 10,000 of the weapons registered in the state.

"There's a lot of trees here," Babiarz continued. "Hitting it would have been a miracle."

I squinted in the direction the bear had gone. After a pause that felt sufficient for reflecting on a deep knowledge of firearms—which I by no means had—I replied in solidarity.

"That's a really tough shot."

Babiarz looked relieved. He went back to talking about the bear. It was out there still, his Moby Dick. He was sure of it.

Can bears be calculating? Babiarz and other Grafton residents I spoke to sure seemed to think so. Dave Thurber, a Vietnam War veteran who lives up the road from Jessica Soule, recounted how, one dark winter night, he had a feeling that something wasn't right. He peeled back a corner of the curtains covering his living room windows and peered out at the front lawn, where he spotted a bear delicately licking sunflower seeds from a bird feeder. When a car approached, the bear flattened itself against a snowbank like an escaping prisoner evading a watchtower spotlight. After the car passed, the bear resumed eating.

Rumors of the bears' cunning had planted unsettling questions in the minds of Grafton residents: How close are we to a bear *right now?* Could one be just beyond someone's front door or hiding behind a nearby tree, casing a pet or, worse, someone's child?

I put the question of bear intelligence to Ben Kilham, a wildlife biologist and leading expert in ursine behavior, who happens to live about 20 miles from Grafton. Before he became interested in bears, Kilham designed guns. Now his personal website features a photograph of his head and upper torso protruding from the entrance to a bear's den. He has adopted and raised dozens of orphan cubs, which he releases into the wild and tracks for thousands of hours apiece. He has been bitten and scratched more times than he can count, but never seriously. State wildlife officials speak of him reverently, and his fame has gone global. In an Imax documentary released in April 2018, he's featured as a bear whisperer helping China reintroduce pandas into the wild.

Kilham suggested that if I really wanted to learn the truth, I should read a book he wrote titled *In the Company of Bears*. The book paints a picture of bears—worrying or inspiring, depending on your priors—as the Einsteins of the wild. According to Kilham, bears have a highly developed sense of self. They can also count to 12 (higher than chimpanzees), transport and use tools, observe societal bonds that include a rudimentary sense of justice, remember the distant past, calculate the likelihood of future events, and, if necessary, ask other bears to care for their offspring. Kilham also asserts that bears can screen foods for palatability by mouthing them and inhaling their scent. He came to the idea after noticing cubs gently manipulating leaves, mushrooms, and frogs with their snouts. Kilham developed a working theory that bears have a special sensory organ about the size of a jellybean embedded in their palate, which he dubbed the Kilham organ. He finally proved its function when, he told me, he "boiled a half-rotted bear head and found what I was looking for."

Kilham comes across as the Jane Goodall of bears, uniquely positioned to understand the species. Also like Goodall, his insights aren't always backed up by hard data or laboratory tests, leaving him vulnerable to academic criticism. In his book, the only evidence he cites that a bear can out-count a chimp is his experience with one bear, named Squirty, who always seemed to know when Kilham had shorted her one or two cookies from a sleeve of Oreos. Yet formal studies measuring bear intelligence generally support Kilham's conclusions. Bears in captivity have been observed solving problems— moving stumps to use as stepladders in order to access high-hanging fruit, for instance—and distinguishing between different numbers of dots on a screen.

A more enduring critique of animal behaviorists is their tendency to anthropomorphize, or assign human characteristics to the species they study. Here the question is one of intent: *why* animals do what they do. If a bear lingers in the presence of a screaming survivalist, is it calculating its odds of getting fed or shot, or processing a more basic fight-or-flight reaction? It's hard to answer these questions definitively, because we can't read animals' minds. That doesn't stop Kilham from trying, however, nor has it stopped Babiarz and other Grafton residents from ascribing human motivations to the bears prowling around town.

Maybe they do so because it's easier to think you know an enemy than it is to admit that you don't and never will. Or perhaps, as scholars have suggested, anthropomorphism is an evolved trait, a kind of shorthand that allowed primitive humans to interpret animal behavior and protect themselves accordingly. Millions of years later, we still feel the urge to think of animals as basically like us, even if we live an infinitely safer existence; we don't hunt to survive, and we're not hunted. Tested only rarely in high-stakes circumstances, our assessment of creatures as friend or foe can be exaggerated or ill applied— sometimes to comic effect.

One night in the spring of 2009, in a house on a hill overlooking Grafton's somnolent downtown, a sheep farmer named Dianne Burrington was awoken by frantic bleating. She reacted instinctively, throwing back her covers, leaping from bed, and racing to the kitchen for her rifle. Burrington, then in her fifties, grabbed a pistol from a drawer for good measure before bursting out the front door "half-assed dressed" in her nightgown and a coat.

Burrington wasn't a shit taker—she was a shit kicker. If you were casting her in a movie, you'd want Kathy Bates: someone solid, assertive, and able to project a down-home friendliness. Whatever was out there, Burrington would deal with it. A coyote? No problem; she'd shot one before. As for bears, she'd installed an electric fence to keep them out. It hadn't failed her yet.

She sprinted through tufted pasture toward her barn. As she got closer, she realized that most of the braying was coming from Hurricane, her llama. Standing five feet nine inches tall and weighing 400 pounds, Hurricane was the farm's guard animal. Burrington claimed that he patrolled the fence line and kept an eye on the smallest sheep, ushering stragglers into their pens at the end of the day.

He was a noisy animal; when a potential danger stressed him out, he hummed. But the sound he was making that night was more like honking, as if he was sounding an alarm.

Burrington rounded a corner of the barn and saw what had Hurricane upset: a bear, which must have slipped through the electric fence wires like a boxer entering the ring. In the ensuing chaos, as sheep stampeded away in fear, a portion of the fence had been torn from its support on the barn. Now a ewe was tangled in the wreckage, panicking. Juggling her firearms in one hand, Burrington reached into her coat pocket and pulled out a pair of scissors. A few snips and the ewe was free.

By then the bear had fled, with the llama hot on its heels. "Hurricane!" Burrington bellowed. "*No!*" She took off running, too, a distant third in a race toward the fence line separating pasture from forest.

Burrington feared that if the bear turned around, Hurricane would be done for. As she ran, she cocked her pistol. But the bear, flustered no doubt by the llama and the farmer, seemed not to see the thin, electrified wires he was barreling toward. He ran into them full force; their tension bowed and rebounded. The bear caromed back at an angle, spinning across the ground. When it regained its feet, the bear turned to face Hurricane. Burrington looked on helplessly.

She learned something surprising that night: Despite their cartoonish appearance, llamas can fight like hell. They have six pronounced, razor-sharp "fighting teeth" at the front of their mouths for that purpose. In a whir of gnashing incisors and pummeling hooves, Hurricane assaulted the prone bear until it managed to pull itself away, slip through the fence, and disappear from sight. The llama snorted and stamped the ground and brayed some more—this time, Burrington was sure, with pride.

Of the clashes in Grafton's bear war, Hurricane's triumph was an instant classic among dinner-table tales. It elicited gasps of horror and laughs of delight in equal measure. Another attack, though, prompted only frowns and solemn vows of retaliation.

Tracey Colburn lived in a little yellow house in the middle of the woods. She was used to seeing bears in her yard, up in her trees, and raiding her compost pile, where they chucked aside cabbage in what she could only interpret as disgust. Colburn was in her forties, with long brown hair and a youthful face. She'd had a tough go of it; a breast-cancer diagnosis cut her college career short, and a long string of clerical and municipal jobs were unfulfilling. In 2012, she was in and out of work, but she had enough savings to care for her dog, Kai, a Husky-Labrador mix she'd rescued from a shelter. Kai had developed allergies to wheat and corn, two of the main ingredients in cheap dog food, so she was trying not to give him the stuff.

One muggy weekend, the kind where you leave the windows open to welcome even the slightest breeze, Colburn sliced up a cold pot roast and fed it to Kai. Then she let him out to pee. She was startled to see that her small porch, eight by ten feet, was "just full of bear." Two of the animals, young ones, were down on all fours sniffing the deck. A bigger, older bear stood right in front of Colburn. Kai rocketed at it, and Colburn screamed. The bear lunged at the sound. "They move like lightning," she told me.

The bear raked Colburn's face and torso with its left paw. Its claws dug into one forearm, thrown up in self-defense, and then the other. Colburn, who'd fallen onto her back, tried to push herself inside but realized she'd accidentally closed the door when her head thumped glass. "She was going to frickin' kill me, I just knew it, because her face was right here," Tracey said, holding her hand about eight inches in front of her nose. "I was looking right into her eyes."

Kai must have bitten the bear's rear legs then, because it jerked away from Colburn. The two animals started snarling and fighting in the yard. Colburn regained her feet and scrambled inside the house, shaking from adrenaline. She looked at her right hand. It didn't hurt, but it made her stomach turn. The bear had unwrapped the skin from the back of her hand like it was a Christmas present. The gaping hole showed ligaments, muscles, and blood. Colburn looked around her kitchen and picked up a clean dishcloth to wrap the wound.

Kai, only slightly injured, came trotting back toward the house; the bear was nowhere in sight. "Huskies prance. He come prancing out of the shadows, big grin on his face," Colburn recalled. "Like it was the most wonderful thing he'd ever done." But she was worried that the bear and its cubs were still out there, waiting for her. It was a terrifying prospect, because she needed to go outside. She didn't get cell reception in her house, and she couldn't afford a landline, so there was no way to get in touch with anyone to help her stanch the blood pouring from her injuries.

Carrying a lead pipe to defend herself, Colburn made a desperate run for her white Subaru, only to realize, once she was safely inside, that her mangled right hand couldn't move the stick shift. Reaching across her body with her left hand, she got the car into gear and puttered down the driveway. She rolled along until she got to the home of a neighbor named Bob. When she rang his doorbell, he stuck his head out an upstairs window.

"I've just been attacked by a bear," Colburn said, breathing heavily.

"Hold on," Bob replied, and he ducked back inside. A few seconds later, his head popped back out.

"Uh, you're kidding, right?" he asked.

Colburn conveyed, in painful shouts, that she was most certainly not kidding, and Bob quickly gave her a ride to the fire station. John Babiarz happened to be on duty. "Those *goddamn* bears!" he kept repeating. He called emergency responders, who whisked Colburn in an ambulance to the nearest hospital, then he phoned the Fish and Game Department. The person on the line was incredulous, like Bob before him. "It's been a century since we've had a bear attack on a person," the man said, referring to the whole of New Hampshire.

"I'm *here*!" Babiarz yelled back. "I *see* the blood!"

Doctors told Colburn that her body would heal. When she was released from the hospital, a warden from Fish and Game showed up at her house to erect a box trap in her yard. After he left, Colburn peeked at the single pink doughnut resting inside. That night she heard a bear banging on the side of the trap, but the next day the doughnut was still there. A few days later, the warden decided that the trap was useless, packed it up, and took it away.

Colburn thought about the bear all the time. She wondered how often it had ventured into her yard, onto her porch, and up to her windows without her knowing. Not like a Peeping Tom. Peeping Toms were people, and bears, she now knew for sure, were nothing like people. "If you look at their eyes," she told me, "you understand that they are completely alien to us."

* * *

At least one theory of aggressive ursine behavior supports the take-away that bears are monstrous. Jaroslav Flegr, a biologist at Charles University in the Czech Republic, studies *Toxoplasma gondii*, a proto-zoan parasite that lives inside warm-blooded animals and reproduces inside cats. (*T. gondii* is the reason pregnant women are told to steer clear of litter boxes.) When the parasite gets into an animal's brain, the effects can ramify through the central nervous system. Flegr explained that infected people can become less risk averse. Men with *T. gondii*, for instance, have higher levels of testosterone and less regard for authority than they otherwise would.

Homo sapiens aren't the only species that *T. gondii* can cause to act strangely—black bears are at risk, too. A study from the *Journal of Wildlife Diseases* found that 80 percent of black bears examined in a lab tested positive for the parasite.

It's compelling to imagine that a horde of bears, zombified by a brain bug that triggers risky behavior, is terrorizing a small American town. But that's more likely the stuff of science fiction than of good science. A more probable explanation for bold bear behavior is bold *human* behavior—which, in Grafton, means people embracing individual liberty. And one person's freedom, it turns out, can be another's burden.

Take the case of two women I'll call Doughnut Lady and Beretta, for reasons that will soon be clear. (Neither wanted to be named in this story.) They both live deep in Grafton's forest, and Beretta's house is just down the hill from Doughnut Lady's. When I met her, Beretta spoke in a sharp, clipped way, and she favored pronouncements like "My handyman is such a leftist" and "Do not write a story glorifying it." The "it" in this case was her neighbor's behavior. Beretta suggested that Doughnut Lady was treating a serious threat like it was all "fun and games."

For some 20 years, dating back to around the time that Jessica Soule's kittens were gobbled up, Doughnut Lady had been feeding Grafton's bears. She was now in her seventies and owlish, with glasses and a no-nonsense demeanor. She told me that she started feeding the bears accidentally; they stole grub from her two cows, Princess and Buttercup. Then, several years ago, she felt sorry for the bears and got into the habit of feeding them directly. The ritual was this: Every day at sunrise, and again in the late afternoon, she tottered outside with two buckets of grain. Up to eight bears at a time waited for her at the edge of the forest, where she poured the grain into two piles and topped each one with six sugared doughnuts. The animals ate in an orderly fashion, side by side on the ground, and then the cubs would clamber up nearby trees or Doughnut Lady's satellite dish.

The number of bears grew, and food costs ballooned. Doughnut Lady didn't want to admit how much the enterprise cost her— "I'm embarrassed, I really am," she admitted to me—except to say that it represented a significant portion of her monthly budget. But the bears were darn cute, and they never once bothered her cows. Doughnut Lady showed me a homemade calendar she'd compiled featuring pictures of the bears.

Hadn't she been worried that she might fall down in the midst of her unusual chore, leaving her vulnerable to animals the size of sumo wrestlers? In a tone that suggested I was being silly, Doughnut Lady said that the thought hadn't fazed her. Not because she was sure-footed. Indeed, she told me that she fell frequently in winter, when the ground was slick with ice.

I soon learned that there were four or five other families in Grafton who fed the bears, in defiance of state recommendations. Fish and Game was intolerant of such generosity. If you fed one bear, the department said, more bears will want to be fed, and once a bunch of bears get accustomed to food and its human sources, they'll keep coming back whether you like it or not. Fish and Game recommended that, in addition to not deliberately offering bears tasty snacks, people should use airtight trash cans, keep meat scraps out of compost piles, and take down bird-feeders in early spring, when bears emerge from their dens.

Late one night in 2017, the long-simmering debate about bear feeding took on added urgency when Beretta heard noises outside her house. She grabbed her gun, the brand of which you can guess, and went to investigate. Paw prints littered the ground, and she was sure she knew which doughnut-fattened creatures had left them. This wasn't the first time the bears from up the hill—a "sleuth" of them, to use the correct collective nomenclature—had gotten too close for comfort. Once, when she was preparing to leave the house for a shift at a volunteer job, she'd been stymied by several bears prowling in her yard, blocking the route to her car. Beretta had called her boss to say that she'd be late, due to unforeseen bear. On more than one occasion, she'd seriously considered shooting a bear and turning it into a rug, but she never acted on the impulse; fashioning the style she really wanted, with the bear's head intact, would be too expensive.

After discovering the paw prints, Beretta called Grafton's police officer to complain about her neighbor's feeding habits. He said he couldn't help, so Beretta called Fish and Game, which agreed to look into the matter. That's how a uniformed warden wound up on Doughnut Lady's doorstep.

Like many Grafton residents, Doughnut Lady referred to Fish and Game as "F and G," but she put her own spin on the name, so that it sounded like "effin' G"—as in, "The effin' G came to attack me." The warden showed her a printed copy of the state's public-nuisance laws and told her that her daily feedings could lead to prosecution.

"You deserve a budget cut," Doughnut Lady told him before slamming the door.

Angry, she called a lawyer, who said that while a legal case against her wouldn't be airtight—the state would have to prove that her actions, not some other cause, were clearly the root of a defined problem or danger—she should probably stop feeding the bears. What if they hurt someone? She was sure they wouldn't, but she wanted to avoid further scrutiny. The next morning, she didn't go outside for the morning grain dump. She felt terrible. Doughnut Lady couldn't look out her window for fear of making eye contact with the hungry bears waiting for her.

"So that was it," she said, her eyes moist.

Then, brightening, Doughnut Lady suggested that she could try a new strategy. She could plant blueberries and other calorie-rich flora that bears enjoy. She hinted, too, that she could stretch the definition of *planted*. Take sunflower seeds, for instance: Bears loved them, and she could scatter them on her property however she wanted. "I could just put them on the ground," she mused, "and they're planted."

* * *

Fish and Game contends that "the majority of human/bear conflicts can be avoided," to the tune of 86 percent, if people act responsibly with their grub. It was no surprise to learn that, in 2012, the year Tracey Colburn was attacked, New Hampshire suffered a drought that limited the animals' usual fare of bushes, berries, and bugs. Fish and Game got more than 1,000 bear complaints that year, many of them describing animals anxious to get their paws on human food.

Regardless of the reasons for the attack, some locals saw it as a breaking point, a violation of the line between man and nature that demanded recompense. The day after the incident made local news, Colburn stood on her porch and watched as a pickup truck bumped up the dirt road past her house. Inside the cab were several men. The bed held a large wooden box containing hunting dogs, whose acute sense of smell and loud baying would lead the men to their prey. The men didn't acknowledge Colburn, and she never saw them again. She was fine with that; if an illegal bear hunt was happening, she didn't want to know about it.

I very much wanted to know about it, so I asked around. As soon as I did, I got what I learned to be a mainstay of small talk in Grafton: friendly advice. It came in various forms, like "I'm a proud gun owner" slipped with a smile between someone's descriptions of their pets. Tom Ploszaj, a scruffy guy who lives in a trailer in an encampment where the preferred method of keeping bears away is pouring cayenne pepper all over the garbage, explained the subtext to me. "There's a lot of places around here where they'll never put a shovel into the dirt," Ploszaj said. "You don't want to find one of those places." I had no idea what he meant, so he clarified: "If you ask too many questions, you might be in a hole in the woods, and no one's going to find you."

It never came to that, but getting answers was still like pulling teeth. During one of my trips to town, a pair of men standing on the wooden porch of the Grafton Country Store told me that an illegal posse had hunted and killed 13 bears in one day. When I pressed for details, the men clammed up, as if suddenly remembering that they shouldn't brag to a journalist about breaking the law. Another resident said he knew about the vigilante hunt and opposed it, but would never have put up any resistance. "It's like being a German in Nazi Germany and not wanting to kill the Jews," he said. "You hear about it, and you know it's happening, but you just don't want to think about it."

I asked the town's police officer, Russell Poitras, about the posse, and he said he didn't know anything about it. Would it have been possible to hear the bear hunt, I asked—all those gunshots fired in the woods? Sure, Poitras said, but gunfire was to Grafton what traffic is to a big city: background noise.

Another local resident, who asked not to be named because she feared repercussions, was more helpful. She told me that one day, in the middle of winter, when hibernating bears were easier targets than they were during legal hunting season, she answered a knock at her door. Standing there was John Dodge. He spoke of "us," and the woman understood that Dodge was there with a few other men. They were probably behind him on the road, bundled up inside their trucks and away from the freezing air.

Dodge told the woman that the group wanted to kill a bear whose den was inside a hill on her land.

"I got nothing to do with it," she replied.

"We need to know if we can get on your property," Dodge explained.

"What I don't know won't hurt me," she told him with a shrug. "I won't look out my window."

After that she heard gunfire in fits and starts. She stayed inside and didn't peek out, as she'd promised. A few days later, Dodge told her that the posse had finished its work, which had included much more than shooting the single bear on her property. "He said they got them, emptied them out," the woman told me. "He said it was 13."

Would Dodge or the other men talk to me? I wondered. "They agreed that they're not going to," the woman said. Word had gotten around about the questions I was asking, and an omerta was in effect. This surprised me less than the revelation that I'd already spoken to Dodge some months prior. His door was one of many I'd knocked on while first sussing out tales of Grafton's bears, before I knew about the posse.

"I just moved here," he'd said. "I haven't seen any bears." Then he'd shut the door.

In fact, I learned, Dodge was raised in Grafton and had lived alongside bears his whole life. Armed with this knowledge, I drove to his house, parked across the road, and approached him when he came into his yard. Rangy, with a sun-browned forehead, skullcap of white hair, and mouth that cut a straight line across his skeptical face, Dodge listened while I explained that I wasn't trying to get him in any trouble—I just wanted to know the story.

"I still ain't going to talk to anybody. I don't want nothing to do with it," he said. "You can explain it, but I don't want to get involved with it."

Dodge denied taking part in any posse. He added that he's part Cherokee, and killing bears was a violation of that heritage. Then he offered me some friendly advice: "If you find out about this bear hunt that you keep mentioning, you're going to have a problem." I took him to mean that the members of the posse would wield some brand of street (forest?) justice at me and anyone who snitched. I thanked him for his time and walked toward my car.

"Just leave me out of it," he called after me. "Because a war's going to come, and I'm going to be right in the middle of it." What role he'd play exactly he didn't say.

It's easy to see locals like Dodge as foolhardy and eager to use the bear threat, whether real, imagined, or embellished, as an excuse to live out action-movie fantasies. But when I looked under the hood of New Hampshire's law and order, I found deficiencies—the kind that people might take as evidence that they needed to act on their own.

Budget troubles in recent years have forced Fish and Game to reduce its staff size. Wardens, of which there are 32 statewide, are stretched thin. They handle upwards of 600 bears complaints annually, among thousands of other calls, and Andrew Timmins admitted that it can be hard to do much more than keep track of the number and type of reports. When I asked him if I could review the department's paperwork on the Colburn attack, he said that none existed. "Given the magnitude of the work, sometimes details slip through the cracks," Timmins wrote in an email, speculating on why a responding warden didn't write the incident up. "I can tell you from experience that there are times when I would not have time to do the same."

To a journalist, it was a frustrating answer. I imagined it might be the same for people who prefer that bears not devour pets, destroy property, or get violent with innocents like Colburn. "If the government won't do its job, the people will," Babiarz told me one day.

But what *is* the government's job in the eyes of a citizenry that exists on a political spectrum from lightly libertarian to all-out anarchist? Only a well-funded, organized state agency can efficiently safeguard communities from bears, and Grafton is full of people who tend to support the depletion of government coffers. Babiarz, I realized, probably didn't want a state agent coming to his farm to capture or kill the chicken-eating bear. More likely, he wanted New Hampshire to lift restrictions on his right to shoot the animal or, if he felt like it, to feed it chocolate. That was the state's job: to protect his freedom.

"I feel, on my property, I have the right to defend and protect," Babiarz told me. "If I see a problem bear, I will deal with it. We can argue about it in court later on."

Driving around Grafton, I passed dilapidated houses that stood like rotting teeth against a yawning green mouth of New England forest. Other fossils of town history were submerged in the intruding wilderness: platforms that once held church revivals, cemeteries in various states of senescence, foundations of long-abandoned homesteads. This, nature's relentless fecundity, molded the town's Great Bear Drama—a mix of luring, feeding, shouting, shooting, and storytelling. History also played a part, as did politics and culture. Vital, too, was the prism of individual experience.

One day I found myself thinking of C. I. Lewis, a New England–based philosopher who wrote a book called *Mind and the World Order* in 1929. At the time, his college-age daughter was dying of leukemia. Lewis used the term *qualia* to describe the unique properties that someone senses during a life event. His daughter, for instance, likely felt pain, the weight of her body, and the speed of time in ways that he, at her bedside, could not. What did qualia mean, Lewis wondered, for the concept of shared reality and objective truth?

Perhaps Grafton's relationship with bears was a huge bundle of qualia, stacked like cords of wood. Every resident's experience looked awfully like the one next to it, as if cut from the same tree, and they were all bound by the ties of a communal existence. Yet up close, each one was distinct, shaped in various ways by ferality and freedom.

Late in the spring of 2018, I visited Grafton one last time. At the end of the day, in a deepening dusk, I steered my car up a rocky dirt road and around tall, twisting trees toward Tent City. I wanted to talk to the survivalists again, to see whether their bear troubles had faded or intensified in recent months. I got there later than I'd intended and could barely see the camp in the gloom. I made out the finished barrier, more motley than originally conceived: a crude network of chain-link, metal gates, and picket-fence sections, all of it trussed together in a common function.

I reached the road's end; I would have to walk from there. Rolling down the window of my car, I squinted at an indistinct shape moving in the woods. Was it a survivalist, foraging for mushrooms or firewood? Or was it a bear, foraging for something else? If I couldn't tell what it was, would the survivalists know I was human when they saw my figure approaching their camp in the creeping darkness? If not, would firecrackers or worse come flying my way?

I spent a long moment considering unwanted consequences, whether wrought by man or by beast, and the fact that danger, like beauty, is in the eye of the beholder. Then I rolled up my window and drove back the way I came, leaving Tent City to another restless night.

ANDREA LONG CHU

■

I Worked with Avital Ronell.
I Believe Her Accuser.

FROM *The Chronicle of Higher Education*

THE HUMANITIES ARE ABLAZE. This month the *New York Times* reported that the Title IX office had found Avital Ronell, a professor of German and comparative literature at New York University and a superstar in literary studies, responsible for sexually harassing a former student, Nimrod Reitman, now a visiting fellow at Harvard. A lawsuit filed by Reitman fills in the details. Leading feminist and queer scholars like Judith Butler, Lisa Duggan, and Jack Halberstam have defended her—or at least deflected criticism.

I believe the allegations.

Last year I worked as a teaching assistant for Avital Ronell. I hadn't sought out the appointment; I am a doctoral student in comparative literature at NYU, and that semester I was, per the handbook, guaranteed a teaching job. A few months before the position began, I received an email from one of my professors informing me that Ronell's other teaching assistants were "all taking her class and working hard to familiarize themselves with her particular methodologies, texts, style, and so on." I was "encouraged" to do the same. I was told this was "an important part of the process with Prof. Ronell." After all, there were other students eager to replace me.

This was not abusive, obviously, only irritating. The lightly mobbish tone of the email—"this is a nice job you got here, shame if something happened to it"—was jarring. In theory, at least, teaching assistants are junior colleagues, not employees, and I had thought that my position was guaranteed. Then again, given the things I'd heard about Avital from other graduate students over the years, I wasn't all that surprised. (Except on formal occasions, she always went by that one name, "Avital," like Plato, or Cher.)

Eventually I kissed the ring. I attended a session of Avital's seminar and visited her in office hours. Her manner in that meeting was odd, wounded. "I just wanted to make sure you and I are OK," she told me with a concerned look, as if we were recovering from a nasty fight. "Of course we are!" I exclaimed, tripping over myself to reassure her. Avital softened. She had just wanted to be coaxed, like a deer to a salt lick. She smiled. I smiled. This was the process.

The course was called "Outrageous Texts." Like most purportedly edgy things, it was less edgy than it imagined. In practice, *outrageous* mostly meant some dead white dudes with weird sexual hang-ups. Sometimes we mixed it up; the dudes were still alive. When we did read women (four of the 15 writers assigned), Avital still mostly talked about men. Her lecture on Valerie Solanas's *SCUM Manifesto*, like the introduction she wrote for Verso's edition of that book, focused on Nietzsche and Derrida.

It is not illegal to read men. Avital is a Germanist and a deconstructionist who has made no serious contribution to feminist scholarship. That's fine. But when news media report that she is a feminist—"What Happens to #MeToo When a Feminist Is the Accused?" read the *Times* headline—they are factually mistaken. This is a professional distinction, not a political one. Personally, Avital may be a feminist, in the Taylor Swift sense of a woman who doesn't like being oppressed, but professionally, she is not a feminist *scholar*, any more than every person who believes that humans descended from apes is an evolutionary anthropologist.

In class, Avital was waited on by her aide-de-camp, a graduate student who followed her around the Village like Tony Hale on HBO's *Veep*. If the energy in the room was not to her liking, she became frustrated. During one session, she abruptly stopped the lecture midthought, blaming her students for making her feel drained. It took a beat for anyone to realize she was serious.

We were sent on a 15-minute break. That afternoon, quite without knowing it, like burrs attaching themselves to some passing animal, the students had been persecuting Avital. As far as I could tell (given that we had no prior relationship), I had done the same when I had failed, during my coursework years, to give much thought to her at all.

It is simply no secret to anyone within a mile of the German or complit departments at NYU that Avital is abusive. This is boring and socially agreed upon, like the weather.

Stories about Avital's "process" are passed, like notes in class, from one student to the next: how she reprimanded her teaching assistants when they did not congratulate her for being invited to speak at a conference; how she requires that her students be available 24/7; how her preferred term for any graduate student who has fallen out of favor is "the skunk."

Process: Wild things live in this word. These stories come from sources who strongly wished to remain anonymous, fearing that to have their names attached would threaten their chances in an already desiccated job market. But even if this was just gossip, I would believe it. When it comes to the American academy, I trust raw, red rumor over public statements any day of the week.

Academic celebrity soaks up blood like a pair of Thinx. A letter to NYU's president, Andrew Hamilton, a draft of which leaked in June, argued that Avital's "brilliant scholarship" qualified her for special treatment. The 51 signatories included giants of feminist theory like Judith Butler and Gayatri Spivak, as well as my department chair—and the professor who emailed to "encourage" me to play nice with Avital. (Butler has since issued some tepid regrets.)

Meanwhile, on social media and on their blog, the queer-studies scholars Lisa Duggan and Jack Halberstam dismissed the blowback against Avital as neoliberalism meets sex panic meets culture clash, straight people apparently being unable to decipher the coded queer intimacy of emails like "I tried to call you a number of times, unfortunately couldn't get through, would have liked to leave a msg" [sic].

That Avital's defenders are left-wing academic stars is not particularly surprising if you've spent much time in the academy. The institution has two choices when faced with political radicals: Ax them, especially if they are graduate students, or promote them. Make them successful, give them awards, power, enormous salaries. That way, when the next scandal comes along—and it will—they will have a vested interest in playing defense.

This is how institutionality reproduces. Even the call to think critically about power becomes a clever smoke screen. There is a whole dissertation to be written on intellectuals using the word *neoliberal* to mean "rules I shouldn't have to follow." "If we focus on this one case, these details, this accuser and accused, we will miss the opportunity to think about the structural issues," wrote Duggan. This *was* code. It meant, "You can talk about structural issues all you want, so long as you don't use examples of people we know."

In a milquetoast take for *The New Yorker*, Masha Gessen applauded Duggan as a model of "academics doing their job: engaging with things in great complexity." Of course power is messy. But there is no complexity in studying forests if you can't recognize a tree from a few feet away. This is not wisdom; it is an eye complaint.

Structural problems are problems because real people hurt real people. You cannot have a cycle of abuse without actually existing abusers. That sounds simple, which is why so many academics hate it. When scholars defend Avital—or "complicate the narrative," as we like to say—in part this is because we cannot stand believing what most people believe. The need to feel smarter is deep. Intelligence is a hungry god.

In this way, Avital's case has become a strange referendum on literary study. Generations of scholars have been suckled at the teat of interpretation: We spend our days parsing commas and decoding metaphors. We get high on finding meaning others can't. We hoard it, like dragons. We would be intellectually humiliated to learn that the truth was plain: that Avital quite simply sexually harassed her student, just as described. Sometimes analysis is simply denial with more words. Sometimes, as a frustrated student in a first-year literature course always mutters, the text just means what it says it means.

My department has been largely silent since the news broke. Faculty members have said nothing to us. Upset and ashamed, my fellow graduate students and I speak with one another cautiously. We heal, or don't, alone. People I know are afraid to make any public comment, even on Facebook, where they are friends with older, richer scholars who might one day control their fates. Even I, who have by extraordinary luck options outside of academia, fear what being vocal will bring.

A culture of critics in name only, where genuine criticism is undertaken at the risk of ostracism, marginalization, retribution— this is where abuses like Avital's grow like moss, or mold. Graduate students know this intuitively; it is written on their bones. They've watched as their professors play favorites, as their colleagues get punished for citing an adviser's rival, as funding, jobs, and prestige are doled out to the most obedient and obsequious. The American university knows only the language of extortion. "Tell," it purrs, curling its fingers around your IV drip, "and we'll eat you alive."

Avital conducts herself as if someone somewhere is always persecuting her. She learned this, I imagine, in graduate school. No woman escapes the relentless misogyny of the academy. The humanities are sadistic for most people, especially when you aren't a white man. This is understood to be normal. When students in my department asked for more advising, we were told we were being needy. "Graduate school *should* destroy you," one professor laughed.

The irony is that those who survive this destruction often do so at the cost of inflicting the same trauma on their own students. Avital, now a grande dame of literary studies, who Reitman alleges bragged to him of a "mafia"-like ability to make or break the careers of others, still feels persecuted. She makes it the job of those around her to protect her from that persecution: to fawn, appease, coddle. The lawsuit against her reads as a portrait, not of a macho predator type, but of a desperately lonely person with the power to coerce others, on pain of professional and psychic obliteration, into being her friends, or worse.

It's possible that Avital genuinely believed that her student loved her, that he wanted to protect her from the scary, hostile world. In that case, the alleged assaults would have literalized the romantic tone she required he use. "Hold me," they would have said. "Make me feel loved."

There is a phrase for all of this: cultish subjection. It comes from a book called *Complaint*, released this year, in which the author writes of graduate school as a kind of indentured labor. "I was a painfully earnest baby scholar," she recalls, "dedicated, conditioned for every sort of servitude, understanding that doing time, whether in graduate school or as part of a teaching body, amounted to acts—or, rather, passivities—of cultish subjection."

The author's name is Avital Ronell.

HOLTON ARMS CLASS OF 1984

■

FROM *StandwithBlaseyFord.com*

September 17, 2018
To the United States Congress:

WE, OF THE HOLTON ARMS CLASS OF 1984, are writing on behalf of our friend and classmate, Dr. Christine Blasey Ford, to attest to her honesty, integrity, and intelligence; and to contend that her decision to provide information pertaining to a sexual assault is not a partisan act. It is an act of civic duty and the experience she described in her letter needs to be seriously considered. We represent all political parties and we support Christine bringing this matter forward.

Christine has had to weigh the personal cost of sharing her experience against her own conscience. We recognize that this has been an extraordinarily difficult decision and admire her courage for being willing to speak her truth when it would have been easier to stay silent.

As sexual assault violates a woman's most fundamental rights, it must be considered a failure of character at any age—regardless of the subsequent accomplishments and power attained by the offender. It should not be dismissed as youthful bad judgment, however aberrant it may be.

In light of Christine's experience, we hold our elected officials responsible for conducting a more thorough and comprehensive review of this Supreme Court nominee. Having taken this courageous step, Christine deserves your due consideration on this serious matter.

We stand with our friend Dr. Christine Blasey Ford and admire her honesty and resolve on behalf of our nation.

Respectfully,

Allyson Abrams Bergman
Robin Bostrom
Ana Coyne
Amy Englehardt
Andrea K. Evers
Holly Huelsman Fuller
Sandra Engle Gichner
Daphne Holt
Jenny Yerrick Martin
Francine Laden
Kim Litle
Monica McLean

Samantha Semerad Guerry
Estela M. Radan
Martha Mispireta Shannon
Lisa Shapiro
Laura Simms Smith
Kendra South
Dana Stewart
Julia Kogan Tanner
M. Sydney Trattner
Virginia White
Stacey Kavounis Wilson

KATE GASKIN

■

Diagnosis in Reverse

FROM *32 Poems*

First, the witch turning from the door
made of spiced cake

and sugared almonds. Then the birds
offering the bread back

to the forest floor, the children
skipping backwards into the gaunt

yawn of the house as the mother's
long hunger begins

to soften, her hearth dark with smoke.
And then a spark,

the children in the back orchard
eating apricots heavy

with juice. Pale cream in a bowl. A vase
of primroses. Foxglove stirring

outside the open window. The father
coming up the summer path, easy

with evening. Hansel humming.
Fresh bread and long light, long light.

VIET THANH NGUYEN

■

On True War Stories

FROM *The Massachussetts Review*

An excerpt from Viet Thanh Nguyen's original personal essay On True War Stories, *with graphic illustrations by Matt Huynh.*

A WAR BROUGHT ME FROM OVER THERE TO OVER HERE

PEOPLE LIKE ME, THE VIETNAMESE WHO FLED
TO THE UNITED STATES AFTER THE WAR'S END,

WERE LIVING PROOF OF THE SUCCESS OF
ONE OF AMERICA'S GREATEST DESIRES,

TO WIN THE HEARTS AND MINDS OF OTHERS.

I HEARD A DIFFERENT KIND OF WAR STORY AS I GREW UP AMONG VIETNAMESE REFUGEES. THERE WAS THE ONE ABOUT A MAN WHO HELD UP A MOM AND POP SHOP IN A SMALL VIETNAMESE TOWN WITH A HAND GRENADE.

OR THE ONE ABOUT A MOTHER WHO FLED THAT SMALL TOWN WHEN THE COMMUNISTS ARRIVED,

TAKING HER SONS BUT LEAVING BEHIND HER ADOPTED TEENAGE DAUGHTER TO TAKE CARE OF THE SHOP, BELIEVING SHE WOULD SOON RETURN.

MOTHER AND DAUGHTER WOULD NOT SEE EACH OTHER AGAIN FOR TWENTY YEARS.

OR WHAT ABOUT THE TIME THAT MOTHER AND HER HUSBAND OPENED ANOTHER SHOP IN SAN JOSE, CALIFORNIA, AND WERE SHOT ON CHRISTMAS EVE IN AN ARMED ROBBERY?

OR HOW THEY CRIED WHEN THEY RECEIVED LETTERS ANNOUNCING THE DEATHS OF THEIR PARENTS IN THEIR LOST HOMELAND?

OR HOW THEY WORKED TWELVE HOUR DAYS EVERY DAY EXCEPT FOR CHRISTMAS, EASTER AND TET?

BUT WHAT IF WE UNDERSTOOD IMMIGRANT STORIES TO BE WAR STORIES?

AND WHAT IF WE UNDERSTOOD THAT WAR STORIES DISTURB EVEN MORE WHEN THEY ARE NOT ABOUT SOLDIERS, WHEN THEY SHOW US HOW NORMAL WAR IS, HOW WAR TOUCHES AND TRANSFORMS EVERYTHING AND EVERYBODY, INCLUDING, MOST OF ALL, CIVILIANS?

GARTH GREENWELL

■

The Frog King

FROM *The New Yorker*

IT WAS TOO EARLY FOR THERE to be so much light, so that when I woke my first thought was of snow. We had pulled the drapes before sleeping but they did almost nothing to darken the room, the snow caught scraps from streetlamps and neon and cast them back up. It was bright enough to see R. still sleeping beside me, cocooned in the blanket I had bought after the first night we spent together, when I woke shivering to find him bound tight in the comforter we were sharing, swaddled beside me. He repeated the word all that day, apropos of nothing, swaddled, swaddled, he had never heard it before, the sound of it made him laugh. He would sleep for hours still, if I let him he would sleep the whole day. He loved to sleep in a way I didn't, sliding into it at every chance, whereas almost always I slept poorly, uneasily, I woke finally with a sense of relief. He complained if I woke him—I'm on holiday, he would say, let me sleep—but he complained more if I let him sleep too long. We only had ten days together, his winter vacation, which he had decided to spend in Sofia while everyone else he knew went home. Mornings were my time to work, to spend with my books and my writing, my time to be alone; I would get up soon but for now I kept looking at him, his face bearded and dark, smoothed out by sleep. It was all I could do not to touch it, as I did often when he was awake, cupping his cheek in my palm or reaching around the curve of his skull. He had shaved his head at the end of the semester, I liked to run my hand around and around it until he ducked and told me to stop, annoyed but laughing, too; even annoyance was part of the pleasure we took in each other, we were that early in love.

I was still groggy with sleep when I turned in to the main room, and I stood uncomprehending for a moment before I realized that R. had rearranged things in the night. He had moved the table to the middle of the room, and had placed my winter boots on top of it, beside the little tree we had bought earlier that week. Sticking up from the boots were packages wrapped in newspaper, his Christmas gifts for me; he must have hidden them somewhere after he arrived, he must have gotten out of bed in the night, careful not to wake me, he must have been quiet as he moved the furniture. I caught my breath at it, I felt a weird pressure and heat climb my throat. I felt like my heart would burst, those were the words for it, the hackneyed phrase, and I was grateful for them, they were a container for what I felt, proof of its commonness. I was grateful for that, too, the commonness of my feeling; I felt some stubborn strangeness in me ease, I felt like part of the human race.

He had seen snow for the first time that winter, and he loved to be out in it, to stand with his arms outstretched as it fell, his mouth open to the sky. We went out that afternoon, the snow already tracked through but still lovely; the streets were quiet for the holiday, all the shops were closed. We were wearing the scarves I had found when I opened the presents under the tree, which were long and knit in the same pattern, one yellow and one blue; we wouldn't ever be boyfriends who wore the same clothes, R. said, but one shared thing was acceptable, having one shared thing was nice. We didn't go far, just halfway down the block, where I whistled, a short upward swoop I repeated three times, the usual signal. She might not be here, I had said, she isn't always, she goes other places or maybe somebody takes her in, but she came quickly enough from her usual spot around the back of the building. She was beautiful in her way, tawny and medium-sized like most of Sofia's street dogs, too skinny and with mange along one side. She was happy to see us, I thought, happy as she always was to get attention, though she lacked the confidence of some of the other dogs; she stayed near the wall, wagging her tail but not coming too close at first. Even when she let us pet her she tried to keep her distance, cringing in a sidling motion that brought her body within our reach but kept her head angled away, a mixture of eagerness and fear. Somebody had taught her that, I thought, somebody had beaten her, or many people had, but not in this neighborhood, here everyone was kind to her, she was a sort of communal pet. She lost some of her shyness when R. pulled the packet of treats out of his coat pocket, clumsy in his mittens, which he had to take off before he could tear open the packet and pull out one of the strips of leathery meat. She started whining when she saw it, prancing closer, and he crooned her name, Lilliyana, though that didn't mean anything to her, it was just a name he had invented, it suited her, he thought. *Ela tuka*, he said, a phrase I had taught him, come here, and he held out the treat so she could take it, which she did by stretching her neck and pulling back her lips, taking hold of it with her front teeth, like a deer plucking a leaf. He had bought the treats the night before, when we were buying supplies; she should have Christmas dinner, too, he said. She let us pet her more vigorously then, finally coming close, even pressing her side against his legs as she begged for a second piece, which he gave her, though that was all for today, he told her, there would be more tomorrow. She seemed to accept this, she didn't keep begging once we turned away, as most dogs would have, I thought; she disappeared behind the building again to whatever shelter she had found.

We found the tree by chance one late afternoon. We were in a part of town I'd never seen before, on the other side of the city center, looking for a German supermarket, a chain that was popular in Western Europe but that had only the single store in Sofia. It was less a store than a warehouse, really, there weren't shelves but huge bins people pawed through, everything mixed together, a dozen kinds of chocolate bars in one bin, toothpaste and shaving cream in another. The chain had its own brand of food, and R. was craving something from his life in Lisbon, a frozen lasagna, and when we found it in an oversized freezer case he clutched it to his chest with happiness. It was a long walk from the store to the metro, longer because the sidewalks were caked with ice; R. scolded me as we walked, telling me to take my hands out of my pockets, to keep them free in case I slipped, as for whatever reason I did often enough; if it had been night he would have passed his arm through mine to keep me upright. R. saw the trees first, in the window of a little shop that was full of Christmas decorations. Even from outside you could see how cheap they were, all metal wire and plastic bristles, but R. insisted that we needed one, and ornaments, a box of lights; I want to have a real Christmas, he said. It was maybe three feet tall, it hardly weighed anything but it was cumbersome, I held it in both arms like a child as we walked. I felt a little ridiculous sitting with it on the train but R. seemed proud, he kept one arm around it to hold it steady on the seat between us. When we got home, he wanted to trim the tree right away, and he opened the box of tinsel to find that it was far too large, we hadn't been paying attention, it was meant for a much bigger tree. He laughed as he wrapped it again and again around the branches; she was swaddled now, he said, it would keep her warm. Her, I repeated back to him, inquisitive, mocking him a little, and this gave him an idea: she needed a name, he said, and he decided to call her Madeleine, I don't have any idea where it came from but he loved to say it. He liked to give things names, I think it was a way of laying claim to them, and he called out to her every time he passed, almost singing it, Madeleine, Madeleine. He saved the box of ornaments for Christmas Eve, little glass balls we hung from hooks on the branches, tucked among the tinsel. We knelt to arrange them, and when we finished R. sat back on his heels. Isn't she beautiful, he said, taking my hand in his, but he answered the question himself: she is, isn't she, I think she's beautiful.

We went to Bologna because it was the cheapest place we could fly: there were tickets for forty euros, a price I could afford. We packed a single carry-on each, anything else would have meant a fee, and rode in a cab to the airport's old terminal, which the budget airlines used. It was my first time leaving the country. During breaks, when the other American teachers left for places near or far—Istanbul, Tangier, St. Petersberg—I stayed behind; I didn't want to travel, I said, I wanted to be settled in a single place. I studied Bulgarian, I read, I wandered the streets downtown. But I did want to travel with R., to leave Sofia, where even when his friends were gone there was a pressure of secrecy, where it was too dangerous to hold hands in the streets, to kiss in public, however chastely, where everywhere we had to keep a casual distance; I wanted to be with him in a place where we could be freer with each other, a place in the West. It was my gift to him, a getaway, a bit of romance. We arrived at the airport early enough to be first in line for the unassigned seats, and sat in the front row, where there was extra room for our legs. Even so, my knees almost touched those of the single attendant who sat facing us, strapped into her foldout seat. She spoke English with an accent I couldn't place, not Bulgarian but something Eastern European, and she smiled slightly, kindly I thought, when the plane started down the runway, thrusting us all back, and R. moved his hand to cover mine where it lay on my knee.

We booked the cheapest hotel, too, a chain a good way from the city center, with a bus stop outside for getting to town. We arrived too late for any exploring, we'd have to wait until morning to see the city. It was hard not to feel depressed by our room, which had the corporate airlessness of such places, comfort sterilized of any human touch. It was on the second floor, overlooking the parking lot. It's not exactly a dream of Italy, I said, meaning it as an apology, but R. laughed, he drew the curtain across the glass and pulled me to the bed. Who cares about the view, he said, the bed is nice, that's all that matters, you should care about the bed, and then we were both laughing, one on top of the other.

The hotel's one luxury was the breakfast we found the next morning, a buffet of eggs and sliced meats, yogurt and fruit, a table overloaded with cakes and tarts. It was early still—we had set our alarms, we wanted the whole day for the city—and I needed coffee first, which meant a complicated machine with a digital screen, then waiting for the paper cup to fill. When I turned back, I saw that R. had covered our table with little plates, a sample from each of the sweets. He hadn't left any room for me, and I waited while he tried to clear a space for my coffee, shifting the plates around until one almost tipped onto the floor, he caught it just in time. I made a little noise, exasperated and amused, and he looked up at me and shrugged. He would take a single bite from each plate, then move it to one side or the other, sorting out the things he liked. I watched him for a while, and then Skups, I said, my tone half question, half disbelief, making a gesture that took in the table with its plates, the room, the other people eating. He shrugged again, glancing around at the assortment of other travelers, businessmen mostly, a few couples. Who cares, he said, using his fork to dig into another piece of something, they don't know me, we'll never see them again, why should I care what they think?

I remembered this later, waiting for the bus that would take us to town. We were the only people in the little shelter at the stop, huddling together against the wind, which was sharper than I had expected; it wasn't very cold but it was cold enough for our coats, for the scarves we had draped around each other before heading out. Then R. stepped up onto the bench, he grabbed my shoulders and turned me to face him. Now I'm the taller one, he said, and bent down to kiss me, not a chaste kiss, he gripped my hair and tilted my head farther back to probe my mouth with his tongue. I tried to pull away, laughing: it was a busy road, we were in full view of the passing cars. But he held me tight, kissing me with urgency, until I realized that exposure was the point, that he wanted to show off, here where nobody knew him, where he could be anonymous and free, could live out an ideal of candor. He leaned into me, pressing his pelvis into my stomach so I felt his cock hard between us; it turned him on to show off like this, I had had no idea. I gripped him, using my body to shield us, I gripped him hard with both my hands through his jeans. I started to undo his belt, wanting to meet him in his daring, to show him I was game; and he moaned into my mouth before he pulled back and pushed my hand away. *Porta-te bem*, he said, slapping my face lightly and laughing, behave.

The bus left us in the Piazza Maggiore, where there was a huge wooden statue in the center of the square, a cylinder painted an uneven green. The bottom half was featureless, the top carved into the torso of a frog, regal and upright, his lips drawn back in an expression at once benevolent and severe. Two arms crossed at his stomach, four long fingers hanging down from each; above the half-lidded eyes there was a crown with four prongs. Cables stretched down from the statue's midsection, securing it to the pavement; wooden barriers marked off a space around it. It would be burned, the man working at reception told us back at the hotel when we asked, it was the tradition, the old year burned at the turn of the new. I remembered something I had seen in a movie, Fellini maybe, a stuffed witch on a pile of kindling and old furniture, the trash of the past, the promise of an uncluttered future. I wondered why we didn't do it in the States, where we love to pretend to start afresh, where we love to burn things down. There was nothing like it in Bulgaria, either, where New Year's was celebrated at home; families gathered in apartments and at midnight they set off fireworks from their balconies. It had frightened me my first year, the sound ricocheting off the walls as the little bombs fell into the streets below, where everyone knew not to be; they were impassable for a good half hour. Which was the opposite of clearing away: all over the city the explosions came down and nobody swept them up, the wrappers and casings littered the streets until the heavy spring rains. It wasn't a traditional statue, the man told us, there was a competition each year, artists submitted designs and the winner had his work displayed there, in the center of the city, for a week before it was burned. For us the frog is a symbol, the man said, it means poverty, here in Bologna, in Italy, so it means to burn poverty. You know the crisis is very hard here, he said, the austerity is very hard, it would be good to burn it away. He had apologized for his English, but it was very good, less stiff than he seemed in his jacket and tie; he was young, mid-twenties, a college student in a university town. You should go, he said, it's a party, there will be music and lots of people and you can watch the fire, it's something you should see.

There was so much to see, too much; I walked around in a daze of looking. We moved in and out of churches crowded with paintings, huge and smoke-darkened, the ceilings crammed with color, I got tired of trying to see them. R. was full of zeal, he wanted to see everything—who knows when we'll be back, he said. The dilemma of vacations, the exhaustion of the last chance. Everything became unremarkable, nothing moved me, it was all a blur of perfection. I wanted to get the bus back to the hotel, I wanted to rest my eyes. But just one more thing, R. said, paging through the guidebook we had bought, and he led me to a small museum, a house converted after the artist who had lived in it had died. There were just a few rooms, open and uncluttered, the walls painted mercifully white; it wouldn't take long for R. to make his circuit. I followed him, barely looking at the paintings, which were small and unremarkable, or remarkable only for their plainness. They were quiet and unambitious, minor, I thought at first, still-lifes and modest landscapes, interesting mostly for having so little to do with everything else we had seen; the painter had spent his whole life in this city but seemed indifferent to the examples it offered, to the virtuousity and gorgeousness it prized. I found myself looking longer, looking more slowly, I let R. walk on ahead. The same subjects appeared again and again, household objects, plates and bowls, not filled with flowers or fruit but empty, set against a plain background. I stopped in front of one that showed a pitcher and cups, white and gray on a tan surface, behind them a blue wall. Something held me there looking, something made me lean in to look more closely. The cups were mismatched in color and in shape, the pitcher rose oddly elongated behind them, the whole painting was eccentric, asymmetrical. There was a kind of presence in the painting, I felt, I could sense it humming at a frequency I wanted to tune myself to catch. I liked the seeming naïveté of it, the way the simple figures had been simplified further, purified or idealized to geometrical forms, almost, but rendered bluntly, imperfectly. And the brushstrokes were imperfect too, visible, haphazard, the paint distributed unevenly, inexpertly; but that wasn't right, really it was striving for something ideal, that was what I felt, the frequency I wanted to catch. What I took at first for blocks of color dissolved when I leaned in, were modulated, textured, full of movement somehow, not the movement of objects but of light, which fell across them gently, undramatically. But that's not right either, it didn't fall across them, there weren't any shadows; I couldn't locate the light at all, or tell if the scene depicted morning or noon. It was as if the objects emanated their own light, which didn't move from one quadrant of the painting to another, as real light would, but vibrated somehow, giving a sense of movement and stillness at once. There was a promise in it, I felt, I mean a promise for me, a claim about what life could be.

* * *

Venice was two hours away by train, another unmissable chance. We wouldn't stay the night, the hotel in Bologna was already paid for, we would spend a few hours exploring and then come back. On the train I stared at the fields we passed, which were laid out neatly, in lines I realized I had never seen in Bulgaria; the fields alongside the train from Sofia to the coast were shaggy, inexactly drawn, like the fields I remembered from my childhood, my family's fields in Kentucky, nothing like this clean geometry. I stared at them, hypnotized, and turned away only when I felt R.'s hand on my ankle, calling me back. We were facing each other, I had my foot on the empty seat beside him, and he had hooked his fingers underneath the cuff of my jeans and was stroking me softly, privately, not looking up from his book. But I knew he wasn't reading, he was smiling just slightly, his eyes on the page, he was basking in how I looked at him.

We had no plans in Venice, had done no research. But it didn't matter, just to be there was enough, amid the capillary water and sinking stone; there was a kind of uniform beauty to everything, a blanket wonder. Every corner we turned made R. gasp, every church we stepped into, every statue with its marble frothed up like surf, like the involutions of thought. Fuck these people, R. whispered as we stared at a painted ceiling, fuck them for getting to live in a place like this. He was smiling when I glanced at him but I knew he meant it, or half meant it. He often said that he was born in the wrong place; shitty Portugal, he would say, shitty Algarve, the shitty Azores, shitty Lisbon, it should all have been different, his life was fucked. Sometimes I could bring him out of these moods, I could kiss him and say he had a new life now, his life with me, who knew where we'd end up, in Europe or America, who knew what adventures we'd have, and sometimes he pushed me away or turned his face from mine. We don't get to choose anything, he'd say then, we think we do but it's an illusion, we're insects, we get stepped on or we don't, that's all. When he talked like this there was nothing I could do, anything I did made it worse, whether I got angry or sad or tried to make him feel my own happiness, the happiness I felt so often just looking at him, as he slept or read, or stared into the screen of his laptop. It was an immovable force, this mood that descended on him sometimes, and I worried that it was descending on him now, that it would darken the rest of our day. But it didn't descend. When we left the church and turned blindly around the next corner he pulled me into an alcove and kissed me, his hands on the side of my face. I can't believe I'm here, he said, it's like a movie, I'm in Venice with my American boyfriend. He laughed. My sister would be so jealous, she's always wanted an American boyfriend, and I got one first. And then he was off again, dragging me by the hand behind him. He did this repeatedly, pulling me into doorways and alleys to kiss me, always somewhere a little apart, though we were still noticed, people passing would stare at us or look decidedly away. One heavy old man scowled; a young couple laughed, which I minded more. R. seemed not to notice but I noticed, it was a weird reversal: he was the more open one here, and I was hyperaware, feeling the reflexes of fear though I wasn't afraid, I didn't think I was afraid.

Our only principle was to stay away from the crowds of other tourists who moved in migratory flocks, following the little pennant or flag the guides all held above their heads, tiny bright triangles on long stems. It meant not seeing the important things but I didn't care, their edges were rubbed smooth by too much looking, there was nothing for my attention to catch on in them. I liked the dark streets we turned into better, the narrow paths beside the canals. Even here there were restaurants and shops, nowhere on that island is indifferent to tourists, money from elsewhere is the blood of the place. We stopped on the footbridges and looked at the boats bundled up on either side of the canals, trussed in canvas, their wooden hulls deep shades of blue and green, their reflections darker shadows in the water. It wasn't late but it was getting dark already, at least where we were, the sun had abandoned the narrow alleys to an afternoon dusk. We had left the grand palazzos behind, the churches; where we were now there were plastic shopping bags filled with trash beside the doors. This is where the people live, R. said, a trick of English making him sound like a revolutionary. Then he laughed and pointed ahead, at a bright yellow bag with the letters BILLA on it, its red handles tied off in a bow. It was the store we went to all the time in Mladost, our neighborhood store. I knew it was a big chain, that you could find them everywhere in Europe, and still it felt like a bit of good fortune to stumble across it here.

R. pulled out his guidebook then, with its useless maps, he was afraid we would lose the light before we saw San Marco. He started walking more quickly while I hung back, protesting; it didn't matter, everything was beautiful, everything was something we hadn't seen before and wouldn't see again. But he insisted, increasingly frustrated as the map refused to align with the streets we walked; he was better with maps than I was but not by much. He got annoyed with me for walking too slowly and stopping too often, but I wanted to take photos of everything, the buildings, the canals, the laundry hung out in the damp air to dry, the mask shop with its window of carnival grotesques, backlit through the metal grill that had been pulled down. R. was growing frantic in a way I didn't understand. We would lose the light, he kept saying, as though he were an artist imagining a scene, I want to see it before we lose the light. So I put away my camera and walked more quickly, I kept my eyes on R. to avoid being distracted by anything else. And he did find it, finally, by luck mostly, I think, suddenly we turned and it opened out before us, after the cramped alleys the expanse of the square, beyond it the horizon of water. R turned to me, smiling, and surely it wasn't at that moment that the bells began to ring, it's a trick of memory to stage it that way, but it is how I remember it, the birds flying up, everyone turning to the Campanile, as we did, its top still bright as it caught the last of the sun. Merchants were walking through the crowds, hawking toys for children, spinning tops that burst into LED color as they helicoptered up. All that was new there was evanescent, the toys, the tourists, R. and I; all that was lasting was old, worn dull with looking though still I wondered to look at it, the centuries-old basilica, the bells, the gold lion on its pedestal, the sea that would swallow it; and everywhere also the books I had read, so that look, there, I could almost convince myself of it, Aschenbach stepping from uncertain water to stone.

I had a mind full of useless things, I had always thought, or useless since graduate school, where they had been a kind of currency, the old stories and stray facts that were all that remained of the years in which I had wanted to be a scholar. The books I had read! But in the churches of Venice I found a use for them, I could read the paintings for R., or not the paintings but the stories they told: Joseph of Arimathea, Mary and Martha, Sebastian nursing his arrows. In churches in Bulgaria the paintings were more or less mute to me, but here they made a story I could read, and as I told it to him I saw the pleasure R. took in it, the way he looked at me and then at the painting, I loved to see it. I have a crush on teacher, he said, whispering, and then he smiled his smile that meant happiness, his whole face beaming, turning toward the painting now though I knew the smile was for me. Later, back in Bologna, where we arrived on the last train after all the restaurants had closed—we ate shrink-wrapped sandwiches and chocolate, shared a little bottle of prosecco, all of it from a twenty-four-hour shop near the station—he asked me to tell him more, it didn't matter what. Tell me a story, he said, stretched out in bed as I lay beside him, running my hands across his chest and stomach, feeling his cock grow thick when I grabbed it, tell me another story.

I woke a few hours later too hot, stifling in the bedclothes. I switched on the lamp beside the bed. R. slept so deeply I never had to worry about waking him on the nights I couldn't sleep, when I spent hours beside him reading or writing. But this time he did wake, or half wake, as I lay with a book propped on my stomach; he turned toward me and linked his arm through mine before settling back into sleep, his face pressed against my shoulder. I looked at him for a long time before going back to my book. They could make a whole life, I thought, surprised to think it, these moments that filled me up with sweetness, that had changed the texture of existence for me. I had never thought anything like it before.

I wanted to make him laugh at first, I meant it almost as a joke. We needed to laugh: it had been hard to return to Sofia after our days in Italy, more snow had fallen but by the time we arrived the city had turned gray again, the holidays were over, the cars kicked black sludge from their tires. And now it was his last night in my apartment; in the morning he would gather his things and go back to Studenski grad, his friends would arrive in the afternoon. We would return to our uncertain arrangements, emails and dates that he might break at the last minute or without any notice at all, those were the conditions, they were non-negotiable. He hated it, he said, he didn't want to go back to hiding, and throughout the day his dread had increased and darkened, coloring everything, until by nighttime he could barely speak, he had folded in on himself as he did sometimes; it was hard for me to reach him, to have any effect on him at all. We watched a movie sitting side by side on the couch, I don't remember what it was, something light-hearted, romantic, though he hardly laughed. We never really watched movies together, it was always a pretense, we would kiss and touch each other and then forget the movie, but now it was all I could do to get him to kiss me back. Finally he let me pull him up from the couch, I folded the computer shut and pulled him half resisting into the bed-room. He resisted less there, standing beside the bed, he opened his mouth to me, he let me draw him close and press my pelvis against his. He raised his arms for me to pull his shirt up and off, and I felt the mood shifting already, it lightened as his passivity became a game almost, his passivity and my insistence as I struggled with the buckle of his belt, the button on his jeans; I could feel him almost smile as I kissed him, as he answered me back more in his kisses, his tongue pressing against mine. I pushed his jeans and underwear down, break-ing our kiss to kneel and hold them at his ankles while he pulled his legs free, kissing his cock, which wasn't hard yet, just once before I rose again. He moved to kiss me again but I pulled away, then shoved him back, not hard, he could have resisted but he didn't, he fell back-ward onto the bed. Onto our bed, I thought, which was what it had be-come in those days, not a lonely place but a place that belonged to both of us, a loving place; it was something I could think to myself but not say out loud. I took off my own clothes quickly and then launched my-self on top of him, which made him flinch and laugh, just once and as if against his will. I caught myself with my hands and when he reached out his own hands, bracing them against my chest, I grabbed them one by one at the wrist and pinned them above his head. He made a noise at this, a little growl, interested and interrogative, as I ground against him, his cock harder now, mine fully hard. I lowered my face but dodged his kiss again, teasing him, and instead kissed his collarbone, first one side and then the other, and then the inside of his arm, just below the elbow, where I knew he was ticklish, and then I licked the pit of his arm, slowly, because I loved the taste of him, first the right and then the left, and he growled again. He was harder now, he pressed his hips up against mine, but I lifted myself off him, beyond his reach. He moaned in frustration, he tried to pull his hands free but I held them firm; *Porta-te bem*, I said to him, and then I did kiss him, I put my tongue in his mouth and he sucked at it hard, tasting me but tasting himself, too, that was what he loved, the taste of himself in my mouth. I broke off the kiss and dipped my head to his chest, kissing first one nipple and then the other, which he didn't really like, he tolerated it, and then to go further I had to let go of his wrists, which didn't matter, he kept them obediently above his head. I kissed his ribs and then his stomach, always one side and then the other, keeping a symmetrical pattern, keeping it at his pelvis, too, pressing my lips to his right hip and his left but avoiding his cock, moving quickly. He made a noise of complaint but kept his arms where I had left them, still playing our game. He jerked a little when I kissed the inside of his thighs, he was sensitive there, too, but he didn't try to stop me, he was being good, he let me do what I wanted. But I wasn't sure what I wanted, or what I wanted had changed. I had thought I wanted to make him laugh, that after that I wanted sex, but I didn't want sex, I realized, or not only sex. I had let my knees drop off the end of the bed as I moved lower, soon I was kneeling on the floor at the foot of the bed. He was relaxed, more or less, his legs were outstretched, his feet splayed to either side, but his whole body tensed when he felt my lips on the sole of his foot, which he snatched away, I had to grab it and pull it back. He was ticklish there, too, he didn't like to be touched there. It had been a line drawn early on, when it became clear I was more adventurous in sex, had a wider palette of things that turned me on; I hope you're not into that, he had said, laughing, it's gross, I don't want you to be into that. It was a difference between us, that fewer things put me off, that I could be indifferent to something and still indulge it for my partner's sake. That was what he did now, I guess, when he let me pull his foot back to me, holding it in both hands as I kissed the sole again, the arch and then the pads at the base of his toes, each of them, and then the toes themselves. What are you doing, he said, and I couldn't answer, I wasn't sure what I was doing as I took the other foot in my hands and repeated what I had done with the first. I was moving slowly now, the tone had changed; I didn't want to make him laugh anymore, I didn't know what I wanted him to feel. I kissed his ankles next, at three points, moving from the outside in, from right to left on his right leg, from left to right on his left, which would remain my pattern. Skups, R. said, a question in the way he said it, his name for me or our name for each other. But I didn't answer, I made another band of these kisses, slightly higher than the first, and then another; I would cover him in kisses, that was what I wanted to do, and I would do it even though I could feel R.'s impatience, even as he said again Skups, and then, don't be cheesy, which was his warning against too much affection, against my surfeit of feeling. I ignored it, moving up another inch. It would take a long time, I realized; when you imagine something like that you don't think about how long it will take, how large a body is, how small a pair of lips. But I would do it, I decided, a kind of unhurriedness opened up in me, a weird wide patience I sank into. I strung kisses across him, his calves and knees, his thighs, the flesh firm in the center and giving at the sides. They were places I had never touched him before, some of them, and this gave gravity to the moment, more gravity; I whispered I love you as I kissed him, and then two kisses later I whispered it again, which became a new pattern, to whisper it again and again. His cock was soft when I reached it, as mine was, I hadn't noticed it until then. I almost passed over it, kissing his upper thigh on the right and then the left, but I didn't skip it, I kissed it, too, as I had kissed the rest of him, and said again the words that somehow became more real with repetition. Usually words wear out the more you use them, they become featureless, rote, and more than any others this is true of the words I repeated to R.; even in our relationship that was still so new they had lost most of their flavor. I remembered the fear I had felt the first time I spoke them to him, weeks before, when they had had all their force; I had been terrified, really, not so much that they wouldn't be answered (they weren't, it would be days before he repeated them) as that they would scare him away, that he would startle like the wild thing I sometimes felt he was. But now we said them often, when we left each other and were reunited (even if it was only a room we left, only minutes we were separated). But repeating the words now didn't dull them, it called them to attention somehow, to service, it restored them, and they became difficult to say again; I found myself almost unable to speak as I whispered into R.'s silence, kissing the soft flesh of his stomach, the firmer flesh over his ribs, his nipples and the patch of hair at the center of his chest, his collarbone, the taut skin at his windpipe. His arms were still raised but he had folded them at the elbow, crossing his forearms over his face. I kissed his armpits again, the exposed undersides of his arms, and then (I was kneeling now, my knees on either side of him) I took his arms in my hands and moved them away from his face. He hadn't uttered a sound in all that time, the fifteen or twenty minutes it had taken me to make my way up his body, not since the interrogative of my name, the admonition I ignored; there hadn't been any change in his breath, or none I had noticed, and so I was surprised to see the tears on his face, two lines that fell toward his ears, he hadn't wiped them away. He didn't try to hide them when I moved his arm, or tried only by turning his face slightly, as if he didn't want to meet my gaze (though his eyes were shut, there was no gaze to meet). I paused, wanting to speak, to ask him what they were for, his tears, but I knew what they were for, and so I hung over him a moment before I continued kissing him, the line of his jaw, his chin, his cheek and lips, which didn't answer mine, which suffered themselves to be kissed, his ears, the tracks of his tears, his eyes. It was a kind of blazon of him, of his body, I love you, I whispered again and again to him. And then, when I had laid the last line across his forehead—a garland, I thought, I had garlanded him—You are the most beautiful, I said to him, you are my beautiful boy, and he reached his arms up and pulled me down on top of him, clutching me. You are, he whispered to me, you are, you are.

They used some kind of accelerant, they must have, so that when the three children touched their torches to it (angling their bodies away, keeping the greatest distance between themselves and the fire) the flame leaped up the wood, from the base to the ridiculous crown the whole frog blazed up. And with it there was a huge explosion of sound, air horns and rattlers and little handheld bells children jingled, and above them all human voices, the crowd cheering both the fire and the new year, which had just struck. There were hundreds of people in the square, pressed tight near the wooden barricades that held them back from the fire but more spread out near the edges, where we were; there was space here for people to toast one another, with wine in plastic cups or little glass bottles like those R. had bought for us, prosecco with a twist-off cap. After we drank I leaned toward him and cupped his face in my palm and we kissed. I moved my mouth in a way he liked, kissing first his upper lip and then his lower before I drew away, hanging my arm around his shoulder. And then, as the statue burned—it was huge, it would take a long time to burn—there was another sound, a salute of drums and a burst of guitars, and then the far corner of the square lit up with floodlights, and there was a new shout from the crowd as it shifted toward the platform where the band had begun to play, four skinny boys bent over their instruments. There was a keyboard as well as the guitars and drums, it was an American sound, I thought, which contrasted with the stone buildings around us, with the pagan fire. R. and I didn't move as the crowd thinned further; we wouldn't stay, it was cold and the band wasn't very good, we would watch the fire a little longer and then go back to the hotel. R. pulled away from me suddenly and reached into his coat pocket, taking from it the packet of raisins he had bought earlier with the wine. I almost forgot, he said, it's almost too late. He handed me his bottle and took off one of his mittens so he could open the packet. Give me your hand, he said, so I put the bottles on the ground and held it out to him, taking my glove off as he asked, and he counted out twelve raisins, placing them in my palm in a single line from my wrist to the tip of my third finger, then counting another twelve for himself. It was the Portuguese tradition, he had told me, a raisin for each month of the year that had passed, a wish for each month of the year to come. He looked at me and smiled, Skups, he said, *feliz ano*, and we kissed again. He ate his all at once, tossing them in his mouth and putting his mitten back on before he leaned down for his bottle and turned to watch the fire. But I didn't watch the fire, I kept my eyes on him, though it was cold and I wanted to be back in the hotel with him, in the warmth of our bed. I took my time, I put the raisins in my mouth one by one, thinking a wish for each, though all my wishes were the same wish.

■

Child A

FROM *Sixfold Fiction*

MY MOTHER SLEPT WITH TED BUNDY. It was 1972 and she was a student at the University of Washington. She met him where she worked, in the library. He had tripped in the stacks (in the Feminist Literature section, she would say, as if that were significant) and she had picked up his books for him.

They went out to dinner, had a great time. He was charming, complimented her on the way she wore her hair. When she reached for the bread, he touched her hand. He slid his foot against hers under the table.

He walked her home, kissed her, gently. Brushed a strand of hair out of her face with his finger and kissed her again. She invited him in and when he left the next morning he promised he would call.

Whenever she told this story, as she did often throughout my childhood, she would shake her head, laugh a bit too loudly, and say, "Blown off by Ted Bundy! I'm the luckiest woman alive."

How exactly do we become our parents? We get our eyes, our bone structure, our curly hair, and our crooked toes from them, but that's not it. We get our mannerisms too. The way she turned her head chin first, the way he stood with one shoulder slightly lower, that nervous way she tapped her right foot in public. We catch ourselves in the mirror raising our eyebrows as he did, pulling on our earlobes like her.

* * *

Our father left when I was three. They had just bought a small house in southern Indiana to be near my aunt Debbie, but after only a few months he moved out, went to the other side of town, closer to the distillery where he worked. A year later he was killed in a late-night run-in with a train. I only have a few pictures of him, but it's clear I have his eyebrows. Stephie is fair-haired like Mom, but I have hair everywhere and it's dark and coarse. Before my first co-ed pool party, Mom made me put on her bikini, even though I was planning to wear my Ramones T-shirt the whole time, and while I stood with my arms and legs spread apart in the bathroom trying not to cry, she used her electric razor to shave off all hair that could be seen.

"Can't have my girl looking like a Yeti," she said.

Stephie watched from the doorway.

Aunt Debbie said my father was a dreamer. She said he fell in love with Mom fast and hard.

She told me Dad played the saxophone in a blues band in Seattle, that they had a record deal in the works when he met Mom. They met at a club and by the end of the night he was in love. Two weeks later they were married. That's how it was with her, Aunt Debbie said.

Mom never talked to us about him. I never even knew he was a musician.

"I don't think he meant to do it," she said as I stared at a picture of him with his band, his head tilted to the side as if he had heard something in the distance. Didn't mean to kill himself, or didn't mean to fall in love with Mom? I thought of asking. But I already knew that there was no difference.

We knew Mom was different for as long as we knew anything. It wasn't her moods or her disappearances or her drinking or that she broke things and laughed too loudly, or that she only ate bananas if they had been blended and refused to allow us to wear the color green, that sometimes she locked us out of the house—those things were just the Mom we knew, the Mom normal. Yes, she was different than our friends' moms, but she wasn't different than our mom.

On Wednesday nights we had picnics in her bedroom. She would pack a basket and lay out a blanket on the floor and we would eat tuna sandwiches with our pinkies in the air, laughing at Mom's British accent.

Once she sewed tags in all of our shirts, so no one but us could see them. They said, *I am here*. In every shirt. I still have one in the back of my sock drawer.

When one of us was sad, Mom would climb into bed with us and sing the song about the mama and baby fishes who lived in a meadow pool, the verses building to their tragic end: "Swim," said the mama fishie, "swim if you can," and they swam and they swam right over the dam!

She always started soft, and then each repetition was a little bit louder, and a little bit louder, until we were all bouncing on the bed, collapsing in a pile when the fish swam right over the edge.

All of that was normal, the loud and the soft and the crying and the laughing, and the knowing when it was time to call Aunt Debbie.

But it was the way other people, mostly our friends' parents, looked at us when we weren't with Mom that wasn't normal. It was the questions, whispered to us in the grocery store or outside of the school or at friends' houses:

"How you doing, honey?"

"Sweet things. You'll let me know if you need anything, right?"

"Be strong, baby."

A few years ago, Stephie called me crying late at night. She'd been drinking.

"It's a real song," she sobbed. "It's a real song, and there were three little fishies, and she didn't make it up." I didn't know why this was making her so upset.

"It's *all over* the dam," she almost yelled through the phone, "not *right over* the dam!"

Most of my friends know who they will become by looking at their parents. They see how their eyes will age, how they will lose an inch to bad posture, how they will settle into their bodies, become sturdier first, then frailer. They have models, maybe not perfect, but rough prototypes to help them plan or prepare or push against. I am now older than my parents ever were. I am the model, the one they could have become had life been very different.

On the night of my 44th birthday I got more drunk than I'd ever been before. I had made it. I had outlived them all. I had been counting down the years until I could believe I would no longer become them.

Once, when I was ten, Mom, Stephie, and I piled into the Renault, an old blue station wagon Mom had bought from Aunt Debbie's ex-husband, and went on a three-state hunt for Smartfood popcorn. That's the way she told it later, as if three states was a crazy feat even though we lived in the corner of Indiana, five minutes from Ohio and ten from Kentucky. We bought every bag we could find in every Kroger's or 7-Eleven until the whole cargo area was full of black and yellow bags, and Stephie was close to buried in the back seat, and it was after midnight when we crossed back into Indiana, over the bridge, singing, laughing, windows down so we could yell into the night. She told us it was good luck to yell into the night, to let it all out for the stars to hear.

"We're the luckiest girls in the world!" she screamed to the stars.

That same night Mom tried to kill herself for the first time. I heard a glass break and found her in the bathroom. I called 911 and the doctors told me I had saved her life. They told me if I had waited just five more minutes she would have died. Just five more minutes, they said, as if I were a hero.

I wrote a report on Ted Bundy my senior year in high school. He was born in a home for unwed mothers in Vermont, raised by family members in Philadelphia, and then moved with his mother to Washington. He dated, went to college, graduated with a degree in psychology. He drove a white VW Beetle. He was accepted at law school, just like I would be years later.

The older I get, the more I look like my mother. Except for the hair. I saw myself in a restaurant window a few weeks ago on my way to the firm, and for just a moment I thought she was there, inside, watching me walk by. We have the same confident posture, the same turn of the head, the same eyes, set deep and just a little too close together.

I remember getting ready for a middle school dance in Shelley's basement when Mom showed up. I heard her upstairs in the kitchen asking if she could see me. She ran down the stairs, Stephie in tow, dressed in jeans and a tank top, no bra, her hair beneath a blue bandana and her John Lennon glasses perched on her small nose (Stephie has her nose).

"Josie!" she said, pulling me away from my friends, who stood with make-up brushes in hand, half-dressed. "Be a doll and watch your sister, will you?" She put her hands on my shoulders and looked at me without seeing. Then she kissed me on the forehead (high like hers) and ran back up the stairs. Stephie was crying.

She was gone for ten days that time. Stephie and I took care of ourselves for the first few until we ran out of food.

Those eyes, so deep, just like the ones staring back out of the restaurant.

When I was seventeen and Stephie was fifteen, she screamed out the window of her room at Aunt Debbie's as I walked away, "At least I know who my father is!"

Stephie is 42. She lives in Cincinnati just across from an indoor farmers' market where she and her boyfriend go every weekend to buy fancy cheese. When she called me last month to tell me she was pregnant, she had been drinking.

"I can't have it," she said.

"Does Mike know?" I asked.

"No. I'll take care of it before he finds out."

"Are you sure?"

"Jesus Christ, Josie. Yeah, I'm sure. I'm not doing this."

"But maybe it would be okay," I said, taking a beer out of the refrigerator. "There's a chance, you know. There's a good chance you'll be okay." I opened the beer and sat back on the couch.

"Yeah, and there's a chance it skips a generation, in which case this baby is fucked. Both our parents, Josie. Both. Not very good odds. I'm saving everyone time and heartbreak." I pictured her baby, pictured holding it in my arms, watching it breathe, cupping its tiny skull.

We stayed on the phone for hours like we used to in our twenties. After a few beers her voice sounds so much like Mom's.

The train didn't even stop. It wasn't until kids found his body that they knew there had been an accident. For a while, I wondered how it was possible to hear a train coming and not be able to get out of the way.

One summer when Stephie and I were both back in town for a wedding, we decided to go down to the tracks where Dad was killed. It was late, and we brought a half-empty bottle of whiskey. We sat on the hill behind Benny's Gas & Grill, our shoes kicked off, Stephie leaning against me. The grass was damp from late-night dew, the air starting to cool. I could smell gasoline, the memory of fried food, and behind that the yeasty odor of the Seagram's distillery. We hadn't been back to town since Mom died, no reason to return. We talked about places we missed, people we hadn't seen since moving to Aunt Debbie's.

We heard the train before we felt it, and we felt it before we saw it.

"Let's see how close we can get," said Stephie, scrambling to her feet.

We ran down the hill until we were ten feet from the track. I grabbed Stephie to keep her from going any closer and we stood, arms locked together. The light cut through the night and the sound grew. We weren't at a crossing, not close enough to town and too late at night for warning horns or flashing lights. Just the sound of metal rushing toward us in the dark. Stephie took my hand, entwining our fingers like we did when we were kids, and we took a step closer.

"One more!" she yelled over the sound. It was physically difficult to step toward the tracks, as if magnetic fields had formed around our bodies, but we did it, together, dresses blowing, hair swirling. We tipped our heads back and howled into the sky as the train passed.

And then it was gone, and it was dark, and we stood clutching each other, aware of exactly how close we had been.

In my college biology class we learned about Punnet Squares, a model of inheritance. The professor talked about dominant and recessive genes and made us list some of the most commonly passed-down traits: eye color, hair color, cleft chin, widow's peak, freckles, free and attached earlobes. We looked at photos of mothers and fathers and children. We read about genetic mutations. We made charts to determine the likelihood that Child A would have blue eyes, red hair, a cleft chin.

I can't decide which is worse, to know or not to know. To hear the train coming or to stumble drunk into its path. Is it worse to kill yourself or to kill someone else? Is there a difference?

On January 24, 1989, when I was sixteen years old, Ted Bundy was executed, found guilty of killing somewhere between 30 and 100 women.

I am guilty of killing only one. I was sixteen, just home from school. The door was open, which was not so unusual. Stephie was at band practice and wouldn't be home for at least an hour, and I just assumed Mom had forgotten to close it. Inside, the house smelled of bananas and dish soap. I stood in the entry and breathed, shut the door behind me. Everything was so still.

She was on the kitchen floor. The ceiling fan was on and the afternoon sun coming through the windows cast shadows on the tiles as the fan circled. I watched the shadows cross over her legs, circle around, cross over again, like birds circling a field, slow and steady, determined. I remember thinking it was odd that a circular fan could cast shadows that were oblong. I remember thinking I should be able to figure out why, based on angles and diameter. I remember thinking I could use the angle of Mom's leg to calculate circumference.

I remember thinking I should call 911, that it wasn't too late to save her again.

But instead, I cleaned. For the next hour, I put away dishes, emptied the bananas out of the blender, washed it. I threw away the bottles, first the glass one, then the small orange plastic one. I started a load of laundry, picked up the living room, swept the hall. I returned to the kitchen and cleaned up the vomit, took the trash out the back door and into the garage.

I can remember all of that, every detail. I can see it all every time I close my eyes. I remember the door the dishes the bananas the laundry the blender the trash the fan the smell the door the bottles the garage the blender the dishes the garage.

"She's dead," I said when Stephie got home. I was sitting on the porch, my knees tucked under my chin.

Stephie dropped her flute case.

"Real?" she asked. I nodded. Her knees gave way and I caught her. Held her. Told her it was going to be okay.

There's a picture of Ted Bundy I keep in my desk drawer, beneath envelopes and old letters. It's a clipping I found going through Mom's things after she died. It's 1978 and he's standing outside a news conference in Tallahassee. He's in his prison jumpsuit, leaning casually, his right arm against the wall and his left disappearing behind his back. He's looking slightly away from the camera, his eyes focused and his lips set in what's not quite a smile. His chin is smooth. His hair dark, no freckles, attached earlobes, like mine.

Stephie looks so much like Mom that it hurts sometimes to see her. I watch the way she pretends to be brave, the way she smiles all the time, even when she's sad, the way she laughs too loudly and tells stories as if they were Homeric epics. I know she drinks too much, like me, loves too hard, sings when she shouldn't, still rolls down her windows and yells at the night.

"Am I like her?" she asked me a few weeks ago. We were sitting on her couch and she was curled into me like a child. She had just told me she was going to have the baby, that they had decided to roll the dice.

"Kind of," I said. "But just the good parts."

"Would you want it to be different?" she asked. "I mean, if you were Queen of the World, would you change any of it?"

"That's a stupid fucking question," I said, and we laughed.

I would change one thing, I think. I would go back to that day in the kitchen, and I would tell my sixteen-year-old self to give it one more try, that this time could be different, that this time we could find a way to make everything better. I would tell her to dial 911 one more time, to shake her mother's body and pound on her chest and ignore the tears and snot and vomit and breathe into her mouth until the paramedics arrive to pull her off, screaming. I would tell that scared, angry child that maybe this time it would be different, that people change, that there is no such thing as fate.

But if I couldn't have all that, if I couldn't change what happened, then I think I would go back to that kitchen anyway, and I would watch my sixteen-year-old self brush the hair out of her mother's eyes, so much like her own, and I would tell her I forgive her.

RENÉE BRANUM

■

As the Sparks Fly Upward

FROM *Alaska Quarterly Review*

For affliction does not come from the dust,
Nor does trouble spring from the ground;
Yet man is born into trouble,
As the sparks fly upward.

—JOB 5:6–7

WHEN THE SEIZURE HIT, it moved through him like a wind that only Randy could hear, or feel on his face. He stood up from the kitchen table, and seemed to cock his head, dog-like, before the trembling swept through his body.

I said his name as a question, just as I used to stand alone at the kitchen sink on late afternoons and rasp out, "Randy?" when I'd hear the front door open and shut real quick and tidy. "That you, Randy?" even though there was no one else it could possibly be.

But the seizure was too quick for me. It already stood between us, walling him off, and he crumpled to the floor before I could even set down the plate I was holding: pre-sliced cheese and summer sausage arranged in layers like scales on fish. It was the Fourth of July, and from somewhere up the road came a little gunpowder crackle, followed by a *pop,* and then the air went dead for a second before I snatched up the phone and called for an ambulance.

He'd pulled the paper red-white-and-blue tablecloth off when he fell, and it was over him like a cape, as if he was trying to hide himself. The saltshaker was halved along its seam, and the air-conditioner worried the spilt salt into miniature dunes.

He hit hard when he fell, and there was a little blood. I wrapped the phone cord tight around my thumb and watched his blood catch in the teeth of the tile where it had chipped away into the shape of a crescent moon — a blue Cheshire grin just where his head hit. I tried to keep the 911 operator on the line because suddenly I was afraid to be alone with him.

"It's a white house," I told her. "A ways back from the road."

"Have you checked his pulse?" she said.

And I hung up, unable to tell this stranger I couldn't remember how to touch my own son.

When I was brave enough, I touched his face, said his name again, got a cloth for his head and tucked it beneath like a little pillow. Still, I couldn't bring myself to check his pulse. My hand hovering above his wrist began to blur with shaking, and to calm myself I thought of winter, how I used to scoop snow straight from the windowsill into a bourbon glass. The barn cats slept in the warmest rooms, the radiator vibrating dust into the air, and the old farmhouse filled with flecks of blond pollen left over from summer. Randy'd come in with the mail, set it down on the piano. With snow in the folds of his clothes, he'd make me think of the shepherds on the night of Christ's birth, reeking of livestock but still holy, and with his very first beard on his chin. Not always happy back then, not every day, but peaceful at least.

Another firecracker, kids whooping, and the dog started to bark himself crazy. I could hear him pulling against his chain as if to strangle himself, and calling to him, "Shut *up*, Wyatt," felt ugly. My voice was too loud, my chest vibrating as if it couldn't hold the sound. The chain snapped, and the dog ran into the kitchen, still barking to wake the dead and trailing the severed chain. He sniffed at Randy and tasted the blood on his forehead with a long, primal tongue. I grabbed him by the collar. "Wyatt, you piece of shit!" My voice pitched to shatter. And in the distance, I heard the first notes of the siren. It swelled across the fields, and the space it filled felt measureless. The sound seemed to grow ceaselessly but never draw near, like some last days' trumpeting.

In the hospital, he was a stranger. His face drawn into itself, and his tongue slack in his mouth. I sat in the waiting room with my sister, and her voice lit, bird-like, upon phrases like "clogged arteries" and "blood vessel walls," thinking she was shedding some light. She'd been a nurse for thirty years before her retirement, but her knowledge of the body seemed fable-like now, some hand-me-down legend that was being retold and reshaped in the telling.

"Come on, Daisy. I want to hear it from the doctor, not you."

"You don't want to hear it from anyone," she said.

The waiting room had American flag buntings draped and gathered around the window frames, and I thought this was somehow wrong. This room shouldn't be touched by holidays, by color and celebration — just four beige walls and the blank-field watercolors with murky hay bales. Those little end tables with their pastel lampshades and marbled tissue box covers.

The doctor told us that Randy'd had a stroke, and Daisy leaned toward me to say in my ear, "Young people can have strokes too," as if she were a high school science teacher.

"Shut up, Daisy," I said, and she looked toward the doctor, embarrassed.

I thought Randy would look small in his bed, fragile, but instead he seemed massive. His stomach swelled beneath the sheet and his large shoulders stretched taut the fabric of his hospital gown. He drooled out of the corner of his mouth and the whole left side of his body sagged — his eyelid and the skin over his cheekbones, his lips loosening — as if the flesh were about to slide off. I tried to picture him as a little boy, but the images now had a limp to them, one side sagging.

All the photos of Randy as a kid are gone. Possibly there are a few packed into a shoebox in my ex-husband's trailer in Arizona. But all the rest burned up in that fire eight years ago that took everything. And all I wanted in that hospital room was some sort of proof. I wanted to hold a yearbook photo next to his wilting face, just to say, *Yes, you see? It's still him.* Because I couldn't quite believe it yet.

Then the sheet moved and Daisy touched his face.

Daisy drove me home, and her air-conditioning wasn't working, so we sweated our way down side streets with the windows rolled down. The dips in the road wavered behind bands of heat that swelled and crackled like radio waves made visible.

"Have you called Rick yet?" Her voice was shy, a worried whine beneath the air coming in through the open window.

"No, and I don't plan to," I said.

"I think he deserves to know that his son is," she paused, "not well."

"This has got nothing to do with him," I said, switching the radio on like a teenager to show that the conversation was over.

Daisy kept both her hands on the wheel, and I saw her forehead beading and streaming, but she didn't move to wipe the sweat away. She was always saying that bad things happen in twos and threes, that one catastrophe will link itself to another, and so maybe she was afraid that if she moved or blinked, she'd lose control of the car and we'd find ourselves in a ditch. I felt somehow grateful for her superstition; it was familiar.

"You okay?" I said to her.

"Am *I* okay? Are you—"

"I mean: to drive. Are you okay to drive?"

"I'm doing all right so far, right?"

"Your hands are shaking."

"They're not."

"Fine."

We passed the gravel drive that led out to the place the old farmhouse had stood before the fire, the house Daisy and I grew up in, and where Randy and I had lived for twenty-five years, and I felt the strangeness of not turning there. Something in me tensed, my foot automatically groping for the brake.

That old route home was still awake in me—each familiar movement that had always ended in homecoming. It felt like an equation, carefully worked out and memorized. The town drew back and the long spread of fields opened like an innocent unbuttoning, a mother undressing her child. Then every tree and window and mailbox, each curve and pothole, was before you, then behind you. The whole process of getting home was like breathing on an old map. And there was a sense of rightness in the final turning off of the engine, the key inside the lock, the dim interior with its smell that disappeared within seconds of returning because it had already faded back into something too close to be recognized.

I wanted Daisy to turn around. I wanted to drive out to that patch of burnt earth, as if I half expected the farmhouse might be where it always had been. That I could climb the porch steps, enter the hall, hear Randy open the refrigerator door and whistle while he reached for a jar of pickles. But the car brushed past, so easily—that bend straightening to show cows clustered in a cleft of raw earth.

"Almost home," Daisy said, as if to remind me.

As we passed the place where the house used to stand, we came to the elbow curve where the trees hide the road and the broken guard-rail juts down to meet the blacktop. It was there, on a night more than twenty summers distant, that a drunk couple overturned their car, and walked the quarter mile up the drive to my doorstep.

The man had hammered on my door with some metal bit of wreck-age—a scorched pipe he'd picked up as if to remind himself of his mission. It was three in the morning. His wife had walked through the laundry hanging on the line and it caught some of her blood, the faint pink shape of head and elbow never completely washing out of my bedsheets. And always after, I slept on the fading smear of her.

The woman sat down on the front step of our porch as if she belonged there. She lit a cigarette, leaning back on the heels of her hands, her shoulders naked and scratched. I watched her from between the gray slats of blinds.

At first, I wouldn't open the door. I talked to them from behind it, feeling childish. When I finally unlocked it, standing in the doorway in my new blue nightgown, I saw what kind of night it was—the moon crowing its light onto the fresh dew on the cornstalks, the air grown flimsy like moist silk. There were a few late fireflies, hovering in a daze as if sleepwalking among the corn. The dog whined, his yips growing more frequent and closer together as though something might break loose, explode in a final flurry of light falling like snow—the world ending with a hiss, like the pop of fireworks thinning into crackling streams. Everything seemed desperate, and utterly unaware of its desperation.

The drunk woman sitting on the top step was bleeding from her nose and had a gash along her forearm. She took the hem of my nightgown between two bloody fingers and started speaking non-sense, almost laughing.

"Look at you! Pretty. Right, John? Shit. Like a magazine cover . . . You should sell Mary Kay or something, sweetheart. I mean, I'd buy from you. I'd say, 'God. I wanna look like *her.*' Here's the thing though, honey: we need to use your telephone. We didn't scare you—just need to make one call. Then we'll get off your porch, right, John? Get back to where we belong. We won't hurt nothing, I swear. Okay, honey? Just wanna get outta here . . . She's so pretty, ain't she, John?"

The man was looking at the metal pipe guiltily as if finally under-standing that I could've mistaken it for a weapon. He let it fall into the garden. I could smell their wreckage a quarter mile distant; the stink of burning had followed them while they'd walked along the winding Highway 3. And I smelled the smoke from her cigarette as she sat with the hem of my nightgown in her hand, fingering it with absent reverence as if she thought I was Jesus Christ himself, with some healing power to offer.

I showed John where the phone was, brought the woman a cloth and a Ziploc full of ice, but she seemed to not recognize the items when I handed them to her, hefting the cold bag in her hand as if deciding what it was for. I dabbed at her nose with the cloth and she tipped her head back like a child, then lost interest, pushing my hand away so she could put her cigarette to her lips.

"Can I have one of those?" I asked her, and she made room for me on the top step while John's voice drifted out to us from the hall, making promises into the receiver: "No, man. If you come get us, I'll give you the record player. I swear to God."

She lit a cigarette for me, holding it in her mouth, drawing on the lit match in her hand, breathing a little puff as if testing for mistakes, then handing me the cig. The saliva on the tip tasted like whiskey and makeup and the salty iron of blood that ran down from her nose and, in this light, was the same color as her lipstick.

We smoked together, our breath hovering inside the night's shal-low haze. I wanted to love her without knowing her, this bleeding stranger. I wanted to brush her hair and bandage her arm and hold a bag full of ice over her face. I wanted to live in the halo her drunk innocence was casting around us, the cigarette never burning out, the ice never melting, the fireflies pausing in their drift, permanently lit.

My son came downstairs just then, awakened by John yelling into the phone and the dog barking his warning. And I realized with that familiar guilt that for a moment, I'd forgotten him.

"Go back to bed, little buddy. I'll be up in a minute. We'll sing a song, 'k?" I said distractedly.

"No," Randy said. "No! What's going on? Who is that? Who's that lady?"

I didn't know. I didn't know who she was. So I just told him John was in the hall using the phone because there'd been an accident.

Randy saw the blood on the woman's face and began to cry, his mouth opening to show the gaps his baby teeth had left, his gums freshly bare. I sat on the step watching the spaces in his mouth, frozen for an instant, as if I'd drifted into Randy's nightmare and become sluggish with horror. The stranger's face was turned toward him, blood crusting around her lips like she'd been eating something freshly killed. She sprang up, shedding a warm booze smell as she moved, arms outstretched toward Randy.

"Now, now, baby. Hush now, little one. There, there, nothing to cry about. Everyone is okay, baby. Your mama's okay. John's okay. Darlene's okay. And you're okay, little man. Aren't you?"

She swept toward him, and he backed away, watching the ring of blood around her mouth. I still couldn't move, something in me shrinking. Randy let out a scream, the little dark gaps showing horribly.

"Mama!"

Darlene stopped, stood still, put her arms down by her side. Randy crumpled, and finally I went to him, scooped him up with an "Oh for heaven's sakes," and carried him to the foot of the stairs, where I set him down again.

"You're a big boy now, kiddo. And there's nothing to be afraid of. Now get yourself back to bed."

He wiped his cheeks with the backs of his hands, still sniffling and looking up at my face, which must've seemed shadowy and distant above him. It was cruel, making him climb the dark stairs alone.

I think I'd felt a flicker of something reckless sharing the step, the cigarette, with that stranger, the night fragrant with newness. I'd wanted to keep ahold of it for as long as I could, knowing how brief and rare it was. I tried to grant myself some kind of forgiveness as I watched Randy make his way up the stairs in his little plaid bathrobe that made him look like a miniature old man.

After the stroke, whenever I thought of his wilted skin, and the blood in a circle around his head when he fell, it half-erased the memory of his little face turned up to mine, the toothless gaps showing as he cried. In the hospital, when he first came to, he tried to speak but it was all gibberish, his own private language. It terrified me.

"I feel like I don't know him anymore," I told my sister as we pulled into my driveway. I wished I hadn't said it. It was like it gave her power over me.

"Don't be a bitch," she said. "He's still your son."

When Randy came back home, he'd sit at the kitchen table, his wheelchair pulled up close so that the tabletop divided his stomach into two bulges, above and below. The Fourth of July centerpiece of fake red-white-and-blue carnations in a wicker basket sat there until the end of August, when the cleaning girl started coming. She came twice a week to clean and help me with Randy. The girl was young, and she didn't speak to Randy, although he tried to talk to her, his mouth full of tongue. I told her what to do if he had one of the seizures that were growing more common, and her lip curled in fear.

"I've never heard of a twenty-eight-year-old man having a stroke," she said to me.

"Well, it happens," I told her angrily.

I could tell she was frightened by this, thinking: *It could happen to me*, so I added, "It's pretty rare."

He liked for us to push him up to the piano. We'd each lift one of his hairy arms and let it rest on the keys. A dull twang, the piano gone out of tune. We'd leave his hands there until all the sound vibrated out of the strings, and Randy would grin on one side of his face, a silver thread of saliva dripping toward the yellowed keys. I asked the girl if she knew how to play.

"'Chopsticks,'" she said. "That's all I remember."

"Did you have lessons?" All of his sheet music was in a shoebox in my bedroom. I didn't like to see it laying around, all those notes crowded together like tiny one-legged insects, climbing and breeding, one on top of another — the ledger lines like cobwebs.

"Yeah," she said, popping her chewing gum. "I had lessons, like, ten years ago."

"Were they expensive?"

She shrugged. "I don't know. My parents paid for 'em."

A waste. An obvious waste. We wheeled Randy onto the front porch, and I'd sit with him, a magazine face-down across my knees and the radio arguing with itself in the kitchen.

A pair of Jehovah's Witnesses came by one evening as we sat together, a man and a woman, and I offered them each a cigarette. I liked watching them refuse, the man putting his hands up, palms out as if to say, "I don't want any trouble" and then watching me blow the smoke over the glinting fields as if I were performing a magic trick. They tried not to stare at Randy; he looked at them sideways and gurgled. The man put his foot up on the steps and asked me if I knew what the Bible *really* teaches.

"What are you two doing all the way out here?" I said, squinting toward the nearest town. They looked at each other as if they didn't know how to answer that question and then asked me if I was aware that we were living in "the last days." The sun was setting above the ridge where the fields dipped back into a copse of trees, and there was a late high haze where the air was still warm, making the shades of lavender waver and bleed. There were birds on the power lines bordering the road, and I watched them drift into flight vaguely, like balloons full of helium coming untied.

I thought of the straggling heat of this past summer when lightning would set the fields ablaze from time to time. Farmers would throw down their wet sacks and bend in half to beat the flames back into the soil. There were news stories on the radio of earthquakes breaking things apart and the hurricanes around the gulf, whole universes distant, difficult to fathom in the face of our own natural disasters. I remembered listening to a story about a tornado that killed eight little boys in a summer camp in Iowa, and of course it seemed believable that the world must be ending. It's been ending since it began. I thought of the warmth of Randy's blood as I sopped it up in a dish towel, on my hands and knees, and how brittle the smiling tiles seemed, and the shape the blood made when it was outside of him. *Ma'am, are you aware that we're living in the End Times?*

"Yes," I said to the Jehovah's Witnesses, taking a long drag that made me cough. "Yes, I believe that."

They seemed pleased, their nods tidy, their smiles neat and controlled. They were dressed to make people think of Sunday mornings, the man buttoned into a blue pin-stripe, his tie flecked with gray and red, and she wore a soft cotton dress; the flowers on the fabric seemed blurred, as if seen through rain, pink and gray like the flesh of a salmon. My eyes watched the smears of flowers, settled on her stomach, where I thought I saw the faintest swelling beneath. She might have followed my eyes, let her hand rest there and rubbed a little the way that children do when they've eaten something good.

They stood with the light of the field falling behind them, a brightness gathering in their hair. Her hair was the color of new pennies. I wondered if she would carry that color into old age. The young man felt in his back pocket, pulled out a pamphlet and handed it to me. It showed a mountain landscape, a young couple sitting in a field of poppies, while moose and wolves seemed to mingle peacefully behind them. In the foreground were baskets full of pumpkins, apples. A caption read: "All Suffering SOON TO END!"

Looking at the picture, I felt truly weary. I stared at it, felt the Witnesses waiting for something, for me to look up, to say, "Please, I want to hear more." Randy made a noise, something urgent in the back of his throat, a pleading. I held the pamphlet out so he could see it, so he could see what happiness looks like. His noise didn't stop, it grew, rising upward as if the image of the couple in their field had made him think of a song. The Witnesses seemed uncertain, waiting for Randy's song to end, trying to make their softly attentive faces register patience, compassion.

I started to talk over him, not waiting for the noise to subside, almost shouting to be heard, "There's a dragon at the end, am I right? And a lake of fire? I want to hear about the different-colored horses, the lamb with eyes beneath his wings. I'm listening."

The sweat of my hands had made the thin paper of the pamphlet moisten and bubble. I looked down at the moose touching noses with the wolf, the pumpkins glistening, and it all struck me as so absurd that I started to laugh a little, an eerie little chuckle. Randy echoed, the left side of his face trying to lift into laughter, but struggling against the dead muscles. The couple seemed to be waiting, politely, for us to stop, their hands clasped in front of them. I suddenly felt ashamed; here were these people trying to offer hope and we were laughing at it.

"Hush now," I snapped at Randy.

I met their eyes again, and everyone was solemn. Randy kept very still. They passed me a Bible and told me how the world at its ending is like a woman in labor, quoting scripture frantically, their faces lighting up as they spoke about the apocalypse. They wanted these things to hurry up and *happen*, for Christ to come in his armor, to "restore."

"But the point," the man said, "is that God offers second chances, up until the very end. But once Christ comes with his sword, there'll be no more second chances."

"You have to acknowledge your failings and seek forgiveness," the woman said, her hand hovering above my knee, not quite touching. She seemed to tremble, very gently. "Once you've repented, God wipes all the past wrongs away. They're forgotten."

"I don't think it works that way," I said. "You can't just say you're sorry and start over."

"That's how God's grace works," the man said. "Saying you're sorry is the first step toward salvation."

"Salvation." I wanted to hear the word in my own mouth. My eyes drifted back to the picture. It didn't look silly anymore. Their idea of paradise made sense — somewhere peaceful and full of good light, the wolves coming to lick your hands, apples falling softly from their branches.

They had more to say, but I told them I was tired.

"Maybe you can come back another time," I said. "And we can talk more then."

I don't know what made me say it. I liked their fresh and eager faces. I liked the smell coming from the woman's hair like clean earth.

They assured me they'd be back, and waved in a vague and friendly way as they walked to their car. I put the Bible in Randy's lap after they left, open to one of the scriptures we'd read with the Witnesses:

1 *Thessalonians 5:3 "For when they say 'Peace and safety!' then sudden destruction comes upon them, as labor pains upon a pregnant woman. And they shall not escape."*

When they were gone I felt sorry that they had given their names and that I had told them mine without saying, "This is Randy. This is my son."

When the cleaning girl came the following morning, she glanced at the pamphlet on the kitchen table, said nothing. She was tidying and seemed to hesitate, wondering if she should throw it away, or put it atop the microwave with the unopened bills.

"Just leave it," I said, watching her.

It took both of us to lift him each morning from his bed to his wheelchair. His weight was immense between us, an arm draped across each shoulder, and feeling his head roll toward mine. He often left a patch of moisture against my neck that I did not wipe away, let it dry in the dim air of the kitchen while I did dishes.

The cleaning girl was nineteen, wore her hair long as I had at that age, and once when we lowered Randy into his wheelchair, he batted at the swing of her braid, like a huge clumsy cat. She pulled back, fidgeting with the braid with one hand, looking at me as if expecting an apology.

"He likes your hair," I said lamely. This, I remembered, is how new mothers speak about their babies.

"He thinks you're pretty," I added because I knew it would make her uncomfortable, and I was angry just then, resented our need of her. I resented all the intimacy she shared with us—this stranger who buttoned his pajama top, wiped his chin. She was always wandering the perimeters of the room, forcing dust to take to the air with the vague brush of a cloth while I sponged his chest, the suds clinging to his thick hair. I would look over at her and she'd avert her eyes while I pulled down his pants to clean the limp curl of his penis.

It was always dark in the house, keeping the curtains drawn, the lamps switched off. After we moved him into the wheelchair, she would make coffee, and I would feed Randy applesauce, scrambled eggs, white bread dipped in smoke-colored gravy.

One morning, as we struggled with the sag of his body while neither acknowledged his reek, he grabbed at her long ponytail to steady himself, her head jerking back before he dropped into his chair.

"Why not just leave him in bed," she said. She rubbed at her scalp, huffing.

I wanted to slap her across the face, but said only, "Because that would be cruel," then realizing, as I said it, that many things are cruel and we do them anyway. *Because I still want to think of him as my son.* This is why we wheel him from room to room, tuck the bib deep in his collar when he sits at the table, dress him in his favorite T-shirts, images spread across his wide chest of running wolves and guitars and women astride motorcycles, hair blowing parallel with the road.

"Either wear your hair in a bun tomorrow," I said sharply, "or cut it off."

I remembered Randy's little baby fist caught in a tangle, reaching up from the changing table, and laughing in the midst of pain, as I shouted "Darn it, Randy!" while separating us.

The next day she wore a handkerchief that covered her whole head.

"You look older," I said.

"I *feel* older," she said, and that may've been the closest we got to friendship.

He was a good boy, always. Only once did he come home drunk, and once brought a girl over for dinner that I hated. She was permed and spray-tanned, kept referring to her and me as "us gals" whenever Randy left the room, and her perfume made it impossible to taste the roast I'd prepared. Afterward, when I told Randy openly I didn't like her, he grinned and said, "Just give it time." But I never saw her again after that.

His jobs would take him away from home for weeks, sometimes even months at a time—construction work or towboat crews, trucking. Often he'd come home with something for me, just a small thing—a silk scarf with all the faces of the presidents on it, a pair of beaded moccasins, salt 'n' pepper shakers showing a tiny Grand Can-yon meticulously painted. This went on until he wrecked his shoulder at a worksite three years ago, started collecting compensation. That was around the time the house burned.

Each time he came home, he looked a little more like his father—getting thicker around the waist, his chin loosely doubled, the layers of fat solidifying around him. A part of me was vaguely worried that, like his father, one time while driving his truck across country, he'd find some girl that he wouldn't want to leave again. But, I knew, this would be normal for a young man. I waited, and he always came back home. I think now that he worried about leaving me for good, because I'd already been left once before. We didn't speak about his father. That absence wasn't an absence anymore, he'd been gone so long. But we were united by that long-ago act of desertion, knitted closely through the years by circumstances neither of us had chosen, the shape of our family solidifying into mother and son and no one else.

When Randy was home, I would cook. In the high heat of summer, I would let him smoke indoors. We'd sit in the kitchen playing cards and drinking sweet tea, cutting thick slices of braunschweiger and smoked Swiss that we'd layer on fresh-baked bread with mustard from the Amish store. In the winter, we'd scoop snow from the windowsill and pour root beer over it, sometimes whiskey, crisp and sparkling brown. We played poker, rummy, blackjack, using candies in gold wrappers to place bets. Once he called us "two fatties," laying down his hand across the table, just a pair of threes, laughing: "Two fatties with bad luck." He played piano, and I never sang until he asked me to, finally sitting on the bench beside him, never for the space of more than two songs, and we'd sing something rich and mournful, the kind of melancholy that is all the sweeter because it's not your own. He had a good voice that continued to deepen each year. I still sounded like a shy schoolgirl when I sang, the voice small, as if pleading to go unnoticed.

I thought this was enough. That motherhood was no more than maintaining a home in the son's absence, setting food in front of him when he returned. This was all I offered. Randy never complained.

The only time he ever came home drunk was several months after he'd injured his shoulder. As soon as he won the court case, he bought himself a motorcycle, and that night he'd driven it into town to play pool with some of his old high school buddies. I heard the motorcycle in the drive throwing up gravel, the tires skidding, and the pinging of the rocks as they fell against the house. He came in, his body slack with alcohol, shoulders slid forward beneath his jacket, pulling off his helmet to show the fever in his cheeks, the hair clinging in stripes across his forehead.

"Come in here, Randy." He was a teenager again. No, that's not true. He'd always been such a good boy. He was his father, lazily defiant, filling the whole doorway as if blocking me in. It was late. I'd fallen asleep reading and now awake I felt ready to punish him, punish him for staying so long.

"Where have you been?"

"Playing pool." He leaned against the doorjamb, lazily clicking his lighter on and off, the flame brightening the sheen of sweat on his chin.

"Where?"

"At Gabby's. Why?" He took a step toward me, seemed to flounder, and steadied himself by putting his hand on an end table. He tried to cover up his stumbling by picking up the little bronze clock that sat there, examining it, and saying casually, "It's not even that late."

"You reek of booze, Randy. I can smell you from here. Is this how it's gonna be from now on?"

"How what's gonna be?"

I remember searching his face for something and losing track of what it was. He was, I realized, always new each time, each time he came through the door. A different son. Holding him in my arms as a baby, pulling back the blanket to look at his face and not finding any resemblance to myself, to his father. He was something separate.

"You're drunk."

"So what? You're acting like I'm twelve years old or something."

I stood up, a paperback sliding from my lap. The thud of it fell between us. I moved toward him.

"I'm ashamed of you," I said. Hearing the word neat and flat on the tongue like a wafer, looking him in the face. This was the first time I'd said it, but I'd never said I was proud of him either. I don't know if anyone ever said that to him.

He stood there, swaying slightly, his face opening a little to my words, then closing up again, narrowing. His cheeks went rosy, polished with sweat. He swallowed, and I wondered if he was keeping himself from vomiting, trying to maintain the balance of his insides.

I was thinking of his motorcycle in the drive, thinking about how easy it would have been to drift from the road, smack the guardrail, the metal ripping the denim of his jeans as if it were butter, and the flesh parting beneath. His body taking to the air. I thought of the drunk couple that night so many years ago. I felt their recklessness standing before me again. I felt jealous and slighted. I wanted to reach up, cup the flesh of his face between my palms, press gently then harder, forming it into something else. I wanted to touch him. How long had it been? He wasn't speaking, or seeking any escape from me, and so I kept going.

"Nothing to say for yourself. Not a word, huh? Coming home drunk to look me in the face and drool like an idiot. I can't even look at you. You're turning into your father."

I had never said any of this before to Randy. I turned away from him in shame. He reached for me, clumsily grabbed the fabric of my favorite blue nightgown, jerked me back around to face him. His breath was a raw, grainy heat—sheaves of wheat being incinerated. He held the fattest part of my arm firmly, and I think there were bruises afterward, the size and color of dimes where his fingers gripped.

"Because I had a few drinks, suddenly I'm Dad? Why don't you tell me what's really bothering you, huh? What are you afraid of? That I'm gonna leave you here and you'll have nobody but Aunt Daisy bringing over table scraps every few weeks? There is no contract that says I have to come back. There is *nothing* keeping me here."

He was still holding the clock in his other hand and he suddenly let go of me, and pitched the clock through the front window. The pane shattered inward, the pieces skittering toward us over the floorboards. Bits of glass still clung to the frame like jagged teeth, the smaller crunch as they loosened and fell continued while Randy spoke:

"I hate it here," he said, a note of pleading behind the rage. "I hate this fucking house. I always have."

"Then why do you keep coming back?" I said, a little fleck of my spittle landing on his upper lip.

He looked at his empty hand, the place where the clock had been a moment before. Then his arm dropped like dead weight.

"Someone has to," he said, and I blinked at him blankly.

"Because if I didn't, you'd have no one," he barked, his face close to mine. There was a long pause as we both just stood there, the glass crunching faintly as he shifted his weight. Then very quietly, his voice light and vibrating, he said, "Because you're my mother."

In early September, I woke one morning to the sound of hands cricketing on the piano keys, an empty clacking where most of the strings had rotted away, a sound like toothless gums chewing. We'd moved the piano out onto the front porch to make more room in the living room for Randy's hospital bed. And afterward, the rain would get in, the sound growing damp, eerie, like a piece of underwater wreckage dredged up. And the spiders built their nests, so that bumping against the keys would send swarms of tiny bodies scurrying, like the crowded notes on Randy's sheet music come to life.

We let these things go to waste, with so much still left over.

But sometimes late at night, the trio of high school kids who'd follow the railroad tracks with their paper bags shaped like whiskey bottles would climb up on my porch, drawn from the road by the bulk of the piano. They'd try to push a tune from the keys — a series of chords, sweetly mildewed with notes missing, probably "Chopsticks." I'd hear them from my bed. I think they thought the house was abandoned, and I never did anything to dispel this myth. It certainly looked empty now, even up close, the rickety sinking of the roof above the porch, and the peeling paint that curled like dead leaves along the soggy, driftwood-colored siding.

On that September morning, I woke to the sound of those damn kids trying to coax "Heart and Soul" from the rotting keys, and I was suddenly angry, throwing the covers off, and almost wrenching the screen door from its frame. I wanted them to know that we're here, that they can't just crawl up onto my porch with their caterwauling and pretend that Randy and I don't exist. *We're still here, goddammit.* But standing in the doorway watching the gravel drive spit curls of dust toward the first lilac sprigs of dawn, I saw that no one was there. I watched something dark scurry beneath the porch—a rat maybe, who'd been nibbling at the moist wood of the stripped-bare piano keys. The rat made me even more angry than the thought of the teenagers had, and I turned back into the house, feeling alone.

The morning was still dark along the edges, and the living room was gray with a spreading half-light, milky between the blinds. I stood, and there was a silence so heavy that I snapped my fingers beside my ears, just to hear a noise. It was the sort of quiet that follows the whir of the air conditioner after it goes off, or a refrigerator's hum—sounds that, through routine, get disguised as silence. I stood awhile, finally understanding what the absence meant, the sound that was missing. I couldn't hear Randy's breathing.

I crossed the living room toward him, feeling a fear finally shift that had been there a long time, unnoticed, stranded in my chest like some long-dead tree tipping over. I stood over Randy, and looking down I saw that his eyes were open, dust or sleep in his lashes. He lay on his back staring up at the ceiling, and my pulse quickened in my ears, but I said nothing. I put my hand on his chest and I thought I felt him shiver, but he still didn't blink. And I waited, and his face sharpened as my eyes adjusted to the faint light, and I prayed only that his eyelids would flutter downward and open again. I took a breath, as if to show him how.

I just let my hand rest there, on the coolness of his pajama shirt, as if I were trying to impart power or blessing, but it was only because I was afraid to move. I saw that the buttons were done all the way up to his chin, and it seemed so unnatural, obvious that he hadn't dressed himself. He never wore pajamas before his stroke, and this was the sort of childish touch that we, his caregivers, had added because it seemed necessary. A man no longer had the freedom to sleep naked when he couldn't dress himself.

My hand moved, shaking, to unfasten that top button—the fabric pulling away to show a ringlet of chest hair at the hollow of his throat. And then my hand slid across to the side of his neck where his pulse should be, and the silence of his flesh seemed to add to his massive weight, his body pressing upward beneath the sheet. And I felt the gathering weight of all those past silences when we seemed to move through and around one another without speaking—those times before his accident when our paths might cross walking from one end of the house to the other.

I thought of him as a child, lying on his stomach beneath the kitchen table with an ink pen. And even before he'd learned how to read or write, he'd spend hours filling blank notebooks with page after page of long squiggly lines, holding the pen awkwardly. And when I asked him what he was writing he said, "Songs," and that was all. I asked him to sing me one, but he just shook his little head and passed me the notebook. My eyes followed the squiggles, and I wanted to find something there, but there was nothing.

I stood over him for a long time, and finally I moved a hand to brush his hair back from his forehead. "Randy," I said, as if trying gently to wake him. I shook him, but his eyes stayed empty. "Randy?" but the name didn't seem to fit him anymore.

Up to that day, Randy had layers of seizures. They began to come in pairs. His eyes grew glassy and vacant, and he didn't respond when we spoke to him or placed his hands on the little Casio keyboard Daisy had bought him to replace the moldy piano. What had he ever really wanted? I was ashamed that I hadn't known him well enough to answer that. But I kept trying to offer things he used to love—Butterfingers and Heath bars from the gas station, a baseball cap with an image of Big Foot proudly striding, a Tanya Tucker album sleeve with lyrics printed that his eyes can no longer make out: "Two Sparrows in a Hurricane." As if these things could save him.

The doctor had said that we should begin to prepare ourselves. And I thought about what that meant—it meant I should gather my strength against his absence. And so I began to imagine the spaces he used to fill, empty again—like when he used to be gone for months at a time, working on the river or a construction site. I told Daisy that I didn't want him buried in a graveyard among strangers. So Daisy's husband, Tom, got a permit from the county courthouse to bury him on the land behind the house, where a narrow pasture cuts back, and where Randy quietly dug a grave when the last dog passed away. Daisy and her husband came to stay with me the night before the burial. *For company*, they said.

On the morning that we buried him, the insects were full of voice, the orange lilies raging like the fire that took the house, burning away first the kitchen then bringing down the balcony. We buried him wrapped in a blue blanket to guard against the damp. Inside the stark ash-blonde coffin that my brother-in-law had built, he looked almost newborn—a pastel and watery-pale Christ child in the manger with baby-blue blanket tucked in meticulously around the soft swellings of his body. It was Daisy who pulled back the cloth to look at his face one last time.

My brother-in-law was quick with the spade, the earth already coming down as soon as the crude coffin touched the raw soil. He'd rolled his sleeves to the elbow, and his soft brown hair darkened with sweat as we watched him work in silence. He'd been awake before any of us, making the hole. That day I'd been pulled rough from sleep—no air, as if I'd been kicked in the stomach. I was crying, knowing Daisy and her husband were both awake to hear me. She was already pulling up my weeds, and sweeping the front porch, and carrying the coffeepot up and down the hallway. I'd heard the sound her bathrobe made when she shrugged it on. No grief was ever kept a secret in our house—never shared, only ignored. It had always been this way.

Standing over his body swaddled in blue, I could hear a train keening, spread thin between the hills, the air suddenly thick with the sound as with birdsong, blackbirds and water thrushes. The train whistle grew in my chest, heavy and rattling, a wail that I couldn't give voice to. I merely stood remote, with my hands clasped behind my back, feeling that train go through me.

The sun was this wash of warmth on my neck, my pores opening to it. I would not look up from the hole where he was, but neither was I looking into it; my eyes lingering at the rim.

I heard the sound of tires on the gravel, coming up the long drive, and Daisy and Tom were looking in that direction, shading their eyes, Daisy moving to stand beside me and say in a low tone, "Did you invite anyone else?"

There was a moment when I thought that somehow, impossibly, it was Randy's father—that, even though I hadn't spoken to him in eleven years, even though there were thousands of miles between us, he knew, had sensed, when his firstborn son was gone; knew and made the journey. But this, of course, was foolishness.

The car pulled up to the house, and I watched as two figures got out—a man and a woman. They were shading their eyes too, and not coming any nearer, as if they could see the grief coming off of us like waves of heat above the blacktop. We, all of us, just stood like that, staring back and forth beneath the little visors we made with the palms of our hands, a small triangle of shadow erasing our eyes. I recognized them, finally, as the Jehovah's Witnesses that had come a couple of weeks ago to tell us about the End.

Daisy said, "Do you know them?"

I told her who they were, and Tom jogged over to them. His mouth moved as he spoke calmly and seriously, all the worry of death something to be dealt with patiently, with a measured gesture that cleared the strangeness of it from the air. The dirt had crusted over the knees of his nice trousers, and I knew Daisy would brush them afterward, fold them neatly over a hanger before driving them to the dry cleaner's, who would have no idea of the source of the stain, of the grave dug in Sunday clothes.

I watched Tom explaining that my son had died. The woman's hand moved from her forehead to cover her mouth in that classic pose of shock and horror. She shook her head, the copper hair falling forward. She looked like a high school drama teacher trying to demonstrate for her class "receiving bad news." I allowed myself to hate her for a second, as if there was only so much grief to go round, and this unexpected stranger was sopping it up, taking a little for herself. The man was looking at his feet, and he looked very young from that distance. He couldn't be much older than Randy.

They started to get back into their car, and I broke from Daisy, her grip lingering on my arm as if pleading with me.

"Wait," I said, and they hovered, half in and half out of their car.

"I read the pamphlet," I told them. "The one about suffering."

They stood, shielded from me by the open car doors.

"We're very sorry for your loss," the woman said, her voice steady and soft.

"His name was Randy," I said. "He was a good boy."

I waited for them to speak, and the silence seemed long.

"We'll pray for Randy," the man said, finally. And something in me came loose then, crowding forward, breathing itself awake—a defeat so whole it felt like it belonged to more than one life. And it did: mine and his.

"I don't want you to pray for him," I said, moving a step closer. "Your prayers don't mean anything to me. I just want you to look around you. What do you think is happening here?"

Daisy came up beside me, laid a hand on my arm. I pulled away. She moved closer, again touched my elbow. I felt I could never escape her touch. I looked at her. "Don't touch me," I said, and her hand dropped.

"You were right," I said to the Witnesses. "The end came and the second chances are over. Just like you said. That's what's happening." My mouth went dry and I thought I'd been struck blind, the light too strong, blurring and swallowing sight.

"And I knew, I *knew* it was coming and still I didn't tell him."

They were silent. I couldn't see them. I wanted them to understand, and so I tried again.

"I never told him. That I was proud . . ."

It felt like I was choking. They looked at one another, as if each sought permission to speak from the other. Finally the man said, "God forgives. He only wants you to ask."

"I don't want God's forgiveness!" I shrieked. "I want my son's."

I knelt, the gravel sinking into the flesh of my knees. Daisy knelt with me. I was whimpering. The woman was saying that God's thoughts were not our thoughts, that we can't comprehend His ways, but Daisy interrupted her to say, "You need to leave."

Before the car doors shut almost in unison, I could hear Tom saying in polite tones, "She's very upset right now. Maybe it's best if you left." Then something quiet from them. ". . . We'll be praying . . ."

I heard the sound of the gravel moving. They were trying hard not to drive away too quickly, and I thought of Randy coming home on his motorcycle, thought of all I couldn't take back, and I hid my face in my sister's body while Tom went back to the spade, and the dirt moved, the earth closing up again with a grainy, breathless sound.

* * *

I'd forgotten to tell the cleaning girl not to come anymore, so she showed up one final time, standing in the doorway, shifting her weight back and forth. I told her that Randy was gone. She chewed her gum and said she was very sorry. She asked if I needed anything, and I briefly imagined sitting down vacantly at the kitchen table while she shuffled over the tiles, making coffee, peripheral to my grief.

But in the end, I didn't invite her inside. I said only, "No, I'm all right. You go on home." And she left.

After the cleaning girl didn't come anymore, the afternoons were filled with this constant hunger, electric in the stomach, and elsewhere—an itch for motion in the soles of the feet, a hand closing into a fist then opening again. I thought of hair itching for the scissors, growing too long for itself, pleading to be cut free. Before the mirror, I avoided my eyes, twisted gray strands into something small, forgettable at the nape of the neck. We are too much for ourselves—the body spreading out, seeking its end, the mind retreating until we remember that prick of fear that began with darkness. Once sight was introduced at our beginning, darkness was fearful ever after.

I thought of the crust forming at the corners of his eyes that I would wipe away, wipe each morning with the corner of a damp cloth. As a child he had ear infections, the white crust climbing upward toward the hairline, a lichen tightening the scalp. He would scratch and sob as I pulled his hand down, flakes scattering beneath his nails, and spreading a cream that smelled of nothing. The crust itself held all the smells of a child's body—that dampish scent of the skin that forms over a cup of warm milk. In the mornings, he left bits of himself on his pillow, the air full of him, mingling with dust motes and cat hair in the light falling sideways through the upstairs windows.

I wish we had *talked* to one another. It was as if I'd become so used to his infant silence that I never sought to replace it, not in all our years of proximity. I remember being so aware of his breathing, always loud even before the stroke, the air coming up from the lungs audible as he sat alone on the love seat, the pages of a motorcycle magazine rustling beneath his fingers. There used to be a long, steady warmth that came from the part of the room where he was. It made me think of walking into a stable, and you can sense the horses in their stalls, the swish of long hairs shifting, the sound of their breath moving through the velvet of their nostrils—their nickering so gentle and knowing. This is what Randy was for me—this presence that drifted in and out of the room, soft and animal. And just as the horses are a part of the stable itself, defining the space with the gentlest movement, so I realize, I thought of Randy's body as a part of the house.

He was like the floors responding to my step, my voice would reach for him, "I've just opened a tin of peaches," and he'd move to stand in the doorway, the creak of him coming back.

"I know. I heard the can opener."

"Like a cat," I'd say, taking down the little glass dish that was reserved only for things of that color: halved peaches, mandarin oranges in syrup thick as motor oil, apricot preserves, pickled carrots, persimmons brought new from the tree, the skin puckering back from the flesh. This glint of dying sunlight, edible, through crystal, represented an occasion, a moment to be shared, just as cake and candles represent a birthday. And I knew Randy was grateful for these moments without him saying so. I knew he respected that the crystal dish had its use. But after the farmhouse burned, things no longer had designated uses. There was a foreignness to every item, the new house so vacant that at first I imagined I could always see my breath, a little cold cloud, even in summer, and the hills rolling back from the fields like frozen waves.

I never felt at home again after the house burned; I never felt that warmth in the chest as you draw back into the space that belongs to you. And Randy's presence in the rooms had a different feeling—something heavy, the sounds making me stiffen and tense. He smelled like a stranger, a new cologne, something coming from beneath his arms, sour and dense. I didn't open tins of peaches for him anymore.

I never really knew him—not as a child in his little bathrobe, not as a teen full of some sweet residue of heartbreak that I saw bubbling faintly, amber-colored, then hardening like sweetgum. Then, not as an adult either, when he found his silence. It followed him wherever he went, retreating only when the piano opened up to him, retold its cravings and worries beneath the soft meat of his fingers. Then finally, the silence overtook him completely, so full and fierce that it swallowed him whole until he was lost inside it—big and slow and floundering, his hands limp on the keys but maybe still hearing some tiny voice within that said, "God gives grace to the humble."

He extended that humble grace to me, and I failed to recognize it. I failed a thousand times. The world assumes that every woman is somehow equipped to be a mother. That God has given each a love for the spoiled-milk smell of her child's skin. But if this is true, why did my hands pull back from the flakes of skin, his hands reaching for me with the crust beneath his fingernails. Why did I never ask, "Who and what do you want to be, Randy?"

He wanted to play piano. He wanted to ride motorcycles. He wanted to grow old, I think. And in the end, he had none of these.

In recent dreams, Randy makes a beautiful ghost. Last night I saw him crying on the window seat with his face glossy like an oil painting. The air around him was ripening into a glow, bluish and slick like a kerosene lantern, and fragrant, his teenage smell of orange rind and cheap tobacco. "Sweetheart," I said, my hand in his hair. "Sweetheart."

I awoke hungry, my knuckles aching. I thought I heard the piano; sometimes those drunk kids still come up on the porch to play it. But it was just the wind chimes outside the kitchen window, creaking and clanking with rust starting inside the long metal pipes.

And when my dream of Randy had snuffed itself out, with my hand separating the strands of his hair, I lay in bed listening to a sudden screaming chorus of frantic adults combing the fields behind the house for a lost little girl. She'd probably wandered off in her sleep again; it was not the first time this had happened, with the parents and neighbors shouting shrill, one after the other, to fill in the gaps between the half-second-long silences. They sounded like coyotes, the pitch building as the little girl's name was repeated in a chaotic rhythm, desperate and pleading. The arcs of flashlights moved through the curving mist and the beams drew insects but no lost children. I fell asleep again to their frenzied cries, and in my mind saw the tiny body of a drowned child just before dropping off to sleep again. Tomorrow, I thought, I'll ask Daisy if they found her.

But I forgot to ask when she came in the morning to bring me fresh bread and preserves, tomatoes from her garden and a bag of bird-seed.

When she came, I was sitting on the porch swing smoking a ciga-rette that tasted like the fermenting air—a flavor of rust and rotting wood and faintly of the gunpowder of detonated firecrackers. I could hear them popping, tiny crisp pavement explosions a half-mile off, almost like the distant cracking of knuckles.

"What's that noise?" Daisy asked, halfway up the steps, the plastic bag she carried shushing against her thigh.

"Firecrackers," I said. "Some kids been setting 'em off all morn-ing."

"What do you think they're celebrating?"

"Probably nothing. Just being kids."

She went into the house, and I didn't follow her.

I sat and smoked, listening and thinking of the time Randy's fa-ther brought home a box of fireworks he'd got at the state line, driv-ing across the river into Missouri where it's legal to buy and sell them. The evening was dewy and fragile, and he set them in a row in the backyard beneath the trees. He was drunk and bent in half, his arms swinging as he lit them, and they exploded in arching lines, foun-tains of sparks that settled in the upper branches of the trees and illu-minated them, their leaves like the tissue of paper lanterns, the skel-etal limbs drenched in lightning. There were blue and green peonies and spiraling horsetails and white rings and long-burning yellow dia-dems, all ripping the trees to shreds with the glowing sparks and tat-tered leaves settling on the roof and littering the backyard. Randy hid his face in my clothes, and the smoke was drifting, a thin gray veil over the ragged trees, a haze that painted everything out-of-focus. I don't remember being angry. But I watched Randy's father through the murk, bent in half, laughing wildly, a pungent, hysterical cackle like the earsplitting shriek of the fireworks. The house didn't burn that night, and it was then that I stopped believing the house *could* burn; we'd sidestepped disaster so deftly. But I was wrong.

I could hear Daisy clattering around inside the kitchen, the gentle music of her swearing to herself when she dropped a jar of preserves on the floor. It had rained the night before, and the roads still shimmered, glossed with damp leaves. I sat very still, breathing smoke, and the screen door creaked. Daisy came out to say, "Don't you light another one of those. Breakfast is almost ready."

"Daisy," I said then, a sudden need welling like dew. "Would you let me borrow your car?"

"What for? Did I forget to bring something?"

"No, I just wanna go for a drive."

She looked at her hands, worrying with her nail at a patch of dry skin. "Where you driving to?"

"Nowhere. I just think it'd be kinda nice."

"You're driving out to see the house, aren't you?"

"I didn't really have a destination in mind."

"But there's nothing out there, Lydie. Nothing to see."

Mosquitoes bred in potholes as flecks of light scattered over the driveway like bread crumbs. I watched the flecks widen and shift on the backs of frayed leaves.

"There could be something," I said, shrugging.

That afternoon, I took to the road shyly, as if afraid it had forgotten me. My hands on the wheel were weak and shivery. I followed the road that runs parallel to the railroad tracks where the bracken has thickened over time, the berries nodding, secretive. Deer hovered among the ferns where the underbrush reeked of lake water and moss and sunlight going stale on the undersides of leaves.

I drove to the place where the house burned down. Turning up the drive where, on that day, Randy and I stood for hours, drenched with sweat and dizzy with a gray, throbbing smoke-blindness. The house fell while roosters crowed. We watched the paint on the mailbox peeling back in filthy, bubbling curls while firemen tried to drown the flames. The dog barked and strained against the length of rope that Randy held, his yips crisp and measured as the ticking of a clock. And with my hand on Randy's shoulder (his shoulder was always within reach no matter how tall he grew), I waited in my faded blue nightgown for the final sound, the beams and walls falling charred and silent. At the time, I kept trying to go back, turn my mind to some memory of the fields naked without the flames, of Randy's chubby face looking over the back of the sofa. But the fire burned an afterimage that swallowed sight, and something rose with the ash, shuttered in all that heat and punctuated breathing—the way a house breathes when it is being erased.

Coming over the hill in Daisy's car, I could see the black patch with grass growing up through the charred timbers—weeds in a rim around the rot where wood lice swarmed and quarried. The trees behind and the distant hills seemed beaten back, and the air was stagnant as it is in marshes and graveyards. There were long, gaunt tracks in the earth where moles had burrowed.

I remember Randy's father once coming from the fields with a tiny dead mole in his hand. He held it out for Randy to touch. The mole with its pink claws folded was almost grinning, its nose like an eye that would not stay closed. I thought of the darkness of its sunken furrows and upward curving tunnels beneath us, its small unseeing face, its moist, velvet blindness made permanent. Randy felt its little silken body with a finger—touching death on the cheek, and I think Randy was crying. He was very young.

In the clearing, the moles still kept away from the dead patch where the house stood, and I too kept my distance, watching the shapes the blackened wreckage made against the landscape. I realized I was trembling. I couldn't remember if I'd trembled on the day of the fire, like Moses before the burning bush, when God spoke with a voice like thundering water: "Draw not nigh hither: put off thy shoes from off thy feet, for the place whereon thou standest is holy ground."

I wasn't wearing any shoes that morning. I was barefoot in my nightgown—my feet raw against the gravel of the drive. It had been a savage, voiceless moment—waking to fire from deep sleep, to find it nuzzling and twining up the wallpaper. Everything receded away, foreign, unknowable. I saw the clock by my bedside and the remnants of a half-eaten apple on my dresser and I didn't know where I was. Randy was calling my name from down the hall. He was not calling, "Mother!" He was calling my *name*. Smoke filled my mouth like a dry cloth, and I pulled down the mirror on the north wall as I felt for the door.

The house seemed weightless as it burnt, a fluttering eyelid. I was hungry as I watched the still-lit cinders, thinking of the pit of my stomach as a blank face, blank canvas—the sheets of laundry on the line, singed by the hot breath the house exhaled when it collapsed, and smeared with the rough hands of the smoke. I felt like a tunnel, a chimney for the billowing heat and smoke. Randy reached for my hand but it was limp in his grasp.

I asked one of the firemen if he could tell me how it had started.

"It looks like it started in the kitchen. Stove probably. You must've left a burner on before you went to bed."

And that's all he said about it, swishing water in his mouth and spitting it between his boots. Something in me shifted when he moved back toward the truck, and I turned to Randy, my eyes tired from watching the flames.

"What do you know about this?" My voice becoming a hiss.

"I don't know. You make tea almost every night. Maybe you forgot to switch the stove off. It happens all the time."

His voice was toneless and empty, and there was a mildness in his face, as if he were watching the sun come up rather than our home being destroyed.

"I know you know how it started," I said. I was watching the side of his face while his eyes never left the flames.

"It was an accident," he said, the flesh of his neck quivering as he spoke.

"No. There are no accidents."

He turned toward me. "That sounds like an accusation, Mother," he said. I noticed a small, faint scar at the corner of his mouth and couldn't remember how he got it.

"Call it what you want, Randall. But right now I want *you* to tell *me* why this happened."

"How can I know that, Mother? I am not God."

"Randy, do you think this is some sort of justice? Are you trying to punish me for something?"

"What are you saying? Do you think I did this? On purpose? You think I burnt our house down?"

"I don't know. I don't know you anymore."

"That is *insane*. You are fucking insane."

Randy turned away, but there was nowhere for him to go. He started walking down the drive toward the highway.

"Where are you going?" I followed four steps behind.

"Do you even know what you're saying anymore?" he cried, over his shoulder.

I caught up to him, grabbing a handful of T-shirt, pulling him back; the heat coming off the house could be felt even here.

"What do you want from me?" he yelled, his mouth wide and dark. His face had taken on the color of the flames, and the smoke had made his eyes water. He was rubbing his face with his hands, watching me. I was silent.

"What do you want me to say?" he pleaded.

"I don't want you to say anything."

And in the end there was no speech. Only the dead weight of his hands on the piano.

The house where I was born, where Daisy and Randy too were born, sent up its ash, and I watched it burn until there was nothing. I stood rooted like Lot's wife, a pillar of salt turning back to watch Sodom in flames. I watched the house changing shape, the heat squeezing like a fist closing, the roof buckling, the siding breaking out in boils, the thunder of beams falling inward like the noise of the fireworks hissing and fracturing the trees. I remember every new shape the house took as it fell and how the sky changed color. The smell was so familiar, as if I'd lived this fire a thousand times in a thousand dreams, and this was merely the last time.

At the end—only a skeleton, the framework, a faint outline traced in charcoal pencil, flames still lapping at the foundations in a weakening grip. And the firemen stood with their hats pushed back, drinking water from bottles, and winding up the hose like a huge fishing line. And I shivered in my nightgown, the moon a faint grin over the crowns of hills, the wood huddled together, a steaming black bundle with the embers glowing from the kindling like scores of hard, smoldering eyes, unrecognizable. The insects prattled in the brush, and fireflies rose like the last sparks flying upward.

As I stood motionless in the dawning silence, after watching the house destroy itself, piece by piece, I heard Randy behind me whispering to Daisy: "I've never seen anything so beautiful," and I remembered how he'd hid his face when his father set off all the fireworks.

Today I stood as I had then, facing the blemish where my house used to stand, and I thought: Yes, he was right. The house was beautiful as it burned. I remembered the heat on my face, holding my body in place and Randy stooping a little with an ear turned toward the burning as if listening for music.

I moved toward the wreckage, lifting a bit of earth sown with ash and sifting it in my hands. I wanted to gather all the things that are left: bits of broken china, pieces of pipe and brick, coat hangers mangled into twists of barbed wire. I've done this before, many times, searching for something, some token. Perhaps the little bronze clock. I stooped and dirtied my hands.

Guilty and breathless, I thought maybe I could be heard here. I knelt in the rubble and lifted my face to the lowering clouds. I didn't know who or what could hear me, but I breathed the words up. They left me like smoke. I longed for any kind of forgiveness, the smallest sprout starting where the house had been, a rent in the clouds, the light of dusk catching the curve of something—the coiled mattress springs of the bed he had slept in for many years. This felt like enough, for now.

Empty with hunger, I finally turned away, driving home with the road leaping and a train throwing itself headlong down the tracks alongside me. The coyotes yipped their worship of a fresh and clammy moon as nightfall reared up to swallow the light. The rush of the sweating evening surrounded me, and I felt that I was seeing myself reflected in heaven's depthless lake, the stars hidden and blind. And I felt that I would never sleep again.

In the beginning, Randy's father and I waited for trains together. We'd sit by the tracks, they'd pass, and afterward, we'd move homeward through the darkness with the porch light glinting in the distance like a beacon. We'd drift back toward the trailer park, coming through the ugly glade strewn with empty beer bottles, mattresses exploding their lice and tufts of bedding, all covered over with a gangrene lichen of bile and semen spoiling in the shade. On long-past nights, frantic couples had dragged the mattresses down from the junkyard a half mile away, then let them rot there, to come back again and again with the young night owls hatching and, in their first moments, smelling the stink of new sin.

It was there, by afternoon light, Randy's father and I waited for trains. On the afternoon I'm thinking of, he had asked me what I thought we'd look like when we were old, while the black and orange caterpillars were migrating across the clearing, down the embankment to touch the railroad tracks—black metal grimed with tarnish, and the backs of the caterpillars leered with yellow eyes. Someday, I thought, as moths, they'll come back to this place, gray wings like sinister flower petals, drained and ashy, moving like eyelids in sleep above the semen-soaked mattresses, where the moon reached its clean fingers that wouldn't fit through the leaves.

That summer, the caterpillars had hatched in their massive, screened nests, moving down the trees and up from the lakes, an exodus of thousands. The ground was wriggling with them, the bristling hair of their thin hides, and you couldn't walk without stepping on them, bright innards exploding over the sidewalk in tiny fat lines. The guts, once outside, were exactly the size and shape of the creatures, like an army of caterpillars turned inside out. I thought: *Be fruitful and multiply;* I thought of them as one of the ten plagues of Egypt—the caterpillars dying beneath our feet with a sound like overripe fruit being crushed.

While the caterpillars moved, we listened in the clearing for warning of the train's approaching passage.

"There must be thousands," I said, watching them crawl, disgusted.

"Doesn't make any sense to me," he said flippantly, as if I had been speaking another language, a string of untranslatable sounds, guttural. He sat on a bucket turned upside down, while I sat on the stone with the tree growing over it, the trunk forming a backrest like a primitive throne.

We always left before there was any inkling of darkness, when the afternoon turned like wine changing shade in the light. But that day, by some weird magic, we saw the train before we heard it, its bulk appearing suddenly before us, moving slow and soundless. We listened for the heavy sound of its movements but they were muffled, as if a throaty groan struggled behind a gag. We watched it move, the coal cars like the silent, rhythm-less caterpillars in slinking migration. We waited for the train to end, realizing that the afternoon had snapped off, night reaching up, moths skitting away from the eyes of silenced birds. In the fresh and sudden darkness, I spoke, my voice moving with the train in the same hushed thunder, telling him that I was pregnant.

"What?" he said, lines of fear on his face.

I told him again.

He stood up, knocking the bucket over, and underneath appeared the tiny, perfect skeleton of a dead rodent. The sight of it filled us both with fear. He was already running, leaving me beside the tracks, where soon the ghosts would come, along with the deviants, the drunkards, the desperate couples dragging their mattresses through the gaps in the forest where no deed could be overheard. I followed, calling after him, and lost a shoe in the dusk. We floundered, my one bare foot bleeding, and finally emerged dewy and cobwebbed, watching mild kitchen lights flutter where the trees thinned, coming home cowardly and bright-eyed.

∎

Arabic Lesson

FROM *The Indiana Review*

SHADAYDAH HAD PASSED OUT in his chair at our kitchen table, though I'd seen my father give him his insulin before his morning espresso. My father drew the medicine into the needle from a plastic jar that looked just like the one he used to deworm the sheep back on our farm. My grandfather was much easier to inject. We never had to run after him flapping our arms, to herd him into a pen, to hold him by his spiraled horns as my father jabbed the needle into his skin. Shadaydah simply rolled up the plain white sleeve of the loose *salwar kameez* he wore every day, and spoke in low tones to my father, words that sounded like he was clearing his throat, but softly. When they spoke like this even my father, with his hands rough from farm work, seemed gentle as he stuck the needle into Shadaydah's arm. This was the miracle of Arabic, and it belonged only to them.

It was when my father was reading the Sunday paper that Shadaydah had gasped, "Sukar, sukar!" and slumped in his chair. I've never known whether *sukar* was Arabic for sugar, or whether Shadaydah had secretly harbored his knowledge of this English word and had, in a moment of desperation, revealed himself.

I ran to the counter and filled a glass with a little water and a few tablespoons of sugar. My mother had pulled my grandfather to the floor and was trying to pry his mouth open. She didn't notice me standing by her side, holding out the glass of sugar-water for him to drink. Perhaps it was no longer needed, now that his tongue had swollen to three times its normal size and could no longer fit in his mouth, now that my mother was pulling out his dentures, now that she was pressing her mouth to his.

I thought what I might say to my grandfather, should he die there on the floor, and the choice was easy between the two Arabic phrases I knew: "peace be upon you" and "pass the bread," though neither seemed to be quite right.

MADDY RASKULINECZ

■

Barbara from Florida

FROM *Zyzzyva*

THE MOST VALUABLE personality trait for a pizza boy was having a car. Alison had an old, bad car, which was good, according to the other pizza boys: if she had never had a driving job before, then she wouldn't be aware of the unprecedented trauma that the car would go through, and the practicality of owning a beater.

The pizza store was not clean, but it was white. The pizza boys were Eric, Casey, Malcolm, and Alison. The manager of the pizza boys was Miles, whose face had begun its middle-age spread but who was really no older than twenty-five. Miles orientated her about her responsibilities while Eric and Casey and Malcolm disappeared patternlessly on pizza deliveries and returned to eat slices of pizza and stare into the small, square television nestled into a ceiling corner like a hornet's nest. It played Mexican wrestling with no sound.

Eric and Casey and Malcolm had a lot of advice for Alison about being a pizza boy. Mostly the advice was about getting robbed, which was an inevitability. They told her not to put the topper on top of the car and to always park directly in front of the customer's house. They disagreed over keeping a gun in the car. Casey and Malcolm had guns and Eric did not. It was against the rules of the pizza store, Miles the manager had told her specifically. The pizza boys agreed he had mentioned it specifically because it was specifically a very logical idea. They agreed it was best to have a fake wallet with a fake driver's license and fake credit cards in it. Eric and Casey and Malcolm were younger than Alison, younger than twenty-one, and all had fake IDs for many of the things they liked to do. Casey offered to get Alison a fake ID and Alison accepted.

They talked to her with their faces turned up toward the corner of the room and dipped pizza into their open mouths. Sometimes one would go deliver a pizza and leave his slice with Alison and her Form I-9. The ridges of his bites would be distinct when he left, and when he returned the cheese would have oozed and rounded them out.

"Assume anyone in a sweatshirt is trying to rob you," Eric said.

"Assume anyone walking toward you purposefully is trying to rob you," Malcolm said.

Phantoms of hatred, Alison thought. It wasn't going to work on her.

The fake ID that Casey brought her said she was Georgina, from Georgia.

"This is so fake," she said. "It's too fake."

Actually, it was real and stolen. It didn't really say that *she* was Georgina, from Georgia, just that Georgina was. And Georgina really was. Georgina looked a little like Alison, although their heights, weights, ages, and eye colors didn't match.

"You aren't trying to trick anyone," Casey said. "It's just something to give over when they want something."

Alison was released into the city with her pizzas. Almost immediately she was made to relinquish the dummy wallet. Casey got her a new fake ID that said she was Constance, from Wyoming.

The work was not interesting, but it changed all the time. Alison was the only pizza boy whose schedule didn't need to accommodate college or a second job, so she was slotted in anywhere and everywhere the other pizza boys couldn't or wouldn't work. On peak nights they all worked. Her hours were different each day of the week, and each week of the month.

She spent a lot of time alone with pizza in her car. Her work was mainly the work of getting to the houses. She had never spent so much time in the car and she had never driven so much at night. Her night vision was either worsening or had always been poor, but the car, the beater, seemed to be coping all right. No need for a map or a plan: her phone spoke directions to her, glowing in her cup holder. The smell of pizza became divorced from the smell of food. It sat zippered into a warm, shiny case like a puffy ski jacket. She sat it behind her in the back seat and looked at it in the rearview mirror every so often to make sure it was secure. She handed it off and her car smelled just the same as if it were still there.

A novel and welcome sensation: Alison was a part of people's lives without them being a part of hers. It didn't take long for people to begin calling the pizza store to place an order and finish with, Send the girl. This meant one of the other pizza boys would go if they were available. If they were not and Alison had to go, the customer would say to her, A pizza girl. That's like something from a porno. The job was only sexual when people standing in the doorways of their homes holding exact change looked at her and said "porno" with their big smiles, and then it was only sexual in the joyless, threatening way of work.

This was not the only type of customer who recognized her. She saw it in the eyes or in the greeting—hi instead of hello—or in a big tip meant to acknowledge and honor their camaraderie. She believed them. It probably was true that she had been to these streets and these houses before. But she was free of recollection.

Again she was robbed. She learned that people would order pizzas to be delivered to empty apartments so that they could rob the pizza boy. She learned that people left the porch light off for reasons mainly sinister, and waited for her out on the porch not out of eagerness to eat. She learned that there was no difference between the fear of a jutting lump in a pocket and the fear of the metal, flashed. She learned that the cancelled credit card in the wallet soothed and sated them. She learned that teenagers were as huge as grown people, which hadn't seemed true when she thought of the difference between herself then and herself now. Casey got her a new fake ID that said she was Lucinda, from New Mexico.

Alison's body changed. Her posture at the wheel was nearly fetal. Her weight shifted in the way of the sedentary: downwards. Her belly acquired a bisection across it like a C-section scar from where it folded over on itself. But she wasn't getting altogether fatter. Her face thinned, and her breasts shrank. All of her bras puckered open off her flesh and pressed out against her shirts like the gaping, hard-shelled mouths of two begging baby birds.

Casey gave her a big stack of new faces. Bulk discount, he said.

Nights when it rained were peak nights. All the pizza boys were deployed at once. There was a sense of pleasant outcastliness in being made to travel more the more other people didn't want to. She drove out into the county.

Deep in a shitty neighborhood she hit an animal. It was nothing she'd ever done before but she knew immediately what had happened from the heft and shift of the car. She got out and couldn't see anything in the rain. Your destination is on the right, said her phone from inside the car. Her shoulders became damp in the rain, but she couldn't find the animal she'd hit. She turned the car around to point the headlights in the other direction and the phone said, Your destination is on the left. She thought: what if she had hit a cat and it was the cat of the person who had ordered the pizza, and she would have to deliver the bad news and the pizza both?

But really it was a groundhog. She found it then. Nobody's. It looked like it was shivering but it was only the rain pelting its fur all over; it was plenty dead.

The person who had ordered the pizza sent their child to the door with the money. The child was five or six, a son.

"PIZZA," he said into the house, which looked entirely yellow from out in the dark rain.

"Can I speak to an adult?" Alison asked.

He took the pizza from her and went into the house. Alison waited at the open door. She had seen this view of many houses. This was a small one, so she could see a lot of it from out here. A television. Some water damage crawling down the wall. Beige carpets throughout. A row of bobbleheads on a shelf. No books. An ill-lit hall leading out of sight, which a woman came out of.

It might have been Alison's glut of fake IDs that suggested to her that this woman was by and large her own type: a white woman with long, brown hair. Neither was she beautiful, but all ugly women were ugly in their own ways. Alison didn't know how long this woman had been an eater of pizza but it took a toll: whiteheads bloomed in the folds between nostril and cheek like clusters of pearls. She was younger than Alison and, because of the acne, looked even younger than that. You have the skin of a much younger woman, Alison thought to say. The title of this joke was "Pizza Face."

She didn't have a pizza body, per se, but she had had a child, unlike Alison, and that showed. She wore the tight, slick ponytail and sweatpants of the shell-shocked night people who came into the pizza store.

For her part, Alison wore her uniform shirt. Clean, as always: for better tips. But at this point very wet.

"I hit an animal outside your house," she said. "A groundhog, I think."

The woman cringed. "What was it doing in the rain? Oh, no."

"It's dead," Alison said. "I wasn't sure what to do."

"Animal control," the woman said. "I'll call. Thank you for the pizza."

"I'm Alison," Alison said.

Highway hypnosis. All the red taillights oozing down ahead of her: slow, relentless, like lava.

Alison applied and reapplied her makeup in the car throughout her shifts. Pizza boy was a job that required no physical upkeep—except to her car. In fact, with a non-zero amount of harassment, the smarter instinct might have been to embrace plainness. But the sexlessness and the solitude dared her to attempt beauty.

House numbers were never visible enough. Astounding that people could live in such close proximity to each other and remain so hidden. "Addies," the pizza boys called them when they complained together. "No addy." They asked each other, How will the ambulance find you in time? Hmm?

Alison stayed in the car when the porch light wasn't on, and called. "Please turn on your porch light," she said. She was becoming bolder. When no one answered her on the phone she would get out of the car and move into the back seat. She would unzip the hot bag and take out the box of pizza and open it. She looked at what kind of pizza these people had gotten. She pried off one pepperoni and ate it herself and then fixed her lipstick.

She knew at once when she had returned to the neighborhood of the woman and her son. It was raining again but the groundhog had been cleared away by someone.

"PIZZA," screamed the boy into his home.

His mother came to the door with the money. Alison gave her five filthy one-dollar bills in change and got all of them back for her tip. "Your son looks just like you," Alison said.

The woman smiled. "Simon. And I'm Hortense."

Alison winnowed herself down. It wasn't hard because she only ate single toppings from people's pizzas, and that only when they deserved it. The only thing on her that swelled and swelled was her ankles. She didn't seem to have any at all. Two logs ending in feet. She underwent a fantasy in which she was taking the hot, insulated package to the hospital as fast as she could, so that it could give birth to the pizza. The title of this fantasy was "Delivery."

She had hoped that ugly women made beautiful sons, and here she was, right after all. The next time she delivered pizza to Hortense and her son, she brought the only offering she could find at the pizza store: an extra plastic pizza saver, a clean one, which she produced from her pocket. "A table for dolls," she suggested.

Simon didn't have any dolls, and his action figures never took meals.

Hortense said thank you and kept the pizza saver for herself.

Alison found that Casey had included a man's driver's license in his bulk order by mistake. Dennis from Arizona. She could see why: the type, white with long brown hair, was the same. She chose this one for her next dummy wallet and looked forward, almost, to its theft. Carrying it in the breast pocket of her clean uniform, she thought what she had thought often: I would have been more beautiful as a boy, or less ugly.

Of course it was taken from her soon enough. The interloper didn't even look at it. These IDs had probably come to her, indirectly, from interactions very much like these, and they were going back where they came from, one by one. Next she would be Barbara from Florida.

Hortense invited Alison into her small home. For what else, pizza. She put in the order over the phone at the pizza store and said, Send the girl. Send her I don't care when. At the end of her shift.

It was pitch-black outside at the end of her shift, which was past eleven. The pizza stayed hot in its swaddle, but Alison checked on it before she went up to the house. She popped one slice of black olive into her mouth and tongued it until it came apart.

Hortense took the pizza from Alison at the door and paid her for it. There was a pile of shoes near the front door so Alison added her shoes to it, making herself at home. Hortense set out paper plates on the kitchen table while Alison touched each bobblehead on the shelf so that they all nodded up at her, frantically and then with fatigue. Simon opened a two-liter bottle of orange soda, which hissed and then overflowed a little onto the beige carpet, and they all ate ravenously. Hortense and Simon chewed their food just the same. Alison didn't know what she looked like while eating. The pizza tasted wonderful.

When they finished the pizza Simon watched Mexican wrestling on TV. It was in Spanish, so none of them could understand. Alison told Hortense that if she let Simon watch Spanish TV often enough, he might begin to learn Spanish from it, being that he was so young. Hortense said that was what she was hoping for.

When it was almost one in the morning Alison put her shoes back on and said goodbye for now to Simon. But when she stepped outside she saw that her car was gone.

"Oh, no," said Hortense.

"The other pizza boys warned me not to put the topper on top of the car," Alison said. "Shit."

Alison called the police and they sent over a young officer to take a statement. She showed him the only driver's license she had, which said she was Barbara from Florida. She told him the registration had been in the car, which was true, and he told her it was more secure to keep it in her wallet in case of a theft like this. He took down the fake name on her fake ID and told her she should get a license in their state whenever she could. He told her it was not likely they would recover her vehicle.

Then Alison called the pizza store and explained what had happened. Miles was confused as to why the topper had been on top of the car after she was clocked out for the night anyway. He didn't feel he bore any responsibility, which Alison was willing to concede. He said he could send one of the pizza boys to give her a ride, but she declined.

What was the actionable difference between a personality trait and a coping mechanism? Without a car, Alison was no longer capable of being a pizza boy. Hortense said she could stay over for the night and she accepted.

There were no extra places to sleep in Hortense's small house, so Hortense had Simon sleep in her bed and offered Simon's room to Alison. "If you need anything, we're across the hall," Hortense said, and then she and her son went to sleep.

It was not Alison's fault what she dreamed that night. It was the pizza. She never ate pizza and she never ate so close to bedtime. Hortense's mouth with its outline of Braille bumps. If she were a slice of pizza she could have decoded this message on her way into the pit: now I will die. Alison got herself all twisted up in the thick pilly sheets enduring this fantasy. If Hortense were to take off her clean uniform shirt. Lay her hands on Alison in the tiny twin bed. Slide her fingers in and draw out something molten and gold.

NATHANIEL RUSSELL

∎

It's Natural

FROM *The Smudge*

Selected comics from The Smudge, *a monthly newspaper published by Tan & Loose Press.*

TYPES OF HUMAN
BUTT ON EARTH
PART TWO

"THE JEFF"

"THE GLADYS"

"STANDARD LARRY"

"BOX BUNS"

"LONGY"

"DIAGONAL DIANE"

"DOUBLE TROUBLE"

"SHALLOW WATERS"

"CONFUSION IS NEXT"

"SIDE SALAD"

UCHE OKONKWO

■

Our Belgian Wife

FROM *One Story*

UDOKA WAS DISAPPOINTED to find that her prospective in-laws' house wasn't two stories tall, with a uniformed guard and a big gate to keep out prying eyes. But though not as impressive as Udoka had imagined, it was still a better house than her mother's. It was painted, for one, and the corrugated roof wasn't coming apart with rust.

Udoka understood exactly what this visit was. When her mother had come home two weeks ago from her trip to Orlu, where she'd attended the burial of a distant relative, singing about God's rain of blessings, Udoka had known that something very good had happened.

"You remember my friend Marigold, who lives in Orlu?" her mother had begun as she unpacked her bag. "I went to visit her and she told me something."

Udoka waited as her mother took out yet another item from her bag: a kitchen towel, a souvenir from the funeral. She handed it to Udoka.

"What did she tell you, Mama?" Udoka finally asked.

"She told me her son is looking for a wife," her mother said with a grin. "The same son that went to Belgium—fifteen years ago? Yes, in 1982, I remember. Marigold told me that her people were thinking of coming here to Umueze to talk to Gloria's family, to ask for Gloria's hand for her son. So I told her, I said, 'Gloria? My sister, don't try it o. That girl, Gloria, is public property. Ask anybody in Umueze Village. That's why no man has come to ask for her hand.'"

"Ah, Mama," Udoka chuckled, "you didn't have to say that."

"But it's no secret. Everybody in this village knows about Gloria." Her mother leaned forward. "Besides, why send a fine man like my friend's son to another girl's house when you are here?"

Udoka frowned. "But Mama, what about—"

"Wait, let me finish. I told Marigold, I said, 'Don't talk to Gloria's people, my sister. You don't want a prostitute for a daughter-in-law.' And when it was almost time for me to leave, ask me what I did."

"What did you do, Mama?"

"I acted as if I just remembered. I said, 'Ah, my daughter sends her greetings. You remember my Udoka? She is now in her second year at Awka Polytechnic.' And she said, 'Oh, tiny Udoka of those days. She must be a big girl now.' Then when she was seeing me off, she said, 'But wait, Agatha. Why can't my son marry your Udoka?'"

"Was she serious, Mama?"

"She was. But you know me, I acted as if it had not even entered my mind. I said, 'That's a very good idea. Let me go home and talk with her.' And that was how it happened."

Udoka shifted her weight from one foot to the other.

"It's a good thing you convinced me to go to this burial, Udoka. If I hadn't gone to Orlu, we would have missed this blessing. See how God works!"

"But Mama, what about Enyinna?"

"What about Enyinna?"

"You know he said he will soon come with his people to discuss my bride price."

"After all these months?" Agatha sneered. "Forget Enyinna. My friend's son, Uzor, he is a doctor, and he lives in Belgium. You want to compare that to a wretched trader at Onitsha Main Market?"

"Wretched, Mama?" Udoka frowned. "His shop is doing okay."

"Ehn, you have said it: 'His shop is doing *okay*.'"

Udoka winced at her mother's deliberately bad impression of her voice.

"You want to manage with a trader that is 'doing okay,' a man who drives a rotten matchbox and calls it a car, when you can marry a doctor making big money in Belgium?"

Udoka considered this. Enyinna was a fine man, but he was no doctor and definitely not a Belgian one. He had never even been out-side of the country and had said many times that he had no inter-est in pursuing a degree—something that had never bothered Udoka until now.

"But—so what will we tell Enyinna and his family? And even our umunna?" Udoka said. "Won't it be a shame to—"

"Udoka, leave shame to its owners. Think about your own life. When Marigold's son marries you, he will take you to Belgium. You will leave that stupid Awka Polytechnic where the lecturers are al-ways on strike. When you go to Belgium, you will attend a proper school!"

Udoka chewed on her lower lip. "That's true," she said. "They will have good schools in Belgium."

"Of course! And guess who will be paying your fees?"

Udoka started to speak, but her mother's pause lasted only a sec-ond.

"Your husband! And when you finish school, you won't even have to work if you don't want to. You can just relax and let your husband take care of you. And you know they don't have sun in those places like Belgium, so your body will be very fresh. By the time you come back to visit me ehn, this your skin that was already yellow before, it will be shining white like that of an oyibo. And you will be talking like them, shiriri, shiriri, as if you are holding water in your mouth. And all these bush village people of Umueze will not be able to un-derstand what you are saying, and they will be asking, 'Is that Udoka? The same Udoka of yesterday?' And I will say, 'Yes, yes, that is my Udoka.'" Agatha laughed, clapping her hands with delight. "And Uzor will be sending me plenty of dollars, and I will expand my shop and hire girls to work for me. And I will campaign for head of the women's group of Umueze, and they will be looking at me every time from the corners of their eyes, because I am the only one of them to have a daughter that lives in obodo-oyibo Belgium."

Udoka watched her mother's face soften into a dreamy, faraway look, one she imagined her mother had worn a lot more before her father's death and the hardships that followed. When her mother gave her a conspiratorial nudge, Udoka responded with a smile.

Udoka's mother had spent the next few days preparing her for the visit, telling her all the things that Marigold would be looking for. Marigold, like any mother-in-law, would want to see that Udoka could take care of a home. She would want to know if Udoka was modest and submissive, or if she was the kind who would want to seize her husband's trousers and wear them. Marigold had said she had a preference for light-skinned girls like Udoka; she wanted a daughter-in-law she could brag about and call nwanyi-ocha, fair lady. It was also a good thing Udoka was not too thin—Marigold didn't like "toothpicks."

Udoka smoothed down the front of her skirt with shaky hands. Her palms were damp with sweat. She stood still as her mother gave her a final once-over and girded herself. "Perfect," her mother said, placing a finger on Udoka's chin and gently lifting her face. Udoka felt a surge of warmth in her chest.

Agatha knocked and the door opened, Marigold's massive frame filling the doorway.

"Agatha, Udoka, our daughter, welcome." She stepped forward to embrace first Agatha and then Udoka.

Marigold led her guests into the living room, where her husband, Mazi Okoro—appearing comically small beside her—set aside his newspaper and rose from his chair. He greeted Udoka and her mother with a smile, peering at them through the thick lenses of his glasses as he asked polite questions about their journey and life in Umueze. Udoka found herself slightly disappointed with the living room. The paint on the walls was fresh and unmarked, but the furniture, though sturdy-looking, was faded. The room was decorated with artificial plants, and an old family photo showing Marigold, Mazi Okoro, and their son, Uzor, hung on a wall. Udoka narrowed her eyes at the photo, hoping to see something of the man she would marry in the scrawny, bug-eyed boy.

Conscious of her every move being watched, Udoka was careful to appear shy (a sure sign of modesty), smiling and averting her eyes each time Marigold or her husband complimented her on her skin or her manners. She could tell that Marigold approved of her attire of an ankle-length skirt and a top with sleeves long enough to cover her elbows. Her mother had made her take out her hair extensions and wear her God-given hair in plaits, and when Mazi Okoro made a joke about women who went into hair salons looking like humans only to come out looking like masquerades, Udoka knew it had been a wise decision.

After a while, Marigold served steaming wraps of okpa on a large platter. "Just something small to hold our stomachs until I prepare lunch," she said as she set it down on the center table. Udoka relished the firmness of the okpa, the way the spices came together in her mouth—the pepper sharp enough to sting but not hot enough to catch in her throat or make her eyes water. The palm oil was the good kind; it didn't leave a gritty feeling on the roof of her mouth. Marigold would expect the same level of culinary excellence from a daughter-in-law.

When they finished the okpa, Marigold invited Udoka into the kitchen to help with lunch, telling Agatha to rest in the guest bedroom. It was an obvious ploy to get Udoka alone, and she felt suddenly grateful for all the cooking lessons her mother had subjected her to as a girl. She would be on her best behavior. Her future, and her mother's, might depend on it.

Marigold's kitchen was impressively modern to Udoka, with its terrazzo floor, tiled work counters, and gleaming stainless steel sink with running water. There was also a gas cooker, which spurted a cool blue flame when Marigold turned it on. Udoka tried to keep her eyes from widening in appreciation. She was not sure how much Marigold knew of her family's financial situation, especially since her father's sudden death eleven years ago, but she didn't want her potential mother-in-law thinking she and her mother were undeserving of her sophisticated son. She wondered what Marigold would think when she visited their house and saw the extent of her family's decline. She was particularly ashamed of the old mud structure that stood at the back of the compound and served as a kitchen, with its walls blackened from smoke, the firewood smell that clung to one's clothes, the lizards playing endless games of hide-and-seek in the rafters.

Udoka reminded herself to focus on the tasks at hand. She needed to make a good impression today so Marigold would overlook anything she might consider less than ideal about Udoka and her mother's status.

"What are we making, Mama?" Udoka asked.

"Egusi soup. It's Mazi Okoro's favorite."

As they worked, Udoka felt Marigold's eyes on her, noting how thoroughly she washed the meat and cleaned the tripe and cow skin. Marigold measured with her eyes how much spice and seasoning Udoka used, how high she set the fire to cook the meat. Marigold, smiling and disingenuous, kept assigning the more difficult tasks to Udoka. When Marigold placed a bowl of live unshelled periwinkles before Udoka, she tried not to show her distress.

"Mazi Okoro likes periwinkles in his soup," Marigold said.

Udoka swallowed. She had never handled unshelled periwinkles. Her mother, whenever she bought periwinkles, had them de-shelled at the market. In her panic, she asked what she thought was a stupid question.

"Should I remove them from the shells, Mama?"

"No, my dear. Just break off the tail end. Use this." Marigold took a small machete from a drawer and handed it to Udoka. "My husband likes to suck the periwinkles out of the shells."

Marigold gave her a low stool to sit on and spread a few newspaper pages on the floor, so she could break off the shells without scarring the terrazzo. She said, "Make sure you don't cut too much or too little off the shell. If you cut too much, the periwinkle will fall out; cut too little, and it will be impossible to suck the periwinkle out."

Udoka took the first periwinkle between her thumb and index finger, held it to the floor, said a silent prayer, and brought the machete down hard on the pointed end of the shell. The end came off with a satisfying snap, and Udoka hid her relief. Marigold watched her work on a few more periwinkles, nodding her approval before turning away to check on the meat.

With the periwinkles cut and washed several times over, Udoka heated palm oil in a pot on the stove while Marigold pretended to arrange her shelves. Udoka added in the onions that Marigold had chopped, fragrant steam from the pot enveloping her face and filling the room. With the onions frying, Udoka poured in the ground melon seeds Marigold had measured out, stirring the yellow paste to keep it from burning. She tasted the mixture after a while, remembering to put the ladle to her palm and not her tongue. When the melon seeds had fried long enough, Udoka added in the meats and stock, tasted the mixture again, added some more pepper, salt, seasoning cubes, and crayfish, covered the pot, and left it to simmer. She would add the periwinkles later and finally, when the pot was almost ready to come off the stove, the ugwu leaves.

With most of the cooking done, Udoka started to tidy up the kitchen, gathering the dirty utensils into the sink and filling a bowl with water from the tap. There was no running water in her mother's house, and so Udoka enjoyed this, the way the tap sputtered to life and let out a stream of sun-warmed water when she turned its head.

Marigold cleared her throat, startling Udoka. She looked up from the sink to find Marigold standing very close.

"My dear," Marigold said quietly, "I want to ask you something."

"Yes, Mama?"

"Are you—?" She gave Udoka's crotch a meaningful look. "When my son knocks at the door, will he meet you at home?"

Udoka looked away—it was the reaction expected from any decent girl when topics like this were raised. She contemplated the dishwashing water. There had been that one boy when she was in her first year at Awka Poly, that one evening, with her panties down and him panting on top of her. "Just the tip. Let me put just the tip," he'd croaked, his eyes bulging like he was choking to death. She had let him (but just the tip), and moments later he shuddered his release, and she shoved him off her so she could look, with dread, for any sign of red on his off-white sheets. There had been nothing, and therefore she could say the words with a clear conscience.

"Yes, Mama. I am a virgin."

"Hewu!" Marigold cried, enfolding Udoka in her arms. "My daughter, you have made me very happy. I didn't think I could find a virgin wife for my Uzor; you know how girls are these days, not like when your mother and I were young. I thank God for my friend Agatha, for bringing you for my son!"

Udoka started to smile, but then she remembered how attractive a little insecurity could be. She lowered her gaze to the floor. "But, Mama, what if Uzor doesn't like me?"

"What do you mean he won't like you?" Marigold scolded gently. "What else can my son be looking for? Beautiful nwanyi-ocha like you, modest and intelligent. I know a good thing, and so does my son. If he does not marry you, it means he won't marry at all."

Udoka allowed herself a small smile. Her mother would be proud.

It was just over a week since the visit to her new in-laws, and Udoka was happy. If she didn't have her Belgian doctor, she would have been worried: about the academic staff at her school who, months since they'd begun, were still on their "indefinite" strike; about her mother having to borrow money from the women's cooperative from time to time to keep her in school. But her Belgian doctor had erased the creases on her forehead. She was in such high spirits that, at the market a few minutes ago, it had been impossible for her to curse back at the butcher when he'd insulted her for haggling too low. "Carry your bad luck and leave my stall!" he'd yelled, waving his knife. Bad luck? Udoka laughed. Bad luck did not fetch one a husband from Belgium.

After their return from Orlu, Udoka had watched her mother, with a feeling of awe and mild unease, as she set about dismantling the wedding plans with Enyinna's family, like a God-sent whirlwind. Within a few days, she had arranged a meeting with both families to call the wedding off. It didn't matter that Enyinna's family was shocked and upset, or that Enyinna, who lived and worked in Onitsha, was yet to be informed of the new developments. With the news broken to Enyinna's family, Agatha had gone ahead and set up a date with the umunna—agreed upon by her, Marigold, and Mazi Okoro—in the coming week for Marigold's family to make their marriage request official. When this was done, and the umunna gave consent, the way would be paved for the bride price negotiation and then the wedding proper. Marigold had said Uzor would be visiting Nigeria in about three weeks, and once he arrived in Orlu, things would move even more quickly. Udoka was more than ready to leave what she considered her old life behind. Her mother, in addition to handling the breakup, had spread the word of her daughter's new suitor all around Umueze, so that some people had begun calling Udoka "Nwunye Belgium"—Belgium wife—telling her to remember them when she entered into her obodo-oyibo paradise.

So far, since the breakup, Udoka had succeeded, through careful effort, in avoiding Enyinna's family around the village. She had begun making her daily trips to the water pump in the afternoons, when the sun was at its fieriest, and she was least likely to run into other people out fetching water. Each time Udoka visited her mother's tailoring shop, she would take a circuitous route of narrow footpaths, sometimes cutting through private backyards and gardens, just so she could stay off the main road and avoid Enyinna's family house, which stood on a side street. Now, on her way back from the village market, she walked quickly and stayed alert, prepared to duck behind a tree or a fence if she saw one of Enyinna's people. She wondered if Enyinna had heard the news by now and told herself that when the inevitable confrontation came, she would face him, bold and unwavering. Because, given the choice, anyone would do as she had.

Udoka swung her bag of foodstuff back and forth and skipped lightly as she turned onto her street, pleased to have avoided her ex-fiancé's family yet another day. The road was unpaved, and a small cloud of red dust rose from the ground with every step she took. They would have real roads in Belgium where she was going, not dust.

Udoka heard a car behind her and stepped closer to the shoulder of the road. But then, recognizing the familiar rattling of the vehicle's engine, she glanced back. Enyinna's brown Volvo, scarred and dented, was unmistakable. Udoka quickened her pace.

"Udoka."

She walked faster, her eyes fixed ahead, ignoring the car now beside her.

"Udoka, wait!"

Udoka ran, her feet pounding the dust. She caught sight of the mango tree that marked the entrance to her mother's compound, and she ran even faster. The car's horn blared, shrill and grating on the quiet street. Udoka pretended there was no Enyinna, no clattering hulk of metal keeping pace beside her, no neighbors following her with keen eyes.

Udoka threw open her mother's squeaky gate and stumbled through. Her mother was bent over the large water drum beside the house with a scooping bowl and a bucket. She straightened up at once.

"Udoka, what is chasing you?"

Udoka ran past her mother and into the house, bolting the front door behind her and leaning against it as she took in gasping breaths. Soon enough, she heard the squeaking of the gate again, and then: "Udoka! Udoka, why are you running?"

"Enyinna, why do you want to bring down my roof with your screaming?" Udoka heard her mother say. With shaky limbs, she got on her knees and crept to the living room window. She lifted a corner of the faded curtain to look outside.

Enyinna, his tone somewhat indignant, said, "Sorry, Mama. I didn't see you there."

"It's not your fault," Agatha said, "since I'm now invisible. What do you want?"

"Mama, they told me you brought your people to cancel the wedding—"

"And?"

"Is it true?"

"It is true. Did they also tell you that a doctor from Belgium is coming to marry my daughter?"

Udoka winced. Her mother's back was turned, so Udoka could not see her face. But she could decode her mother's expression from Enyinna's, like some kind of mirror in reverse. Hurt and anger on Enyinna's face, defiance and mockery on her mother's. She rubbed her wet palms over her churning stomach.

Kneeling there behind the curtain, Udoka wondered how different things might have been had her father not died. More than even her grief, it was the burden of holding the family together that had torn at her mother. Udoka's family had never been wealthy, but with her father's teacher's salary and her mother's tailoring business, they had gotten by. In the years following her father's death, her mother had grown harder, inside and out: more controlling as her hands grew calloused from overworking; more critical as worry lines emerged on her face; more materialistic even as their house crumbled under the weight of repairs they could not afford to make.

As a teenager, Udoka had witnessed creditors accost her mother at home and in public, with curses and, in one case, a policeman. Too many times she'd had to avert her eyes or sneak away so she wouldn't have to see her mother beg for "just one more week," wouldn't have to endure her mother's attempts to reassert her authority at home by being even harder on Udoka than she already was. And so as much as she hated hurting Enyinna this way, Udoka knew the doctor from Belgium was the better choice, because her mother deserved some relief from a life of want, because Udoka herself did not want to live like this forever.

"So it's true," Enyinna said. His face was to the ground, his voice so quiet Udoka had to strain to hear. "I didn't want to believe—"

Udoka felt her throat tighten. Her mother resumed filling her bucket from the water drum.

Enyinna's voice was hoarse when he spoke next. "Mama, please—"

"Enyinna, the family and umunna have accepted Udoka's new husband. Very soon he will come and pay her bride price, and they will do the wine carrying. You had Udoka for almost a year, yet you kept dragging your feet."

"But Mama, it was never like that," Enyinna said, in that high-pitched tone he used when trying to make a case. "Udoka deserves the best. I needed the time to gather enough money so I could give her a correct bride price and a fine wedding. I explained to you, Mama, and you said you understood. I am ready now. I will marry Udoka today if—"

"Enyinna," Agatha said, her voice falsely sweet, "you know the one thing you have said today that makes sense? 'Udoka deserves the best.' And she has it now. Be happy for her. Let God have His way."

"Let God have His way?" Enyinna said. "So you are saying this is God's will because the man has more money than me!"

All the while Agatha had carried on filling her bucket. She stopped now, straightening up to look at Enyinna. "More?" Agatha's voice was soft, and Udoka could tell her mother's face would be wearing that look of exaggerated confusion she feigned so well. "But Enyinna, what money did you ever have in the first place?"

This was her mother's final blow. Proud Igbo man that Enyinna was, there could be no greater gratification than seeing his family well taken care of, protected from a life of poverty, and no greater shame than in being perceived as incapable of doing so.

Enyinna walked away without another word. Udoka listened to his matchbox car rattle down the street.

* * *

The first time Udoka heard the sniggering behind her, she was certain it wasn't at her expense. She knew that sound well; she could read the mockery in it like words on a page. She had made that sound at people before, when she was, like these young women—no, girls—frivolous and immature.

Udoka liked the burden of responsibility on her soon-to-be-married shoulders. She liked that it was no longer proper for her to spend too much time with her single Umueze counterparts. With Marigold having sent word three weeks ago that Uzor had arrived in Orlu, it was important that she didn't give the gossips a reason to start even the smallest rumor about her. Most of the pre-wedding matters—the official marriage proposal, the acceptance, and the checking into each family's background for deal breakers ranging from epilepsy to serious criminal behavior—had been finalized before Uzor's arrival. All that was left was negotiating and paying the bride price, and then the wedding proper.

This man, Uzor, was all Udoka could think about. The strike had ended a week ago and school had reopened, but it didn't matter now. Udoka had returned to campus merely to invite her friends to her wedding and empty out her dorm room. She knew she would not be returning.

Udoka wondered what her husband was like. He would no longer talk like an Igbo man, she was sure. Maybe he wouldn't even remember how to speak Igbo, or he would speak it with a strange accent that would make everyone smile and indulge him. Would he still eat fufu with his hands or, as she hoped, with a fork and knife? And surely, he would be a gentleman, like the men she saw in oyibo films, men who helped with housework and brought their wives breakfast in bed.

The girls giggled again, and now it took a lot of resolve for Udoka not to look in the direction of their laughter and ask what had happened. She would bide her time. She was next on the queue for the water pump. When it was her turn, she would place her bucket under the nozzle, and when she turned around to use the hand-operated pump, she would smile at the girls and ask, with a carefully constructed air of disinterest, why they were laughing.

When Udoka got behind the pump and regarded the three laughing girls like she had planned, she was surprised at the effort they put into straightening their faces. If she were uncertain of her new status in Umueze, she would have felt self-conscious.

"How are you girls?" she asked.

"We girls are fine," the one called Chisom answered. Udoka recognized the other two but didn't know their names.

"What's making you laugh?" Udoka said, concentrating on raising and lowering the pump's handle to let out water.

"Nothing," said Chisom, clearly the mouthpiece of the group.

It dawned on Udoka that they realized she was no longer one of them, and that was why they were reluctant to share their gossip with her. Fair enough; she needed to make more friends from among her equals anyway.

"Nwunye Belgium," Chisom said, "when is your husband coming to Umueze?" Chisom's voice was low, her concern clearly insincere. "Or aren't you going to Belgium anymore?"

Udoka frowned. "What kind of question is that? Of course he is coming, very soon."

"Okay o," Chisom said. "I said I should ask because I visited my cousin in Orlu the other day, and I asked if she'd heard about the big wedding that's about to happen, but she was arguing with me—"

"Arguing about what?" Udoka asked.

The other girls averted their faces, but Udoka could see their shoulders tremble as they chuckled. Only then did Udoka start to wonder. The suppressed laughter, the look of exaggerated innocence and concern on Chisom's face, her tone, at once mocking and deferential. Udoka felt her grip on the pump's handle slacken. Thankfully, her bucket was full.

"Nothing, don't mind me." Chisom's voice retained its sweetness. "It's just that we have been waiting so long to see this our husband, and now people are starting to spread rumors. But we are all very happy for you. We pray for your kind of luck."

"God forbid!"

Udoka wasn't sure which of the other girls had muttered it, but it didn't matter. She needed to leave at once and find out what these girls thought they knew. She stepped from behind the pump to lift her bucket onto her head.

"No, no, no, Nwunye Belgium, let me help you," Chisom said, rushing forward. "You know we need to keep you fresh for our husband when he finally comes."

Udoka was speechless as Chisom lifted the bucket and placed it with exaggerated care on Udoka's head. Udoka walked away from the pump, her hands holding the bucket steady. The girls' laughter followed her, down the footpath and all the way home.

Agatha was not worried. She knew better than silly Udoka, who had come home from the water pump yesterday agitated by something she had heard and demanding that Agatha immediately visit Marigold in Orlu. People could be vicious, and they would tell all kinds of lies when jealousy was eating them up. The only reason Marigold and her people hadn't shown up yet to finalize the wedding was that they were busy preparing to throw the biggest wedding party in the history of Umueze. She had told her daughter this, but Udoka had been insistent. And so here Agatha was, walking through her friend's compound to the front door.

It was when Agatha reached the threshold, wiping her dusty soles on the foot mat, that she realized something was not quite right. Marigold's house should have been swarming with people eager to "welcome" the doctor from Belgium, in the hopes of leaving with gifts from him. There should have been extended family and neighbors offering help so they would find favor with their wealthy relative. But Agatha calmed herself with the thought that she must have arrived at a rare quiet moment, and worried instead that she might be interrupting her in-laws' rest. She knocked.

"Who is there?" Marigold's voice called from within.

"It's your in-law, Agatha."

After a minute, the door swung open and Agatha smiled at her friend. Marigold did not return the smile. Marigold's cool demeanor surprised Agatha, but she continued with a cheerful voice. "How are you, Marigold? I said let me come and see how you people are doing today."

"We are fine," Marigold said, stepping aside from the doorway with clear reluctance.

They walked together into the living room, where Marigold

showed Agatha to a chair and took a seat across from her. Marigold said nothing, so Agatha filled the silence with complaints about the bad state of the roads and the stress of the journey. All the while, Agatha wondered why her friend was acting like someone had poured cold water over her body.

After another long silence, Agatha said with an uncomfortable laugh, "Marigold, won't you offer me something to drink?"

"We have only water."

Agatha's sense of unease deepened. She forced a smile through the panic starting to rise in her throat.

"Why is your face like stone?" she asked. "If I didn't know better, I would have thought you don't want me in your house. Please, call my son-in-law so I can finally meet him."

"Which son-in-law?"

Agatha recoiled at Marigold's sharp tone. "Your son, Uzor," she said. "Why are you talking like this?"

"Why am I talking like this? Agatha, I have found your secret," Marigold said, leaning forward to point an index finger in Agatha's face. "The breeze has blown, and we have now seen the anus of the fowl!"

Agatha shifted to perch on the edge of her seat. "What secret? I don't have any secret!"

"Oh, so you just forgot to mention that you people have mental illness in your family," Marigold said.

Agatha sprang to her feet. "God forbid! It's not true! Marigold, why would you say something like that? You know my family very well. Where is this coming from?"

Marigold heaved herself to her feet. "All we know is that after we thought the checking of your family's background was done, one of our old uncles told us that your grandmother had a great-aunt who went mad. So you people thought that because it was a long time ago, nobody would remember? God has exposed you!"

"It's a lie!"

"So now you are calling our uncle a liar?"

Agatha opened her mouth to protest but Marigold carried on.

"Anyway, let us stop wasting each other's time. My son has already gone back to Belgium."

"Gone back to Belgium?" Agatha said. "Without even seeing my Udoka?"

"What is there to see? The woman he came to marry is from a family of mad people, so he went back to Belgium. Simple."

Agatha stood quiet for a moment, and then she said, "If your son doesn't want to get married anymore, why not just admit it, instead of making up such a big lie about my family? Do you know how many men were lining up at my door to marry Udoka? She left a very successful businessman to marry your son!"

Marigold's laughter dripped with scorn. "I wish you and your many suitors all the best," she said. "It is only mad people that look for other mad people to marry. We will come and see your umunna and tell them the wedding is off. You and your daughter can do whatever you want."

"Better come quickly!" Agatha said. "My daughter was not lacking suitors before your son; I just thought it would be good for our children to marry because we were friends. Now you are putting shame on my family, but it is God who will judge you. Just use your conscience, and don't go around telling people there is madness in my family."

"I have heard you," Marigold said. "Now, please carry your madness and leave my house."

Agatha stood on shaky legs and walked to the door.

Marigold slammed the door, locked it, and bent to watch through the keyhole. When Agatha was gone, Marigold let out a sigh, ignoring the twinge of guilt in her heart. She had to protect her family, whatever the cost. Perhaps, years later, Agatha would look back and recognize this, and somehow she would understand, even if she could not forgive.

As Marigold entered the living room again, her husband emerged from their bedroom.

"I see you're done hiding," Marigold said.

"And I see you decided to go with the madness story."

"It's not like you had a better idea."

"It was your idea to set up this whole wedding thing in the first place when nobody asked you."

"Ehn, go ahead and blame me for trying to help."

"Trying to help who?"

Marigold glared at her husband. "You're talking as if you don't live in this same town. I don't know how it is for you men, but me, all I hear these days is 'Oh my son is getting married, oh my daughter just gave birth, I am going for omugwo.' I can't go anywhere without someone asking about Uzor. 'When will he marry? When will we rub powder for your own grandchild? Is everything okay? Should we be praying?' One day, we will wake up and people will have answered all these questions for themselves. And you know how that goes."

It was decades ago now, but the memory was still sharp for both of them: those long years of waiting and trying before they had Uzor. The rumors had spread like fire: Mazi Okoro was weak; Marigold had tied up his manhood in a bottle; Marigold's womb had bitter water, and no child could survive in it. Even after Uzor was born, it was a long time before they could stop looking over their shoulders, stop searching for the malice lurking beneath every smile that was offered to them.

They avoided each other's eyes as they sat on opposite ends of the living room couch.

"But why is Uzor refusing to get married and settle down, at his age?" Marigold said, as much to herself as to her husband. "There's something he is not telling us."

They let the silence sit with them for a while, and both finally agreed, with themselves and with each other, that no, their Uzor could not be one of those homosexuals they kept hearing about. They had raised him well. Perhaps there was some oyibo girl in Belgium who had caught his eye. Marigold and Mazi Okoro had always insisted on Uzor coming home to take a wife; they would not accept some strange girl whose family and history they did not know. But with their son now nearing forty, an oyibo daughter-in-law would not be the worst thing in the world.

It still seemed like yesterday to Marigold when her Uzor, her doctor-in-the-making, had come home from university to inform her and Mazi Okoro that he, along with two friends, had put together enough money to travel abroad, to Belgium. With nothing more by way of a plan, the boys had set off, Uzor ignoring his parents' pleas and threats of disownment. It would be two years before they heard from him again, via a letter saying he was fine, he was starting a business. In the meantime, when people asked about her son, Marigold said he'd gone to Belgium to complete his medical degree. It would be another couple of years before Uzor began sending money home, money he claimed he was making from "imports and exports." That was the extent of Marigold and Mazi Okoro's knowledge of Uzor's career; the two previous times he'd visited home, he'd been as vague and tight-lipped about his work as he was in his letters.

"There are many things he is not telling us." Mazi Okoro sighed. "You know Agatha's family will not accept this madness business."

"They don't have to accept it, and we don't have to prove anything. It's just a matter of whose story is sweeter and who can make more noise. Me, I've already started."

Mazi Okoro eyed his wife. "This woman, I fear you sometimes."

"Oh, so you would prefer that people talk about us instead of them?"

Udoka and her mother sat in the shade of the veranda in front of their house, sifting through a tray of beans and throwing out chaff and small stones. Over a month had gone by since Udoka's engagement to the doctor had ended, yet people still called her "Nwunye Belgium." "Nwunye Belgium," they would call out, ignoring her ignoring them, "you are still with us in Umueze?" Or "Nwunye Belgium, when you go to Belgium, make sure you ask the oyibos if they can cure madness."

Udoka could not believe how quickly things had changed for her. When her mother had returned from that last trip to Marigold's house and related the details of the visit, Udoka had seen the life she had envisioned for herself crumble. She spent the next couple of days huddled in an inconsolable heap in her room, while her mother tried to coax her into normalcy with steaming bowls of fish pepper soup. Simple tasks like fetching water and going to the market became unbearable, with people giggling and pointing fingers behind her back.

"I saw Mama Enyinna today," her mother said. Udoka knew she was supposed to ask a question, to draw the story out of her mother. She ignored her mother's sidelong glances.

"Did I tell you what she did to me at the last Umueze women's meeting?" her mother eventually said.

"You told me, Mama."

Agatha carried on anyway. "I didn't look for her trouble o. We were discussing what punishment to give to women who don't pay the monthly levy on time, and Mama Caro said that they should be fined two times the fee. So I raised my hand. I said times two was too harsh, that they should just add a small penalty on top of the levy instead, because everybody knows that things are very hard these days. And then Mama Enyinna said, 'I didn't know that things are hard for Belgium people o.' Then she and her friends started to laugh." Agatha put her index finger to her tongue and pointed to the sky. "I swear, I wanted to get up and beat Mama Enyinna very well, use sand to scrub her mouth!"

Udoka kept her eyes on the beans. She wondered what her mother would say if she told her about that afternoon soon after Uzor's family ended the engagement, when she'd taken the two-hour ride to Onitsha Main Market. She'd negotiated her way through the narrow corridors separating the maze of shops, ignoring the calls and outstretched hands of traders trying to get her attention. She found Enyinna sitting on a stool outside his shop, his shop boy beside him. They were talking and peering into what appeared to be his stock book. The shop boy looked up and saw Udoka; he said something to Enyinna. Enyinna raised his eyes and gave Udoka the widest smile she had ever seen on him. Udoka smiled back, hope soaring in her heart. Enyinna sprang from his stool and rushed to meet her. He took her hand and led her to sit on his vacated stool.

"Linus!" Enyinna shouted to his shop boy, who stood mere feet away. "Go and collect a cold bottle of Coke from Mama Doodi's shop. Be quick, ehn! Nwunye Belgium must be very thirsty after her journey."

The smile grew stiff on Udoka's face. She stood to leave, but Enyinna blocked her way, lowering her to the stool with his smile still in place.

"Nwunye Belgium, sit down and rest your feet," he said, his voice still loud and starting to attract the attention of neighboring shop owners. "Linus is bringing the Coke. It won't be as sweet as the kind they have in Belgium, but I hope you can manage it."

Udoka sat, trying to hide her apprehension as she eyed the other shop owners. She knew most of them from her previous visits. They sold the same kinds of cosmetic products that Enyinna did, but there was a geniality to their competition, and Udoka knew he would have told them what she and her mother had done to him. Any doubts she might have had of this were dispelled by the hostility she saw in the shop owners' eyes now. They had always had friendly smiles for her, calling her "our wife," making jokes about stealing her from Enyinna, and buying her plates of abacha from passing hawkers. Today their faces were hard, their eyes knowing. They started to gather in front of Enyinna's shop.

"See, Nwunye Belgium came to visit us today," Enyinna addressed them.

"But Enyinna," one of the men said. "I thought you said she was going to Belgium with one doctor."

Udoka sat examining her sandaled feet and blinking back tears.

"Yes, but something bad happened," Enyinna said, his voice heavy with feigned sorrow. "The man came from Belgium but refused to marry her. Because they have madness in their family."

Exclamations of "Tufiakwa!" and "Madness?" ripped through the gathered shop owners. Udoka couldn't find her voice to say that the rumors were not true. She didn't think it would matter to the men, or Enyinna, anyway.

Udoka sprang up off the stool, tears falling down her face as she dashed through the crowd, laughter and shouts of "Nwunye Belgium" echoing behind her. She cried all the way home, arriving minutes before her mother returned from her shop. Seeing Udoka's swollen face, Agatha assumed she was suffering through another bout of melancholy and sat with her in quiet solidarity. Udoka had let her mother think what she might, convincing herself she was waiting for a good time to tell her about her visit to Enyinna. But now, she realized she never would.

"Oh, Udoka my daughter, we have suffered." Agatha turned down her lips and shook her head. "And that Marigold, going about running her diarrhea mouth, telling people there is madness in our family. God will punish her. God will punish all of them!"

Listening to her mother rain curses on all the people she believed were out to get them, Udoka wondered if there wasn't some kind of twisted truth to the madness rumors. How else could one explain her mother's stubborn insistence on innocence, her willful blindness?

"This is the work of our enemies," Agatha said, nodding slowly. "But don't worry, they will all be put to shame. God will open another door for you. He will bring another good man. A better man!"

Udoka swallowed her exasperation. It *was* all madness: her mother's hunger for the kind of salvation that could come only from a man, and Udoka herself, how readily she had surrendered the reins of her life, letting her mother decide how they, how she, should be saved.

"Mama," she said finally, "I want to go back to school. I've missed many weeks already."

"Okay," Agatha said absently. "I'll give you some money from the shop tomorrow. Manage that, you hear?"

"Yes, Mama."

They sat staring ahead, Udoka still while her mother shook her legs and ground her teeth in misery.

"Udoka, I'm telling you, this is the work of our enemies," Agatha said. "But God will fight for us."

Udoka felt her mother reach for her hand and squeeze it tight. She did not squeeze back.

ROBIN COSTE LEWIS

■

Self-Care

FROM *The Paris Review*

While watching
a movie

with a lovely, unyielding,
Well-founded black female

Character, the ten-year-old
Says, Mom, I love

How fierce
Black people are.

He's read thirty-six graphic
Novels in two days.

(I don't know how
To parent him.

I only know how
To protect him.)

My intestines gorge red.
Warm. I smile at him. Pretend

I don't feel this green leaf of relief, a leaf
Because he's managed somehow

Not to hate himself. Me.
A girl's neck was slit

Yesterday. Every day.
We watch her die

On the platform.

■

The Brothers Aguayo

FROM *Victory Journal*

THE AGUAYO BROTHERS, Roberto and Ricky, like to play a game at the end of workouts called IT. It's basically PIG, only for placekickers. One less letter because placekickers, unlike basketball players, who can shoot all afternoon, have a limited supply of big kicks in their legs. And because when the Aguayo brothers are playing, they never miss.

Just like PIG, you take turns calling your shots. "Sideline, hash, on the numbers," says Ricky. "Wherever you want." You can put the ball at midfield. You can put at the pylon. You can go all the way into the back corner of the end zone and hook it through. "Sometimes you wanna narrow those uprights," says Roberto. "Focus on your accuracy."

"It's really cool to watch," says Ken Burnham, a long snapper at Florida State, where Roberto played college football and where Ricky plays now. "For the first ten minutes. Then you start getting bored."

The games get tense. Almost silent. Their teammates will watch and talk and flap and crack jokes, and then gradually they'll notice they're the only ones talking. "You wouldn't think that they're brothers," says punter Logan Tyler, Ricky's oldest friend on the team. "It's fascinating to watch that dynamic flip, because they are extremely close."

Sometimes Roberto tries to worm his way into Ricky's head, but it's whispered, psychological warfare, not the goofy burns his teammates throw at him. They make fun of his hair, call him Pretty Ricky. Tell him he should be in a L'Oréal commercial. On the cover of *GQ*.

Ricky likes that. Doesn't bother him at all. Tyler likes to imitate the little wiggle-shimmy Ricky does at the start of his kicking motion, a tic
that gets him set, the way Tyler snaps his fingers. That doesn't work
either. Nothing does, really, not even Roberto. He'll get in close. He'll
crowd him. Invade his space. *I know you can make this kick,* he'll whisper, *but can you make it right now?*

On it goes, again and again, until they can't swing their legs anymore.

Placekicking is a compact, one-second motion that requires the
total elimination of distractions—crowds, pressure, idle thoughts—
so that a precise set of muscle memories can take over and fire flaw-
lessly. But in Tallahassee, in late July, in humidity so thick you can
write your name in it, distractions grow out of thin air. The sweat
starts stinging your eyes, and the heat can make you dizzy. Pretty
soon the only sound is *thhhhwomp...thhhhwomp...thhhhwomp,* and
then the ball somersaulting through the uprights. "It can kind of go
on for a while. Too long sometimes," Ricky says. "And then we're
like, 'Hey man, sudden death.'"

Games tend to end the same way: hit the upright with the ball.
"Like calling backboard," Roberto says. "If I hit the upright, you gotta
hit it." He says this like it's no big deal—hitting an eight-inch-thick
pole from 40 yards away—but for Roberto and Ricky Aguayo, yeah,
it kind of is no big deal. "I can call it, and I can hit it," Roberto says.

"This is our craft. This is what we do."

2

The spring of 2016 was a special time for the Aguayos. Ricky, then a
high school senior and committed to Florida State, moved to Tallahassee a semester early so he could start training with the Seminoles
and overlap for a few months with Roberto, who'd already declared
for the NFL draft.

At the draft combine that April, Roberto told *Sports Illustrated* that
his goal was to get drafted in the second round. Everyone laughed. "A
kicker coming off the board in Round 2?" wrote NFL.com. "Keep drea-
min', kid." And then the Tampa Bay Buccaneers did just that, trading
away two picks in order to move up to take Aguayo in the second round,

immediately marking him as the most hyped rookie placekicker the NFL had ever seen. He was 20 years old, and he was a millionaire, and all he had to do was take three steps and kick a football.

Roberto was handing his little brother a heavy legacy. The best kicker yet at a place known as Kicker U, birthplace of Sebastian Janikowski and Graham Gano. Winner of the Lou Groza Award as a sophomore for the nation's top kicker, and secret weapon of FSU's last NCAA championship team in 2013. The name Aguayo already etched in stone before Ricky ever set foot on campus. Roberto could feel it, and he felt responsible for it.

"I'm the older brother," he says. "I gotta represent myself better and show him the way." Roberto understood that Ricky wouldn't be given a chance to get comfortable at the college level. Seminoles fans are, in a word, lunatics. The admissions office at Florida State is located inside Doak Campbell Stadium, if you want to get a sense of the priorities around campus. Tallahassee isn't south Florida, or even central Florida, where the Aguayos grew up, outside Orlando. Tallahassee is the South, the Deep South, where college football is king and you get yelled at on the street if you screw up. Ricky would have to be perfect from day one.

But all summer long, Ricky seemed ready. He showed up in Tallahassee breezy and confident, his long pretty hair almost a rebuke to the supposed pressures of his job and the long shadow of Kicker U. Such a little brother. He had no intention of living up to what Roberto did at Florida State. "He wants to be the best kicker that ever played here," Tyler says. "He competes with his brother harder than anybody."

It was a special summer for the Aguayo family, Roberto and Ricky kicking together, their parents staggered by their luck, both of their boys playing within a few hours from home, their father, Roberto Sr., who tried three times to cross the border from Mexico, who almost died the time he finally made it for good, millimeters from drowning in the Rio Grande, now with one of his sons about to play in the NFL, and the other replacing him at an elite college program, the Aguayo boys booming, a straight climb through the uprights.

It was the summer when Ricky's dream was just getting started, the summer before Roberto's started to crumble.

3

Placekicking has got to be the strangest job in sports. It's debatable, because you can debate anything, but just start with this: Aside from punters, it's the only position in sports where you play what amounts to an entirely different sport than the rest of your teammates. They only touch the football with their hands; you only touch the football with your foot. You score in a totally different spot on the field.

Imagine deciding the outcome of a basketball game by bringing in a kicker to plunk a basketball off the backboard from the opposite baseline. Or the outcome of a soccer game by using a specialist to throw the ball past the goalkeeper.

This is how football works. Everyone plays one game, then the kicker comes in and plays another one.

As a result, placekicking is a job perfectly engineered for breeding resentment. It's not hard to understand. These massive people, magical athletes, blessed with video game strength and speed and instincts, bash each other's brains in for 60 minutes, and then this guy, this stranger, this rando comes onto the field for five seconds and decides whether or not you're a Super Bowl champion for the rest of your life. Someone you talked to maybe a handful of times all season. It's nothing personal—you're just never in the same room with the kicker, or on the same practice field, or with the same coaches. And now it's all up to him?

In the passion of the moment, as the kick sails right, it is a thought that has crossed the minds of every player, coach, fan at least once: *Why is that guy even on the field?*

It's a fair question. It is weird.

For a while, the prevailing stereotype was that the placekicker was only technically part of the team at all. Remember the scene in *Any Given Sunday*, when the steroid-raging pass rusher tosses the kicker out of a bathroom stall like a used tissue—"Kicker! Out!"—to address an urgent case of roid-induced diarrhea? That, we assumed, was how it worked. Kickers were, at best, second-class citizens on their own teams. It didn't help that placekickers looked so shrimpy compared to everyone else—the dad-bod frames, the single-bar helmets. Who wouldn't want to punch that guy when he missed?

Kickers don't look like that anymore. Growing up, Ricky Aguayo played soccer, too, but by high school he was way too big for soccer—too tall, too thick, too muscular. If a kick returner breaks off a big return and sees only an Aguayo brother between him and the end zone, there's a good chance the Aguayo is bigger than him and hits harder. ESPN used to show highlights of kickers getting laid out on return touchdowns; now you're more likely to see the reverse—a kicker flattening some speedy little fidget spinner into the turf.

The stereotype is still there, though, and it's not entirely wrong. Kickers don't get treated like dirt anymore, but they're still an island apart. "It's a little different," Tyler says with a sarcastic smile, proud but with just a hint of irritation. "The specialists are often put to the side and people think that we're not working, and that we're just indoors sitting down or whatever. That's obviously not the case." People—like fans, outsiders? Or teammates? "Outsiders," he says. Then he laughs. "And some teammates."

The special teams unit does plenty of its own walling off, too, though. The difference between what kickers do and what everyone else does on a football field goes down to the cellular level. Tom Brady, who uses his brain more than anyone else in the stadium on game day, ramps up his adrenaline to SEAL Team Six intensity before kickoff by bashing helmets with his lineman. Cornerbacks lose their shit on the sidelines when the offense scores a touchdown.

If you're looking for the kicker, meanwhile, he's probably sitting on the far end of the bench, zoned out, hardly paying attention, like he's waiting for a yoga class to start. "Looking like I am right here—legs crossed, arms up on the bench, just sitting here, just watching like a fan," Tyler says. We're sitting in an office in the athletic complex at Doak Campbell, a long way from the vibe of a Florida State home game. "Ricky does the same thing. He sits next to me."

Kickers don't want to be amped. They don't want their veins coursing with emotion. They want to be cool. They want to be a metronome, set slow. "It's not our job to be emotionally involved," Tyler says. During a game, their job is to "stay mellow. Keep our heart rate down, keep our emotions under control, keep our bodies ready and loose. You can't get tense. You can't start pressing and try to be perfect."

For a placekicker, perfection is not the goal. It's the job. "Bore ev-

eryone to death," Roberto says. "That's one thing Coach Fisher"—
Jimbo Fisher, the head coach at FSU until he left for Texas A&M this
winter—"told us. At first it was kind of weird. Why would you want
to be bored? But you want to bore the coaches, you bore the fans, you
bore everyone with 'Oh, he's gonna make it.' You know, no excite-
ment. Once it's boring, that means you're doing it right."

No other athlete in any other sport aspires to be anonymous. No
kid grows up dreaming of doing something so well that they vanish.
For a kicker, though, or for a punter, or a holder, or a long snapper,
it's usually a bad sign when everyone is shouting your name. "We
want to be forgettable," Tyler says. "You want to be one of those guys
that just goes out there and does what he needs to do, and nobody really remembers you."

By the time he left Florida State, Roberto Aguayo was the most
boring kicker in the history of college football. His NCAA record
for career accuracy—88.5 percent—still stands. But when you're
that boring, that robotically excellent, you can cross a rare threshold
and become a kind of superhero. You acquire a nickname, invari-
ably humanoid, like Greg "Legatron" Zuerlein of the Rams or, in the
2000s, Martin "Automatica" Gramatica. (Martin's little brother, Bill,
also kicked in the NFL for a couple seasons, making them almost by
default the target for the Aguayo boys.) A kicker who never misses,
even under pressure, even in a Super Bowl, from almost anywhere
past the 50-yard line—those guys are super rare, and limitlessly valuable. Only a handful have existed, Adam Vinatieri being the GOAT,
and they're all Hall of Famers, or will be soon, and they're all rich.

By trading up to take Roberto Aguayo in the second round, the
Buccaneers were basically declaring him the next Adam Vinatieri before he ever put on a helmet. He would have to be in order to justify
the price that Tampa paid. Being a solid NFL starter would not be
good enough. Aguayo wasn't drafted to win games. He was drafted to
win a Super Bowl.

The thing is, Aguayo wasn't perfect in college. His senior year,
he missed five field goal attempts, and his longest make was just 51
yards. In three seasons at Florida State he never once missed an extra point, 198 for 198, but the season before he arrived in the NFL,
the league backed up PATs 10 yards, turning what had always been

a gimme kick into a very missable 33-yarder. The hashmarks are in different places on college and NFL fields; for a placekicker, a millimeter of adjustment can turn into a couple feet by the time the ball reaches the uprights.

No one, at any position, comes into the NFL perfect. But the moment Roberto was drafted with the 59th overall pick by the Bucs, a round ahead of where anyone would've guessed, a round ahead of where anyone else would've dared, he had to be perfect.

Not in a year, not in three years. Now.

4

The moment when Roberto Aguayo was fired from the Bucs, barely a year into his four-year contract, aired on national television. He knew the camera was there. He'd seen *Hard Knocks* before. He'd seen this exact moment before, when some nameless kid gets summoned to the general manager's office and told to bring along his playbook. He just never imagined it'd be him in that chair. Not this soon. Not ever. And he didn't know they'd put it on TV a few days later. He didn't know everyone would watch it happen. His friends. His teammates. His family. His little brother.

Ricky didn't see the moment on HBO, and didn't plan to watch it at all, but the next day he was scrolling through Twitter and there it was: the lowest minutes of his brother's life, his brother humiliated for all to see. It angered him that such a painful, private moment got shown on TV, but he tried to take it in stride. "If you're working at a coffee shop," he says now, "and your manager calls you in, you get fired, there's no cameras in there, but it's basically the same thing. Learn what you can, and move on."

"Obviously you want to make everyone proud," Roberto says, "especially your younger brother who looks up to you. But at the end of the day, he knows what the position holds."

So much has been said and written about what happened during Roberto's rookie season that it's become necessary to set the record straight about what didn't happen. He did not get the yips. He did not fall to pieces, or lose his nerve. He wasn't anything like a golfer who suddenly couldn't make a putt, or a pitcher who suddenly couldn't find the plate.

During his one season with the Bucs, Roberto made 71 percent of his field goal attempts, which isn't good enough to hang on to your job as a NFL placekicker, but it's also not anywhere near the total unraveling that people have come to think happened. Vinatieri, who kicked two Super Bowl–clinching field goals, made 76 percent of his tries as a rookie. One more make for Roberto and one more miss for Vinatieri, and they would've had the same season. That's the gap between the two of them as rookies, the difference between being the greatest clutch kicker of all time and being among the biggest draft busts of all time: two kicks.

Vinatieri, though, was not a second-round pick. The Patriots didn't trade up to select him. In fact, they didn't select him at all. Vinatieri went undrafted. He didn't get a $1 million signing bonus. He got plucked off the street. No one expected anything from him. When you're a kicker taken in the second round, Roberto quickly realized, when you're the most accurate kicker in college history, every miss shocks people. Fans got on him right from the start, when he'd miss during drills. Not scrimmages. Drills.

Maybe it got to him. Or maybe he was just new to the NFL, trying to adjust like every other rookie, just like Vinatieri had to. Who knows. It doesn't matter, is the point. Roberto missed a PAT in his first preseason game. Then he missed a pair of field goals in his second. In his first regular season game, on the road against the Atlanta Falcons, Aguayo made all five of his kicks—one field goal, four PATs. But then he hit a skid, too deep and too soon to be forgivable, missing at least one kick in five of his next six games, and cementing him in the eyes of fans, and his teammates, as a flop before November.

Ricky and Roberto talked on the phone a lot that fall, maybe more than ever. "He knew what I was going through," Roberto says now. "He said, 'You're gonna get through this, bro. I understand it.' It's a tough thing to do, and he was like, 'No one else can understand that as much as I do.' He just kept motivating me."

"It was kind of eye-opening," Ricky says, and what he means is: Things going wrong on the field for an Aguayo brother, how easily it could happen. "He never really was in that position. I was just happy to be there for him. It helped me lean on him better and him lean on me."

Up the coast in Tallahassee, Ricky got off to the opposite start, opening his college career with what still ranks as the best game of his life: six field goals in six attempts, 3-for-3 on PATs. The Seminoles needed every kick, coming back from 24 points down in the second half to beat Mississippi.

"From 7:30 p.m. to 11:30 p.m., Ricky was a completely different person," Burnham says. "You could see his confidence increasing. On his fifth, sixth kick he was like, 'Hey, let me get this one. I want this one. Let's get it, let's get it.' It went from the pregame jitters, adjusting to college to, in the end, was ready for the spotlight. It was a big four hours of growth."

It's a remarkable thing, making all eleven of your kicks in a single game; just as remarkable is even getting a chance to kick eleven times in a single game, including six field goal attempts. Plenty of kickers go their whole careers without getting six tries in one game.

The whole night had an electric vibe for Ricky—the next great Aguayo, announcing himself in theatrical fashion. After one make, Ricky dropped all pretensions of calm, steady, robotic kicker cool, pointing an imaginary needle at his forearm and shouting "I've got ice in my veins"—the boast made famous by D'Angelo Russell, who, let's remember, unveiled it in a game against the awful Brooklyn Nets, during a season in which the Lakers would win just 17 games.

It was, in other words, an obvious karmic boomerang waiting to happen, an act of youthful indiscretion at a level where everyone gets humbled soon enough. And Ricky's came fast. One month later, at home against conference rival North Carolina, he missed all three of his field goal attempts during a game in which any one of them could've flipped the outcome. FSU lost by two points, 37–35. "My low point," Ricky calls it. He remembers each miss. Usually he's good about forgetting misses, but not this time. "The third one—it's a rough feeling when you walk to the sideline, I'll tell you that. I just wasn't prepared as well as I could have that week. I wasn't confident going into that game, and it just showed on the field."

He recovered, making all four of his kicks the following week against Miami, and only missed one over the following month and a half. But on November 26, as his brother's woes were hitting their peak, he missed two of his three field goal attempts against archrival

Florida. The Seminoles won in a rout, and the campus was rocking that night, and Ricky was out late celebrating with his teammates. What happened next was caught on camera too: Ricky, a little drunk but nothing unusual for a college kid, passing a fraternity house and getting jumped by some of the brothers.

If Ricky made a mistake that night, it was going back a few moments later to retaliate, taking a few more punches but throwing a couple of his own, in one of those drunken scraps that last a few clumsy moments before everyone falls down or someone breaks it up. In this case, a teammate of Ricky's showed up, a tight end, a much larger teammate, and in the video you can watch one frat guy get tossed into some shrubs like he'd been swept up by a tornado. In the court of public opinion, the frat guys were the clear villains. A kid two months into college, beaten up by his own fans. Ricky wasn't charged by police, or disciplined by the team.

The video footage, though, eventually got sold to *TMZ* and spread widely on Twitter. The ugliest part wasn't even the fight itself. It was watching a white, overprivileged frat guy get up in the face of a Mexican-American kid and lecture him about daring to speak when he's just a kicker and not showing proper "respect." In the Deep South, a white kid telling a person of color to shut up and show respect—the racial dog whistles were everywhere, and it was coming from a classmate.

"It definitely surprised me," Tyler says. "At the end of the day, we're nineteen-, twenty-, twenty-one-year-old kids. We're doing everything that we can to give our best to the school, to the fans. Obviously, it was extremely disappointing."

The Florida game was Florida State's last of the regular season. Their next game was the Orange Bowl in Miami against Michigan, on December 30. Ricky made two crucial field goals, and the Seminoles won by a point, 33–32. His freshman year was over. All in all, a big success.

Two days later, New Year's Day, 2017, was the last game of Roberto's rookie season, but it was not a big success. In fact, it would turn out to be his last game with the Bucs—the last NFL regular season game he's played in to this day.

Sometimes a missed kick matters less than when you miss it. Roberto recovered after the ugly first half of his season, looking much more like the kicker that Tampa thought it was drafting, missing just four kicks in his last nine games. But two of those misses came in the season's final game, and they happened at home, in front of Bucs fans who'd already seen enough of this Aguayo guy, and who wanted back those picks that Tampa dealt for him. It was the team's dumb decision—spending a second-round pick on a kicker was always insane, if for no other reason than that he would've still been there in the third—but Roberto was the one paying the price for it. For someone else's blunder. Take away those two misses at the very end of the season and he would've been Roberto Aguayo again, the kid who hit some bumps early but figured it out and got rolling again. Take away those two misses and he still could've been the next Adam Vinatieri. Instead, it was like a thundercloud that rolled in over him and stayed put all summer.

The 2017 season was a wash for Roberto. After he got cut by the Bucs, he signed with Chicago and hung on there for a few months, but backup kickers rarely last long. He got cut again, signed with Carolina's practice squad, then got cut again. The Los Angeles Chargers signed him this spring, after a season in which they went through four kickers and narrowly missed the playoffs, and he went into camp in a competition with ex-Eagles kicker Caleb Sturgis for the starting job. If you watch him now, you'd never guess what happened in Tampa, partly because he's put it behind him, partly because it was never that bad to begin with. "Oh my goodness, man," Burnham says, "that guy's still got a boot and a half."

Roberto might not get many more chances—he knows that. He's like every other placekicker now, just trying to make a team and hold on to a job. But things could be worse. He's married now, kicks a ball three or four times a week for a living, and has already made nearly $2 million at it so far. He's only 24 years old.

5

Here is what Ricky loves most about kicking:

That split second of impact, this tiny and elemental thing, when the hard ridge on the top of his foot connects with the sweet spot of the ball, about one-third up from the ground. "This big bone right here," he says, rubbing the spot on his right foot. "You can hear it—the perfect thump when you get it on the metatarsal bone. You can feel it too. It goes off your foot so easily and it just jumps out." The pure ball, Ricky calls it. "It kind of gets addicting after a while."

Both brothers got hooked young. Roberto Sr. had them kicking some kind of ball since the moment they could swing their legs. First soccer, then football. Over and over he made them kick. Before practice, after practice. Roberto and Ricky loved kicking, but no kid loves anything that much. Roberto Sr. made them keep going. He tried so many times to cross the border, got caught, got sent back, tried again, then again, and now that he was here, his sons were going to be professional athletes. That was that. You try, you fail, you try again, you fail again. You keep trying until you don't fail. You keep trying until you never fail.

"I'm not gonna lie—he wasn't easy on us," Roberto says. "I look back at it and sometimes I'd be like, 'Hey, Dad, why you gotta be so tough?' Now I know why."

When they were still little, their father built an H-shaped soccer goal in their backyard that could double as football uprights. It wasn't big back there, maybe an acre, but it seemed massive then. If you teed up the ball along the side of the house, in the driveway, you could line up a 30-, maybe 35-yarder. There was a small forest behind the house, so the boys would split the uprights, try to clear the power lines, and then go hunt in the woods for the ball. They'd kick until it was too dark to find it.

By the time they were in junior high, the yard wasn't big enough anymore to hold them, and they lost about a dozen footballs in those woods. For the other parents, whose boys were normal athletes who kicked footballs a normal distance, it was surreal to watch Roberto, as normal-sized as their own sons, his voice cracking just like theirs, swing his leg and crush a ball like that...and then three years later, watch his kid brother come along and do the exact same thing, like a superpower passed down the genetic line. Ricky remembers a Pop Warner game when his coach was riding the kids for their effort, and finally one of the moms in the crowd decided she'd had enough. "Hey, Coach," she called out. "Stop yelling at all the kids, they're not going to go pro—except for Ricky." That's what it was like for both Aguayos. They were special. Everyone could see it.

Lots of special talents reach the NFL, of course, and quickly discover that their talents aren't so special anymore. Even if they're still good enough to hang on—sometimes even if they're good enough to start—their careers depend on making peace, fast, with what they are now: ordinary. Or, as they say in the NFL, "just a guy." It's a slow dawning that happens to some pro football player somewhere every day. Usually it happens quietly, on the bench, or in practice, or almost invisibly on the field, a few missed assignments that only a coach would notice. Few athletes, though, have ever come back to earth so quickly and so publicly as Roberto Aguayo, and it's hard to think of another recent player who's been punished more harshly for it. It wasn't Roberto's idea to get drafted way too high, so high that even his misses in practice got covered on *SportsCenter*, so high that the price could be repaid only with a pound of his flesh. He missed the kicks, yes, but it wasn't his fault that so many people were waiting to pounce when he did.

There were moments during that terrible season when it seemed as if it might ruin Ricky too. After Roberto's lousy preseason, Ricky got booed in Tampa during a road game against South Florida. His disastrous game against North Carolina came just six days after Roberto missed two kicks of his own in a home loss. It always seemed like kicking was in the Aguayo brothers' blood, like predestiny. Was this in there too? Like a poison, or some kind of curse?

It's silly, of course, but sillier things have wormed their ways into athletes' heads and chewed up their nerves. Roberto and Ricky Aguayo, though, just don't think that way. Great kickers don't think that way. For them, there is no narrative, there is no score, no crowd. There is no backyard, no woods, no I or T if you miss, no brother trying to get under your skin. There is only the ball, the kick, the uprights.

If Ricky keeps making his kicks, this will probably be his last season at Florida State. He won't get drafted in the second round; no one is doing that again for a while, certainly not with an Aguayo. But he will get drafted. The question is whether his big brother will still be in the NFL when he arrives. Roberto played well for the Chargers during their preseason, kicking the winning field goal in their final game. But three days before the first game of the regular season, the Chargers went with Sturgis, and they cut Aguayo. He was out of a job again.

This time, though, the circumstances were different. Roberto got 10 attempts during his brief stint in Los Angeles—four field goals, six PATs—and he made all 10.

He was perfect.

SYLVIA CHAN

■

Naked and Vulnerable, the Rest Is Circumstance

FROM *Prairie Schooner*

MY FOSTER FRIEND pushes me into the carpet and slides into the sucker punch before I would have taken it. This is 1999, the end of the twentieth century and the advent of Y2K. Of Destiny's Child's *The Writing's on the Wall.* Of Bill Clinton speaking forcefully over our group home mother's FOX News broadcast. Everything is white in the living room: the walls, the cheap carpet that unraveled with each vacuuming, the couches sooty with grime on the plastic seat covers because Group Mama didn't tolerate our skins on her furniture. Everything untouched yet blanketed in a run-of-the-mill living—a single mother whose children had grown and departed, who had registered to house a group of four to eight foster kids to make ends meet. She was there, but she left us alone, and as the popular media foster stereotype depicts, she was happy with her check; we were all right if we had a home.

The sucker punch throws Evan Isaiah against the fireplace mantel. Before he hits the fire irons, Maria is on him again, digging her nails into his sternum. At fifteen, she is older and bigger than his fourteen- and my eleven-year-old body, but Evan Isaiah, even when his head slumped on his left shoulder, seems renewed. I watch his wiry muscles tighten and relax and then charge straight into her stomach, hitting her below the belly button. Maria oomphs and falls onto her back. Just when I want to believe they'll stop, they're at it again, and all I think is, *how many times will he fight for me, did he not break his body enough.*

I didn't want him to fight. Evan Isaiah would age out of the foster system; we knew his mother, an English teacher who taught Harlem Renaissance poetry, had remarried and fostered her stepchildren. I would have a different fate, a successful opportunity to reunite with my biological family, the less popularized but still irrevocable "take me back" story. I wanted every opportunity for us to both get out on our own terms. Meaning: No fighting. No sneaking out. No punishments or slaps against the wrists for Group Mama to report to the Legislative Court Angels, or our case managers, Child Protective Services, and our parents' attorneys against us.

The brawls were routine. Group Mama retreated into her bedroom when we came home from school or truancy. I was small and quiet, but everyone knew I could read three languages and tell any story so convincingly they would cry. I won over visiting parents with my recitations on Paul Celan and why reading a man who walked out of Auschwitz broke my heart. But I refused to lie. I'd let my mother smile and tell me her truths—that she would never choose a man over her daughter, that she would never let him touch me—and I refused to become my mother.

When the others asked or demanded or tried to force me into writing their papers and coming up with a sob story to win family brownie points, I hid under the bathroom sink cabinet. Nobody except for Evan Isaiah thought to look for me there. And when I emerged, they found me.

All day and night the summer of 1999, I hid and listened to the other foster kids lather their conversations shit talking Evan Isaiah and Sylvia Lin. I remember the slurred juxtapositions of their speeches, how they drifted into the bathroom, used it, and floated away, never pausing to hear that I was there. That, at sixty-eight pounds and four feet ten inches, I fit perfectly and comfortably in the sink cabinet. I remember everything; I dissected every snip at my lisp and my red-brown hair, of Evan Isaiah's blackness and the sureness they felt he pitied me for being unworthy of saving. That's what Maria said while bumping her knee against the cabinet knob: "Can't anyone see she's not a damsel at all? She's a sniper. If any of us will grow up to break grown men's hearts, it will be that little bitch."

I looked at myself in the mirror and saw a girl whom my world seemed to despise: unattractive and fosterless. Undervalued by my parents, who chose their addictions over me. I hated myself. I tried to take up as little space as possible, to go through my days quietly, because why should I speak? I was someone to be left.

When Maria and her boyfriend grabbed me by my limbs, pinning me to a wall or to the floor, I could never fight like Evan Isaiah. I was frantic, and my kicks meant nothing. My sense of worthlessness followed me: I was miserable. I tried to act stupid, and to do better by avoiding my bullies.

I imagined her mouth forming an O as she pinned me down after hours. Group Mama locked the girls in from the outside and kept the boys downstairs—no hanky business. The only way Evan Isaiah didn't think of saving me. Twirling the black cap in one hand, Maria grazed the Sharpie on my limbs: snitch, witch, bitch. Rinse and repeat because she ran out of words and I refused to supply her with more. I didn't scream because I knew she wanted me to protest; she wanted my visceral pain. As a finishing touch, she scrawled FOSTER FREAK onto my forehead.

When Evan Isaiah saw me the next morning, he pounced on Maria after her shower. Tore off a strand of hair. Told her she was better than this. He climbed to the girls' second-floor window every night, perched on the sill, and watched me sleep. Watched the other girls sleep. Maria never laid a hand on me again.

What continued was a kinship between Evan Isaiah and myself: he fought to save me, and I told him no. It bothered me that he was willing to jeopardize his body for mine. Why would I be the one to get out? I didn't want to be saved. I wanted to foster my sense of indignation and pride and fight. I believed in my heroine's journey: the only savior worth writing was me. It had to come from me. Watching Evan Isaiah's reckless compassion—the ways he defended myself and others for any little squabble, no matter how wrong we were—made me want to emulate him. I wanted to love someone so much I'd wear his pain as my own.

When he turns fifteen and a half, Evan Isaiah gets in contact with his birth mother, who wants to help. He gets a new case worker. He is assigned a court advocate, or a guardian ad litem, who visits him twice a month. I see the change in Evan Isaiah's strut, and I know he's hoping for reunification bad.

It's 2001. Dusklight slats fall over his windshield. I blink; can't see through his mom's dirty car. Someone has even scrawled "Crusty mess" on the passenger side. Okay, I'll prod him to wash it in the morning, plus I'm pretty sure Nelson, one of the younger foster boys who looks up to Evan Isaiah, did it. I see Evan Isaiah approaching and I slide over to pop open the driver's door.

He gives me the stink eye. "Why you listenin' to Eminem? Change it to Tupac."

I laugh and fiddle with the radio station till we hear the Bay Area stations. We're eager to paint our ghetto Hayward town red, though he has to bring me back to the group home every night. Even though "Last Wordz" and "Keep Ya Head Up" blast from the speakers, our car rides are mostly quiet.

From group home to juvenile court, we understand two wards of the states—one with a court advocate, bound for reunification with his mother—are tied by circumstance. Friends, families, and strangers give us the stink eye. It's like, what does a black boy and a yellow girl have in common? Why would anyone think we were brother and sister?

I think we are defined by our actions. For me to hear from my group home guardians, probation officers, police, and other administrators I am lucky to be alive—I understand I should be grateful, and I am. But that doesn't make it easy for me to live like I'm always fine.

As a writer who has been called "sick" for teaching blackness and whiteness in 2018, I have never been questioned for my authority. Which is not anything beyond my subjective experiences, or what Evan Isaiah has informed me all along. He always told me it didn't matter I wasn't black: that I listened and felt for him was enough to make me sound like I'd watched it all. Like I'd been in the kitchen with Evan Isaiah when his mother got the news his father was shot in Prince George's County for drunk driving. That's what the cops told her. And it wasn't every girl who "got" that, even though my father had never been pulled over for drunk driving, but for recklessness, mostly under cocaine and heroin. Evan Isaiah admired that I cared for the American life he could live with his skin, even though I had no reason to empathize because I was simply born whiter.

"Why are our lives supposed to be different, just because we were born?" Birth was a lottery. He didn't consider us to be the unfortunate; he saw our less favored bodies as two lives that would make a difference.

When I left Group Mama's home in 2001, Evan Isaiah feared we would never see each other again. "Don't worry," I said. "I'm in the next town over." And Union City and my family's home was five minutes away from Group Mama's house on Sleepy Hollow Avenue, tucked behind the intersection of the old Kaiser and St. Rose Hospitals.

Consider: it's the last time I recite poetry with Evan Isaiah. It's dark and we're outside; Evan Isaiah climbs to my window and lifts me onto his back and we shimmy our way down the tree. Huddled in blankets, I grip a flashlight as he looks at the battered copy of Celan's *Lichtzwang,* unseeing.

"Do you know this will be your ticket out this house?" he says, gesturing toward the original Suhrkamp Verlag edition. "Wish I could read it."

"We don't know if this will work." Our late-night practices—my recitations to him in languages he didn't know—were curated to allow me to become the literate daughter fluent in English, German, and Chinese. What parents wouldn't want to take me back?

He laughs. "Yours is everything a poetic voice should be," he says.

And until we no longer need the flashlight, he watches as I recite the German, and translate the poems into English. We try short ones and longer excerpts, mixed and matched poetic resonances with melodrama. But I couldn't victimize myself, he reminds me. That was why our parents got rid of us; we were burdens.

"And play up the fact that you're translating on the fly, okay? I don't know any girl who can do that." He smiles. "You'll make some boy happy."

"A green, not from here." I stop.

"Go on. That's beautiful. A reminder of who they gave up." He nods and sits up.

"I don't know," I say.

The small stones I wish in my mouth.

"The end, then." He points to the last three lines. "That's how great poetry works. You read the beginning and the end, and if you're hooked, you've sold the rest."

I follow his calloused finger to where it moves back and forth between those three lines. He is right; it is easy. "The orphans buried again and again."

"Just end on those two snippets: A green, not from here. The orphans buried again. And again." He speaks them slowly, almost happily, with his eyes closed. Their long fringes flutter even as he remains still.

"Try it."

It's the same stance he wears in 2010, the last time I see him as a free man.

On May 16, a drunk driver hits my boyfriend and me on the I-5 at 150 miles per hour. We survive. There is some investigation, but the accident is ruled as reckless endangerment, and the drunk driver confesses to being intoxicated, and nothing else. He takes his life within the year. My boyfriend passes six months later in an accidental shooting. From the car accident injuries, I've been sitting in bed for six months and watching the news.

I don't sleep. I fail my physical rehab tests. I'm not laid off because it's illegal to fire a disabled body, but the university pays me workers' compensation and tells me to grade from home.

Evan Isaiah reaches out in July. I'm lying motionless on the couch, tracing curlicues with the hand I didn't lose. The doctors encourage me to learn to use my right hand because it'd take a couple of surgeries to make my left look whole—to reconstruct it. I will never be able to write again.

I pick up the phone call, even though I let it ring for five minutes. He asks how I'm coping. I hear his cat, Siu Mai, meowing in the background. "Syl," he says, "all you can do is recover. You're doing everything right. You know, orphans are the closest to God."

I roll my eyes, and Evan Isaiah, through the phone, calls me out. "I know you're not an orphan," he says, "but you can't deny everyone treats you as if you're an orphan. You want to get things right, but you have to consider that not everyone cares for those details. They hear trashbag kid, and think, her parents must be dead.

"Your mom really is horrible," he adds. "Do me a favor and stop giving her money and bailing her out."

We spend the next half hour over the phone before we talk in person, when I drive to his house and spend the night philosophizing about God, good and bad characters, and the elusive idea of fate—we are born from different circumstances, that's undeniable, but we choose how to live.

I climb into bed with him, turning away. He spoons me and throws his arm over my waist, holding me like he had when we were in group home, and when I was scared I'd be attacked in my sleep. I always fell asleep with his arm rising and falling on me. I thanked his God he still breathed, even as I was sick that whoever would kill me would kill him. *This has to end someday,* I thought. *Someday.*

Evan Isaiah tells me about bullet holes—that's what he remembers and sees in his dreams when he returns to that night. "It is kinda God's intention," he says. "Yeah, I hope none of this is fatal, but I know he creates holes for us to find him."

I'm so lost. "Why are you telling me he needs to take a life in order to sustain yours?" I ask.

I don't tell him I also dream too much about the same holes. In my memories and nightmares, the bullet holes look like pinpricks of blood on a heel, not unlike those of a heroin addict. In the end, children, and then adults like us, are forsaken. The idea that a God could love us, darknesses and all, is laughable.

He doesn't answer. Instead, Evan Isaiah quotes Sebald and Celan and a bunch of literary luminaries; I forget he was the well-read kid. Evan Isaiah compares me to his former "adult" best friend, a girl who's not unlike me in that we have parents who didn't want us. The difference? I'm strong, compassionate, and conscientious—things I've heard all my life. Is that shocking in a former trashbag kid? Maybe. To me, being a model citizen and professional is only part of growing out of the system: I did "good," as Evan Isaiah affirms.

But none of us should be dictated by our escapes from the system.

I wake up three hours later. My eyes are swollen, matted from fitful sleeping. I stumble into the bathroom. In the 4 a.m. light, I see cigarette butts in the sink and in the toilet. Dirty towels in the tub. I decide to hold my pee and return to Evan Isaiah, who is still sleeping peacefully.

I throw on his sweatshirt and tuck him in before driving home. In the shower, I think about what I wanted to say had he been awake: Why are you doing coke? Why do you want to look like cigarette butts and as if your face is so sanded by the substance, you can't promise me you'd shape up? Our books had promised us more when we were younger, that, perhaps, we wouldn't die without end. *We're twenty-five and twenty-two*, I thought. *I'm tired of wondering what the hell is wrong with us.*

His even-limbed frame a beauty, even in sleep. The dawn turning his face blue. His forehead, a sliver of light. It's the same color he wears in 2012, when I'm visiting him nearly every week before I move to Tucson for graduate school, round two. We palm each other over the glass window, sooty with other thumbprints. This is the only time I remember Evan Isaiah having to meet me this way, with a partition between us. "What did you do?" I ask.

He shrugs. "Nothing of consequence," he says.

That has been his answer since he was designated a "condemned A" prisoner two years ago. I could touch and hug him, unless he picked a fight. He was convicted of first-degree murder, rape, and robbery for a woman he assaulted at a gas station on Sleepy Hollow and Hesperian, near my birth hospital and old Group Mama's home.

He didn't keep his finger outside the trigger guard. I imagined he tried to take it back, even when he knew it was too late. I could see him standing over her body and placing her hands on her chest and closing her eyelids—to shut her eyes like a woman.

He didn't try to get far. They caught him later that night, on Mission Boulevard, at the Union City and Hayward junctions. The news said he was trying to make for the hills, but I knew Evan Isaiah didn't care for rich white people. *What the hell would I want with a white picket fence on top of a hill?* I'd laughed: that was never in our dreams.

I wanted to be a jazz pianist. He wanted to be a teacher, just like his mother. What did his mother always tell him? "We write to keep hope," she'd said.

"But I don't want to be a writer," he'd said.

He would relay these last words to me again and again, in the backyard, in the living room, on the way to school. We write to give: it is the inherent right of all writers to experiment with the possibilities of language in ways they couldn't imagine. To impart these juxtapositions of real and unreal to someone else. That's what she wanted for him.

On normal visiting days, I could have shown Evan Isaiah my poetry. I was allowed to bring up to ten pages. I wanted to write for a reader, not for a writer. I wanted them to read my experiences and get them thinking about theirs. Wasn't it obvious?

"Hell no," Evan Isiah says.

He mimics thumbing through the pages, as if we could hold hands across the table. "You know your problem has always been loving those who don't love you. Which is admirable and wild. People love and hate you because you are the most kindhearted person I know. You don't get that they will use this against you—they will call you malicious and stupid and reckless."

He smiles, cocks his head. "And you'll still take it. It is crazy beautiful how relentless you are in your refusal to check your compassion."

Yawning and stretching his arms, Evan Isaiah reveals his tightness in his body. In prison, he'd thinned out. He is still wiry and muscular yet he seems quieter and, I feel, content to settle for next to nothing.

"Only you," he says. "You ain't going to jail. Not back then, not ever."

He asks me to shut my eyes. I feel the religious energy emanating from him; I know this man is going to ask me to pray, or to believe in his God again. I don't have the heart to tell him no—how do you tell an imprisoned man no?—I cannot, after all these years.

With the partition between us, with our hands face palmed to the glass, he recites: "If you love me, keep my commands. And I will ask the father, and he will give you another advocate to help you and be with you forever. I will not leave you as orphans; I will come to you."

I shake my head and stare dumbfounded at him. "Why are you doing this?" I ask.

He bites his lower lip and smiles. "You need it," he says. "Promise me one thing. Don't ever let a man have you believe you need to hate him so much you can't forgive. You can't become one of them—our parents, our failed case managers, our social workers. You can't let hate spurn your body until you're unable to forgive. I can't be in a world where you become inhuman."

He brushes away a strand of hair which has fallen over his forehead. "One day I'll walk you down the aisle," he says. "I'll still be your brother, your best friend, and I'll be your dad if he's not there."

"Really?"

He nods. "Promise." Forget the fact he's in for life.

"Help me figure out what I should say about my family when I get to Arizona," I say. "When they ask where do you come from. Where are your parents."

The prison light catches his face, which tilts toward me, ready to take on the task. He's beautiful.

There are things we do for the ones we love. That's how Evan Isaiah ends our last conversation. A Thursday morning. I'd driven from Oakland at 4:30 a.m. I preferred missing Bay Area traffic so I could be one of the first persons Evan Isaiah would see for his day. I liked sitting in my Altima in the parking lot, waiting for dawn to break and watching the sun spread its horizon over the pink striated sky. The tips of the clouds touching the shadow of the Richmond–San Rafael Bridge reminded me of Evan Isaiah's drawings—he penciled images to match my poetry, even when it was still Celan's.

The drive was just me. I had broken up with my boyfriend because I wanted a clean start leaving California. Evan Isaiah didn't ask about him; he knew. I'd thrown up around Point Reyes; driving in the hills always got to me. *What kind of California girl are you?* I thought he'd throw the quip, as he usually did when he saw me pressing my lips together.

Instead, he reminds me how he'd mailed the CDCR 106 form for first-time visitors to him. "I wanted to meet the love of your life," he said. Two years ago, I'd held the request in my hands and filled it out immediately, never thinking for a moment my boyfriend didn't want to meet Evan Isaiah. I'd paced our Temescal studio, sealed the form, and then cooked a chicken curry for dinner. It was over dinner I'd admitted I'd signed it for him.

It was my turn to laugh. "It sounds stupid," I say, "expecting him to say yes."

"But that's what you wanted," Evan Isaiah replies. "Those who love you will always be around. He would've gotten over the whole convict thing." He grins.

I feel the pit of my stomach growl. It's not hunger; it's the coffee. Or the dry heaving. I feel like I'm on top of the world, talking to my best friend; my body feels otherwise.

"I got a feeling you'll be the last," he says. "You are going somewhere."

He doesn't talk about the dream job: *I want to be a teacher.* No: *I want to save other kids like us.* Neither: *I want to get out of jail.* Even after visiting him for two years, he'd been fine. I thought he made peace with the fact he'd spend his life there because he'd looked at those with him who were angry they'd messed up, and listened to them. Maybe I forgot he was one of them. Maybe, when he was coming off the coke, he saw he was dying inside. Maybe he didn't tell me because he saw I was no longer part of his world; I was outside.

I forget he carried a darkness; I didn't see him when he turned complacent, frustrated, and depressed. I was too selfish to remember at the time I carried my darkness—my conviction of self-abasement and terror—that was his, too.

"Don't say that shit." I think about the times we walked the train tracks on the south side of St. Rose Hospital because it was the fastest way to get to the Dairy Queen or Mickey D's. Evan Isaiah would stride easily over debris and granite, almost dancing on each wooden crosstie. I always heard the train first, or maybe I was the one to admit it. I'd lope faster and cross over the rails long before Evan Isaiah would turn around and jump out of harm's way.

But I never forgot how long it took. His hesitance, until he waited for the train's blast, for the horn to pulse in my eardrums. He knew exactly how long it would take for him to live another day.

"You are going somewhere," he repeats. He holds up his hands. "Talk to me," he says.

"I'm all wrong," I say, biting my lip. "No, I'm not. You're not wrong, either.

"Evan Isaiah," I say. "I love you."

He looks at me, puts a palm against the partition, and waits for me to match him.

Few persons are willing to face death for a principle. On Thursday, December 8, 2016, I receive the "returned to sender" letter I'd mailed to Evan Isaiah a month ago. My stomach flips. I run into my house and look up San Quentin, call, and wait. For a human on the other end.

The reality is he'd passed nearly eight months ago. How could I have been so detached from him? I think about my year—most of it spent with a man who didn't love me, the one Evan Isaiah always cautioned against: a man who looked at me and saw himself a savior. A man who didn't love me for my own.

And I think, before she tells me there was a brawl, perhaps he defended someone. I could see him pushing me to the floor again and taking from the other man's thrust into his own torso. A fatal sucker punch.

I'm still depicting the scene in my mind. The lady on the other end jolts me back with her *Is that all?*

After she hangs up, I call Charlie, Evan Isaiah's mother.

"It's Evan Isaiah," she says, almost matter-of-factly. "He's been in an accident."

"I know," I say. "I already did this. It took me eight months. I am not the best friend he deserves."

It's like we've never stopped talking, even though I was always the short Asian with Evan Isaiah. I cannot ask her about the facts of his death. I don't want her to think about if he was still alive after the rod pierced his torso. I don't ask if he spoke to his assailant when he tried backing away and running for it. I don't ask if he was still conscious when the guards reached him and yelled at one another. I cannot ask if what killed him was his volition in protecting others, always, at the cost of himself.

I want to call his people. I think about Nelson and Maria and Rys in old Group Mama's home, that, no matter the time, we'd find each other because we had been bound by the same circumstance. We loved and hated each other.

I cover my eyes and breathe. "What the fuck," I say.

I feel as if Evan Isaiah and I are still in our tree in Group Mama's backyard, as though our world is visceral: the dirt pricking my legs, the ants crawling over my bare feet and forming a line around me, as if they could obscure me. I can't forget it. What is the physical representation of my hate and grief, of the darkness embodying all the times in Hayward when I'd been terrorized or sexually assaulted and Evan Isaiah had been there to fight for me?

"I know," Charlie responds. "If I had talked to him more," she continues, and I hear the break in her voice. "If I would have stayed with him, he'd be alive."

We are burdens to our parents, Evan Isaiah told me long ago. *That's why our parents got rid of us.* How relentless: that the burden of blame and regret could follow a parent when her son was killed, long after they'd parted from one another.

Recall: Evan Isaiah fights Nelson or Rys or Maria, knocking on their bodies, jumping on them after he'd learned they'd picked on someone else. I would take my anger and frustration and watch him defend me, and forget about trying so hard to fight. I would let him fight for me.

And, perhaps, this is the way he had written all along. I'm eleven and my best friend, Evan Isaiah, is fourteen, and it is two weeks after we became witnesses—two kids tied by being there for the same event. We're sitting in an oak tree tire swing reading June Jordan. Watching the dusklight. He says, "Whatever has to be in our guardian has to be in us. Whatever encouraged him is also for us. We deserve to die."

I didn't agree then and I don't agree now. I refuse to believe we were bad kids because we were cut from different circumstances. And I refuse to believe that to want a family is to deserve to die.

This came from the same person who taught me we don't choose our families. Evan Isaiah taught me to be reckless with my heart, even though it meant I had to learn to be hurt. I think good acts, like good writing, offer the writer's compassion: I would wear my beloved's pain. This is not popular, fostered or unfostered: it takes incredible duress to take someone's pain and live with it. Not get rid of—to live with it.

* * *

Today, I am a court advocate for foster kids, the same woman Evan Isaiah had as his legal and compassionate voice eighteen years ago. I can't believe it has taken me so long to be brave enough to return to the court, to the same system which validated and betrayed me. I think about how every trashbag kid desires reunification with their parents, even when we know it's no good. Better a life with people who love you than none. Better to have my mother drive up in another man's car and to have my father disappear every four months than to know they'd never come back for me.

Court advocacy requires me to listen, and I mean, learn to listen to others' stillnesses and restlessnesses and darknesses, which return to mine. There are fewer rules for this work. Just that I love, period.

It's cleaner this way, like Evan Isaiah grafting his limbs to mine eighteen years ago. Who can represent the tradition out of which we come better than I can? Who can speak for us?

At the oak tree, he would scrub his palms against its trunk. "Does it hurt?" I'd ask.

"I can't get the feeling off my hands," he'd said.

"What feeling?"

"Our names." And, with a pocketknife he'd knicked from Nelson, he'd proceed to scratch "E.I." and "S.L." into the trunk.

Call him Evan Isaiah. Call me Sylvia Lin. We are born naked and vulnerable; the rest is circumstance.

MIKKO HARVEY

■

Spring

FROM *The Indiana Review*

I opened the car door and noticed
a sparrow sitting in the passenger seat.

Howdy, I said.

Howdy.

And I drove for eleven hours, through three states, attended the
funeral, slept on the couch, heard the whispers, ate the brunch,
folded the sheet, hugged, hugged,

and opened the car door and noticed
a sparrow sitting in the passenger seat.

Howdy, I said.

Howdy.

ANGELA GARBES

■

The BabyLand Diaries

FROM *Topic*

I'M PEERING INTO A CRIB in the nursery of BabyLand General Hospital in Cleveland, Georgia. Outside, the air above the rolling hills just south of the Chattahoochee National Forest is sticky and humid, but inside BabyLand, it's cool and scented with baby powder. Inside the crib, two "newborns" in white bonnets—Cabbage Patch Kid dolls with hand-sewn fabric faces, priced at $225 each—stare back at me blankly, as baby coos and cries play on a loop in the background.

Before I can be creeped out by the soundtrack, it is interrupted by an announcement: "Mother Cabbage is in labor! Mother Cabbage is in labor! If you would like to see Mother Cabbage give birth, please make your way to her now!"

This is the moment that the dozen or so people there have been waiting for, myself included. I turn on my heel, with embarrassing urgency, and beeline it through the "hospital"—an immaculately kept white-columned estate that is, in truth, a Cabbage Patch museum–cum–toy store. My shoes squeak on the black-and-white floor tiles. As I'm fast-walking (running seems a touch desperate, even for me) through BabyLand General, another announcement is made: "If you think you are going to get queasy during birth, you may proceed instead to the Fathers' Waiting Room."

I look around. There doesn't seem to be an actual waiting room, so the crowd moves toward the center of the store to see Mother Cabbage—the matriarch of the world's millions of Cabbage Patch Kids, and a towering sculpture made to look like an artificial tree that serves as the portal, i.e., birth canal, through which Cabbage Patch Kids enter the human realm.

At the height of the Cabbage Patch mania of the 1980s, children and adults lined up for hours outside the BabyLand General Hospital in New York City. (Across the country, a few adults were also involved in violent holiday toy-store riots as they battled to procure the precious dolls.) Three decades later, widespread Cabbage Patch mania has dwindled, and this BabyLand General Hospital, in the rural hometown of Xavier Roberts (the original marketer of the Cabbage Patch kids, which closely imitated "Doll Babies" created by the artist Martha Nelson Thomas), is the only one that remains. But the allure of the Cabbage Patch has not entirely faded. Every year, 250,000 people make the pilgrimage to BabyLand General, the centerpiece of which is the towering Mother Cabbage.

Mother Cabbage is a massive object—at least 12 feet tall, though she rises into a domed ceiling, giving her the appearance of infinite height. Like the drive-through trees of California's Redwood Coast, her trunk is large enough to allow passage for BabyLand's Licensed Patch Nurses (LPNs), who move in and about her as they work. Mother Cabbage's many branches comprise a wide, shady canopy that protects a patch of roughly three dozen fabric cabbage heads. Tiny doll faces—mostly white, though there are a few brown ones here and there—peek out of the center of each cabbage. Under the twinkling, multicolored lights that dangle from the branches above, some of the babies' heads turn and move, meaning you'll occasionally find yourself in direct eye contact with one of them as it stares back at you, vacant and dumb. Or perhaps it's staring straight into your soul.

From an upside-down, baby-bottle-shaped container filled with bubbling blue medicine, the LPN pantomimes filling a plastic syringe. "I'm going to give Mother Cabbage a dose of Imagicillin," she explains, dabbing the tip of the syringe in various places around a head of cabbage in front of her, at the base of Mother Cabbage.

I crane my neck to try and see where exactly the Imagicillin is going—the cabbage's spine, à la an epidural? Or perhaps amid her labia-like leaves? But alas, Mother Cabbage is too far away, and Baby-Land doesn't seem to have mapped the human female body to the cabbage/tree body in any rigorous way.

The nurse places the used syringe in an antique, white enameled medical tool tray which holds more syringes, a scalpel, and scissors.

"Don't worry—this does not hurt or harm Mother Cabbage in any way," she says. "It just loosens her leaves before and after her deliveries and helps her not feel any pain at all."

As the nurse talks, I make eye contact with another mother sitting nearby. She's with her daughter, a blonde, pig-tailed two-year-old pushing a Cabbage Patch Kid in a stroller. The mother looks back at me and laughs. We both know better.

Actual human labor is, of course, much more difficult and unpredictable than what happens at BabyLand General, where crystals at the bottom of the Mother Cabbage exhibit begin to glow brighter as the blessed event is set in motion.

It's also not well understood. In fact, there still isn't a consensus among researchers about what exactly makes a body go into labor, or why childbirth—a process essential to all human life—is so demanding and harrowing.

Throughout the ages, women's bodies have been poorly understood—particularly as reproductive vessels—and they have often been subject to myths and wild speculations that were treated as facts. For example, it wasn't until the early 20th century that menstruation was clearly understood to be linked to ovulation; before that, people thought that women bled for no reason, or as a way to release their emotional hysteria. (Roman historian Pliny the Elder wrote: "Contact with [menstrual blood] turns new wine sour, crops touched by it become barren ... hives of bees die, even bronze and iron are at once seized by rust, and a horrible smell fills the air.")

When I ask Dr. Holly Dunsworth if she's surprised that we still don't know what causes labor, she says no—at least for now. Dunsworth, a professor of anthropology at the University of Rhode Island, studies how human anatomy, physiology, and behaviors related to growing, birthing, and raising children have evolved.

"I know enough to know how complicated this stuff is and how difficult it is to imagine how to try and figure this out," she explains. "I don't think it's true we'll never know what starts labor, though."

In other words, yes, childbirth might be difficult to study, but so are many other things—the brain, heart function, epigenetics, erectile dysfunction—and we've figured out ways to do it. It's not just that pregnancy is challenging to study; it's that medical and scientific researchers have chosen not to. There are certainly hurdles to studying the unique and temporary state of pregnancy, in which two bodies share the same real estate. But we should know much more than we do.

During pregnancy, a woman's body builds an entire human being (sometimes more than one) from scratch. It also grows an entirely new organ, the placenta, alongside the fetus. When it is time to give birth, a mother's cervix must expand from zero to ten centimeters, and her uterus, through a series of increasingly strong contractions, pushes the baby down the birth canal and out the vagina, an opening that is noticeably smaller than the baby's head. It goes on for hours, sometimes days, and it's excruciating—that's why we call it labor.

For the last few decades, the difficulty of childbirth has been succinctly explained by an evolutionary hypothesis put forth by anthropologist Sherwood Washburn in 1960. Washburn's hypothesis, called the "obstetrical dilemma," posits that when humans parted evolutionary ways with our primate cousins—when we stood up and started walking on our hind legs—our brains got bigger and our hips got smaller. Over millennia, babies' heads and their mothers' vaginas became an increasingly tight and complicated fit. All this meant ever-more-painful births.

"It's got a lot going for it," says Dunsworth, of the obstetrical dilemma. "It pulls together so many of the stars of our human evolutionary story, or the highlights: big brains, bipedalism, our helplessness as infants." But Dunsworth, who has spent the better part of the last decade testing Washburn's hypothesis, believes the obstetrical dilemma doesn't hold up.

Her research reveals that the onset of the birth process has less to do with head and bone size, and more to do with something more complex: metabolism and energy. Around nine months, she explains, a fetus's energetic needs begin to outpace what a mother's body can supply. (Toward the end of pregnancy, mothers' bodies are operating at a metabolic rate more than two times their usual.) A pregnant woman holds 50 percent more blood volume than normal, and her heart is pumping all that extra blood to move oxygen through her body, as well as that of the growing fetus. It's a lot of work, and a body's metabolism is limited by its ability to handle the extra load. In other words, there is a limit to how long the female body can operate at such a heightened level before birth will need to occur.

"There's a point when you could eat the moon, and you still couldn't gestate or be pregnant any longer," Dunsworth explains. "Metabolism is more than converting calories to energy and building a fetus . . . it's everything. It's being the flesh-and-blood home for this extra person."

Dunsworth calls her hypothesis the "energetics of gestation and growth." This suggests that, after 40-plus weeks of negotiations, labor is the result of an energetic stalemate between mother and child—one that, thankfully, will be resolved by the fetus opting to have its needs met outside of its mother's body.

"A lot of people have perpetuated [the obstetrical dilemma] as fact," Dunsworth says. "It was very difficult to even question this hypothesis until very recently. This is how science unfolds, though: we rethink assumptions that are decades old."

Back at BabyLand General, Mother Cabbage must be checked to make sure she is dilating properly. Presumably they are checking her cervix, but I really can't tell. No one else—not the mothers, the grandmothers, or the little girls—seems concerned, though, or interested in posing the sorts of questions I'm anxious to have answered. Like, for example, does Mother Cabbage have a mucus plug?

The nurse pulls out a pelvimeter, an actual stainless-steel gynecological instrument that resembles the silver electronic claws used to pick up toys at arcades. "We want to make sure [Mother Cabbage] has dilated a full ten leaves apart," she explains.

Another syringe appears and Mother Cabbage is faux-injected in her trunk with a large dose of "TLC." (The nurse also spritzes some behind each of her ears, as though the syringe were a perfume atomizer, telling us that she likes to give herself a dose of TLC every day, too.) She then raises a pair of surgical scissors and begins to spread the leaves of Mother's cabbage head.

My intrigue (and horror) reaches new heights. I stand on my tippy toes and grip the cabbage patch fence, trying desperately to see what is about to go down with this particular magical, mysterious crystal-cabbage-vagina-hole.

"This procedure is what's known as an 'easiotomy,'" the nurse explains. "We are in fact the only hospital in the entire world that performs the easiotomy, though I'm not sure why. We've had no bad results and never once had to perform a C-section—a 'cabbage' section, that is."

Almost against my will, I find myself laughing at the joke, a play on words hinting at the episiotomy, a once-common procedure of making a surgical incision in the perineum (the small sling of skin between the vagina and the anus) to expand the opening of the vagina. Episiotomies were performed with the belief that they could speed a baby's delivery and prevent extensive tears during vaginal childbirth. But research has shown that the procedure's risks outweigh its supposed benefits: the incisions risk infection, and recovery is often more complicated than it would be with a natural tear. Since 2006, the American Congress of Obstetricians and Gynecologists (ACOG) has discouraged the use of episiotomies; health-care providers have come to understand that what female bodies do naturally during birth—rip open, tear—are not merely symptoms of weakness.

"Because women are, on average, slower walkers and runners, we're seen as 'not as strong as men,'" Dunsworth tells me. "You encounter this idea everywhere: that women's bodies are not as evolved, or well-built, as men's." To her, it's a "logical conclusion" based on the overuse of medical interventions (such as episiotomies and C-sections), which have gone from being used only to assist mothers in dire need to commonplace practices, as if women lacked the fortitude to endure their physiology.

I've birthed two babies—both pulled straight from my uterus as I lay on an operating table, each after 24-plus hours of labor. When I was pregnant with my second child and hoping for a vaginal birth after a C-section, an obstetrician strongly urged me to schedule a second C-section at 40 weeks because, she said, it was likely that I have an "uncooperative cervix." I asked her: was there a way to gently encourage it to cooperate? She didn't answer, and repeated the only op-

tion she was offering: to give up on my cervix and opt for major ab-
dominal surgery.

There are no doulas at BabyLand General—none of these non-medi-
cal professionals who provide continuous support to laboring mothers, to massage Mother Cabbage's hips or bring her ice chips to chew
on. The goings-on are also, notably, completely sterile and removed
from the actual territory of birth: the female body. There are no men-
tions of body parts or fluids; even when Mother Cabbage is dilating,
there are no references to uteri, vaginas, blood, placentas, amniotic
fluid, or even umbilical cords.

It's a vision of a "good birth" that is familiar, although perhaps a
bit dated, and it gets me thinking about Shulamith Firestone, the
feminist theorist who, in her 1970 book *The Dialectic of Sex,* imagined artificial reproduction as a possible means for achieving gender
equality and feminist revolution. "To free women from their biology
would be to threaten the social unit that is organized around biological reproduction and the subjection of women to their biological destiny, the family," she wrote.

At the time, Firestone's ideas were widely dismissed as absurd (the
New York Times called her "brilliant" but also "preposterous"). But on
many issues—including the dissolution of the traditional marriage
model and the drastic change in social relationships that would be
brought about by machines surpassing humans in problem-solving,
which she called "cybernetics"—she was almost prophetic, particularly in her observations that reproductive science and medicine did
not actually prioritize women.

"The money allocated for specific kinds of research, the kinds of
research done, are only incidentally in the interests of women, when
at all," she wrote in *Dialectic of Sex.* "For example, work on the development of an artificial placenta still has to be excused on the grounds
that it might save babies born prematurely."

In other words, the fact that an artificial placenta could improve
the mother's life was not really a good reason to do it. The same stan-
dards have not been applied to, say, the development of medication
to improve erections.

* * *

Mother Cabbage is close to giving birth and, the nurse says, she is tense and very anxious. The nurse asks those of us in the audience to help Mother with her breathing. Loudly and slowly, at the nurse's request, we take three deep breaths in and out, in and out, in and out, for a minute or so. It works. Mother is now ready to push.

"Everybody yell, 'Push!'" the nurse instructs.

"PUUUUUUUUSSSSHHHHH!" we scream in unison.

And just like that, the baby is here. How exactly the baby's pliable, vinyl head and limp, fabric body are pulled out of Mother Cabbage's hole is once again obscured by distance, an artificial fence, and so many green leaves. The baby is raised up in the air triumphantly and even begins "waving" at its many admirers. (The nurse acts as a puppeteer.) "It's a girl," the nurse then announces, dangling the doll upside down by its ankles, and patting it firmly on the butt.

Mother Cabbage's baby—Campbell Ella, a girl named after a toddler in the audience—is then swaddled in a pink blanket and taken to the nursery by an LPN to be weighed and measured. Most of the audience has followed, and little girls wait to have their picture taken with the freshly born Cabbage Patch Kid.

Watching from the bench next to me is Amber McConnell, a native of Cleveland who has been coming to BabyLand General since she was a little girl. She's now 41 years old and pregnant with her fifth child. McConnell sighs happily after the completion of the birth.

"This is actually just like labor and delivery," she tells me.

"How?" I ask.

"Well, the nurses and everybody in the room helps Mother with her breathing. And breathing is very important, and you need a lot of people helping and encouraging you."

I can't argue with that, though I tell her it still seems quite different to me.

"Watching Mother Cabbage give birth gets to the easier, magical side of things," explains McConnell, who has brought a friend here for fun to witness her first birth. "When your five-year-old asks where babies come from, you don't want to lie, but you don't want to go into all that other stuff. Here, it's in a more delicate form.

"You really get to see that Mother went through a lot to get the baby here," she adds.

We should see all the work women do to get the babies here, I tell her. Because you have to be really strong to do it.

"Oh, sure," she says, nodding. "No man alive would be able to go through it."

That's what makes labor exceptional: the almost superhuman power required to do it. The uterus, an entirely female organ, is a profoundly forceful muscle ball capable of exerting over a pound and a half of pressure on every square inch of a little fetal skull. The force not only moves a baby down the birth canal, it also thins the cervix and shrinks the placenta, simultaneously squeezing all the blood into the fetus so it can get what it needs to take its first breath outside of its mother's body.

And then there are the forty or so weeks preceding labor, during which the uterus grows exponentially, both in volume and size. A pregnant uterus expands to over forty-five times its usual capacity, growing—to use the fruit-size comparisons favored by pregnancy websites—from the size of an orange that sits deep in the pelvis to a watermelon that will need to displace the stomach and lungs, and eventually graze the rib cage.

As Holly Dunsworth says, "Let's call the whole pregnancy 'labor.' It is all the work of making humans." Even when the mother is a cabbage.

■

Two Poems

FROM *Black Queer Hoe*

Black Queer Hoe

Black Queer Hoe shotguns pbrs on the redline before heading
to a club where she can't afford the water bottles. she yells at her
girls about the dick she just sucked across the slowdragging of the
crowded train. she know people. finesses her way to the front so she
don't have to wait in the cold. she sweats and sweats and throws it
back until she forgets her tab is still open. she scared to be the only
girl in the club in nikes. she wanna take her heels off but she scared
to be called ratchet. she just requested cardi b. she used to care that
niggas didn't want to dance with her. now she turn away niggas who
grab or pull or spent the whole night holding up the wall. she pays
the uber surcharge cause it's better than being followed home. she
gives the address of two houses down in case the uber decides to follow her home. she stands naked in the kitchen drinking juice from
the carton. she too drunk to remember if it's hers.

Black Queer Hoe makes sure her lesson for tomorrow is ready.
checks both her emails and all three of her slack accounts before the
room starts spinning. makes a note of all the work she didn't do to-
night. of all the things she'll have to catch up on tomorrow. sends the
"you alive bitch" text to her girls. thanks someone for keeping her
alive. sets two alarms just in case. writes down the six lines of the
poem that kept replaying in her head. takes her vitamins and birth
control with the water waiting by her bed. she smokes a little so she

doesn't think too long about all the ways in which she isn't successful. checks her credit and debit card balances. regrets nothing.

**open letter to the mothers who shield their daughters from
looking at me**
no ma'am you wouldn't want your daughter to be like me, i sucked
dick this morning and didn't brush my teeth. and yes my hat, neck-
lace, and septum ring all say Bitch. and i used to burn myself and
lie about it. and i've forgot how many men have forgotten my name
but not what i look like bent over. and i curse like a pirate fucked a
veteran fucked a barkeep fucked my mom and had me. and i got tat-
toos in places you didn't even know you could get them. and i touch
women in places you warn you daughter to not let boys near. i've
pierced some of those places too. sometimes i stand naked in my
kitchen. and i sleep with men in relationships. but not married ones
that's too much drama. and i feed off of drama like my uncle and a
bottle. and i do drugs. drug drugs not pot. and i smoke that too. and
i steal from target. imma feminist and i watch punishment porn.
and instead of a list of respectable shit i do, all i'll say is i respect my
elders, see i called you ma'am when I could've called you bitch.

KEITH DONNELL JR.

■

The Gettysburg Address
(Sound Translations 1 and 2)

FROM *Puerto del Sol*

The Gettysburg Address (Sound Translation 1)

Force door of heaven. Seers old as coppers sought forms of disquiet, enumerated cons, each iniquity, a den of cadence true and preposterous, thawed pen marks of fated inkwell.

Who'll weed our graves? Ingrates? Evil wards tasting hot nail gun? Thorny Haitians in old slaveries, hands decapitated, calmed by chores? We charm eternal snakes, fables built of past lore. Weave some to dredge the lake. A fortune, a fat yield as a single resting page. For poets, true seers, their grave lies at abomination's light mist. It is tar and feather, filthy proponents that weeds do resist.

Bet on a farther rest. We cannot medicate—we cannot obfuscate—we cast no shadow under ground. The Brahman, thinning sandalwood to loved powder, paste-consecrating forbearers, people house story too old to deter. Each word whittled, told, not log dismembered, not anymore, one inch can better forehead, what stays adheres. In this forest, bewildering matter, to be dead, cased in air, to come from it, wordage wrought clear, homes honed from snowy language. It is sour for us to be dear, dead-cased with a good asp, tamed to dust. That form bleeds ordered dread, sweet ache in bleak motion. Choose that pause for which they gave the lash. Sooth treasure with indecent poems, that water divinely re-soiled, that tested eggshell cracked in twain. That this Haitian, under trod, shall laugh a new curse of treason—and that gory sent troubles pupil, rides the pupil, corners pupil, shames all princes from their births.

The Gettysburg Address (Sound Translation 2)

Corner store better beers be cold. Our fathers built Fords, honest compliments, annunciations received in lit purity, handed cases to the opposition, that seesaw, hard crooked scale.

Now we are engorged with a greed evil tar, taking every fat ration of any bastion, soaked, weak, almost destroyed, cons de jure. We carve it on a great platter forged of their sword. We halve some to debt the cake with poison, salt the field, a spinal tapping plague or dose. Who dare give bare knives that fat? Nothing right lives in this alabaster city; only pepper weed shows truest.

Butting hard against weakens all delicate—weakens lost sacra-ment—weakens hot tallow—thistle-bound. The cave men, fixing the deck, troubling the air, have celebrated grift, pharaohs over poor pauper to app or distract. This world with bitter cold bore strong tim-ber, what we made fire, what can never go out, what may again flare. As its core, trust the listening. Rather to bleed educated, near to the underworld, with they who bought quarters want boatly passage. It is ample fortune. Be here, dedicated to the Greek tragedy's refraining chorus—platform these onward men, we pay in coin the boatman. To that calm for which they pay the ash dull pleasure of the boatman. Thankfully, here lightly salted, that these dead shall not have fried in vain. Fatten our patience until hog and save a new perch for bleeding. And that glowing scent of the meat, try the meat, tore the meat, shal-lots perfect on the hearth.

DEBORAH TAFFA

∎

Almost Human

FROM *A Public Space*

DAD LAUGHED WITH THE booming violence that always made me look over my shoulder. Of course, he was not in the back seat of my car. He was not on this trip with me. I slapped my cheek and told myself I should stop at the next gas station for coffee. But even then, I looked over my shoulder again, still believing I might find him there.

It was the stupor that follows a long flight and a four-hour drive on a dull Arizona highway. The confusion that arises after a string of bland hotels, too little sleep, and a month on the road. Many have experienced this disorientation when driving through a blizzard, fewer in a sandstorm.

Imagine jumping on the highway exhausted, and as you cross the border into California the steering wheel begins to tug and pull your hand. The wind is blowing hard, and the Imperial Sand Dunes sweep across the highway, pecking your car with a sound more frenetic and violent than hail. You slow to a crawl, but the sand flies forward into the headlamps, and the driving slant of dirt coming at your windshield makes you forget: who you are, where you are, when you started on this journey.

You pull over. When the storm ends, you stumble out and stand beside the road. The asphalt bounces hot breath in your face. You look toward California and see a puddle of water in the middle of the highway. You've landed on some faraway planet. You are an adult and you know the water is a mirage, but imagine you are a child who hasn't learned she's being fooled.

I grew up here on the Yuma Reservation in southeastern California, the ancestral lands of my paternal grandfather. His mother was Shoshone-Paiute, and his wife, my grandmother Esther, came from Laguna Pueblo in New Mexico. My father's clanship is Badger people at Laguna Pueblo for the Keepers of the Water people of the Yuma Nation, yet for all his tribal connections my childhood was confined to our family's southernmost reservation: the Yuma Nation. Holidays were a medley of Native languages, but only my great-grandfather spoke Quechan, the local Yuma language.

I lived in the southern desert for the first six years of my life, and there is no doubt that I prefer the high desert of Laguna Pueblo instead. The Sonoran Desert requires too much of the body to survive. There are cloudless skies and brutal sun, the absence of moisture and shade. Temperatures rise to 120 degrees in summer, yet drop so low at night one can easily freeze.

The desert's primary trait is deception. My childhood home is favored by the Fata Morgana. Long before I understood illusions, I saw castles and ships floating over the horizon. I chased turrets and sails only to see them vanish. The ideas I had about my family back then were confused by loss, Indian stereotypes, and silenced histories. I was small and invisible like all Indian kids are, a ghost child in love with mirages.

We were broken girls. We twisted our ankles sailing off playground swings, toppled out of tamarisk trees, plucked yellow-jacket and broken glass stingers out of our skin. We slammed our fingers in car doors, burned our feet in campfires, and then sat in the waiting room at the Yuma Indian hospital, ice pressed to injuries.

Joan broke her wrist. I broke my collarbone. Lori had a two-inch scar down the center of her chest. Monica slipped through the handrails of a tall metal slide and landed twenty feet below. The reservation was rowdy in the 1970s. Scars were a main source of pride.

Put a little whiskey in Dad's beer, and he got to talking about his friends. Crushed under a fast-moving train. Stabbed in the chest during an alley fight. Propped against a tree at a public park with a hot needle sticking out of an arm. Killed overseas in a land mine explosion. Mom tried to shush Dad when he told us his stories. But he said we needed to know the truth if we were going to survive, to hear how tough the world could be.

Swagger was a great way to get praise. Despondency hung over the reservation, and when tiny kids acted rebellious, adults saw hope and verve. A sassy girl was a girl who might make it, even given the dismal odds. My sisters and I did what we could to impress.

We rejected all things girlie. We painted our dolls' faces with markers, tattooing their chins in the style of our female ancestors. We chopped off their hair, and when they grew grotesque, threw their heads in the trash can and danced their bodies around, calling out like barkers selling tickets to see Geronimo at the World's Fair: "Come and see the Amazing Headless Wonders!" We were unruly Indian girls, not the friendly Thanksgiving Day type who knew how to cook and behave. Our mother said it was too late to teach us any manners.

Dad always said, "Broken bones grow back stronger." He raised us the same way his older brother, Gene, raised him. A father's job was to control the pace of the world's wounding; to dole out the pain in slightly bigger doses each time so his kids wouldn't break under the pressure. This is what I think of when I think of my sisters and me: we didn't get anything for free, and we blossomed because of it, blood flowering into bruises, skin thick and ripened in the Sonoran Desert sun.

The toughness we saw in our elders was rooted in pain, and for this reason I have always considered crying men courageous. I remember an old neighbor bawling his eyes out over his dog, Rocco.

You never saw a dog as spastic as Rocco. He made a play for freedom every time our neighbor opened his front door. "Rocco, you shit!" we'd hear him yell. The screen door would slam, and the chase would begin.

Rocco wouldn't heel, and our neighbor couldn't catch him. It was dodge-and-go for thirty minutes every time, an entertaining show that my sisters and I watched with glee. We scrambled on top of the swamp cooler and cheered Rocco on, loving the way he sidled in and ducked away at the last second.

The downside to our afternoon pleasure was the finish. The longer it took our neighbor to catch poor Rocco, the harder he would kick him once he got him leashed. "You fat old bastard!" we yelled.

Rocco's owner lived alone. He passed us Popsicles through the rip in his front screen door, but only if we'd stay with him for a while after eating. Cold and sticky and sweet, the Popsicles were a treat we never had in our own refrigerator with its week-old refried beans, lard-hardened cheese enchiladas, and Bud Light beer. When we finished he'd come out and wash our hands with the hose. Then he'd gather us around his lawn chair, take one of us on his lap, and crack stupid jokes. We couldn't leave because that would mean abandoning whoever he had on his lap. The rest of us gnawed nervously on the Popsicle sticks until he let the unlucky one go.

"Next time I ain't taking one of those Popsicles," we would swear. Then his jalopy would crunch up the driveway, and we'd see him carrying sacks emblazoned with the words "Del Sol Grocery" to the carport door. Our mud cakes would fall to the ground. We risked plenty for those Popsicles. Our parents gave us strict instructions to stay away from him.

"Don't go near that guy," neighbors warned. They said the only reason he lived in Yuma was because his ex-wife died and left him her house. They said never to trust an Indian who doesn't want to go back to his own reservation.

It was hard to be certain about anyone because we were always moving. We were simultaneously rooted in the land and homeless in it due to the region's history. My great-grandparents received their land in 1884, but President Roosevelt revoked the treaty nine years after it was signed, giving the entire reservation to the Bureau of Reclamation for farm development.

The Colorado River was healthier back then, its water strong. In June, the river rose and burst its banks. When it subsided in July, my ancestors planted their seeds along its irrigated shore. The soil was valuable, and the bureau set aside five acres per tribal member before giving the rest to white farmers. After protesting, my great-grandparents earned an extra five acres each in 1912, but by then the river had been dammed and the old way of planting was gone.

Only four houses could be built on our family's twenty acres, according to federal law. One home every five acres, and by the time Dad started a family, his older siblings had already moved in. With only a fifth of our treaty land remaining, my family lived in duplexes, apartments, and run-down stucco houses, rental properties on both sides of the river.

When the rattler got Rocco, our neighbor's scream ripped the desert. I was hiding behind clothesline sheets in a game of hide-and-seek when I heard him yell Rocco's name. I came out of white cotton to see his shovel moving like a jackhammer as he chopped the rattler in two.

He threw the shovel down and limped over to Rocco. His good leg buckled. We inched closer. Rocco was bleeding out of two puncture wounds and his forehead was starting to swell. "What're you staring at?" our neighbor yelled.

The rock wasn't big, and he only threw one. It struck the back of my hand, and my sisters took off running. Stunned by the pain, I lost them. The memory gets lost, too, at this point, but I always say I ran down to the river. I wouldn't have gone home while I was crying.

I sat there throwing rocks in the water, wishing Dad would pummel our neighbor. I'd seen him knock a guy off his feet with one punch, but he was straightening his life out, and his new docility embarrassed me. Like all the kids in my family, I admired Uncle Gene. He was six foot five and vicious as sin, the object of our uncritical hero worship. He would stagger in with one swollen eye, my younger uncles pale and shaking beside him because they had been his passengers as he raced the train, crossing the tracks just in front of it.

There were, of course, things I didn't understand until years later. I knew that Dad was the second oldest brother in a family of ten kids, that Uncle Gene was five years his senior and the eldest of the entire herd. But what I didn't know eclipsed what I did: Uncle Gene forced Dad to fight one of his very best friends when they were ten years old, and when the friend went down, and Dad wanted to stop, Uncle Gene threatened to beat Dad to a pulp unless he kept kicking. The longer Dad kicked, the angrier he got, until the anger took over, and the kicking felt good, and he cracked two of his very best friend's ribs.

Uncle Gene made his oldest daughter, Peanut, fight as well. He took her to the house of a guy he hated and forced her to fight the guy's daughter. He used to make Peanut, who was only twelve years old at the time, drive him and his friends around the reservation when they were drinking. I never saw her skinny elbow sticking out of the window as she backed down the driveway or heard her begging to stay home.

I didn't know that my uncle Gene was the last person in our immediate family to go to Phoenix Indian boarding school as a child, or that they chopped off his hair, and put him in child-size handcuffs. Perhaps because my parents never finished high school, or because my grandparents were stunned by cultural trauma, I didn't know the history; after the massacre at Wounded Knee in 1890, Native Americans lost their sovereign status and became wards of the US government. Richard Henry Pratt, leader of the Friends of the Indians, and founder of the Carlisle Indian Boarding School, sold his idea of "killing the Indian to save the man" to Congress and kept a catalogue of before-and-after photos: Native kids with long hair and traditional clothing on the left, the same kids with short hair and suits on the right.

I didn't understand that my father's education in a Catholic elementary school further damaged our ancestral memories, or that it ostracized my father from his Yuma peers because his mother's people at Laguna Pueblo practiced an indigenized Catholicism and Christianity was not popular on the Yuma Reservation. Five hundred years of mainstream media including best-selling captivity narratives, Wild West shows, and television Westerns had branded the "Indian" for all time, making him synonymous with wilderness and an antonym for civilization. I didn't know that this meant the more modern an "Indian" becomes, the more society questions whether or not he can claim to be who he is.

Most importantly, I didn't know that one night when my father was sixteen and doing math homework at home, trying to get to bed early because he had a big football game the next night, my uncle Gene called from downtown Yuma and said he needed to be picked up. He'd been in a fight. My dad was sent to fetch his older brother in the family car, and a gang of Gene's friends piled in when he arrived at the address he'd been given. The cops chased them, and Uncle Gene placed his foot over my dad's foot on the gas pedal to try to escape, and my father lost control of the car on the All-American Canal and flipped it into the water. One of their friends failed to emerge from the canal that night. It was the first time Dad got in trouble with the law, and got sent away.

Until I started school, I didn't know Dad had gone to prison. He ended up in solitary confinement, where he nearly went mad, and when he emerged from the hole he washed his face in the sink and looked in the mirror, realizing, finally, that he would never be able to defend his humanity or freedom by fighting for it with his fists.

Unlike my older sisters, who witnessed more of Dad's madness, I was born after his crookedness was finally becoming straight, after any illusion he'd had about who he was in America's eyes had gone to die. Dad was a pragmatist by the time I came into the world, in the final throes of the long spiritual crisis many Natives go through in order to build an identity they can live with in peace. If he knew the atrocities that had been committed against our people over the course of American history, he rarely spoke of them.

Some family histories are so painful they require decades to unfreeze. Understanding the past, for a Native American family, is like sifting through the wreckage of an earthquake. Only fragments are found: leather, bone, broken pottery, indigenous knowledge in shards. Dad and Uncle Gene raged to be seen rather than be thought of as vanished or extinct, but they didn't have the education to contextualize or communicate what they were feeling. The complexities of life for a mixed-tribe Native family in the 1950s has never been portrayed in books, on television, or in the media, and without talking about it at home, we didn't understand our own inheritance. Absent a voice, Mary Rowlandson, Buffalo Bill, the Friends of the Indian, and the Lone Ranger spoke for us, prescribing what we needed.

I mourn my community's broken bonds with the natural world, and the way the Catholic Church dehumanized my ancestors by calling them "heathens." I think of the false righteousness and greed that led leaders of the church to write the Doctrine of Discovery, a law granting land rights to any Christian nation settling an "empty" territory. I resent that the writers of *terra nullius* declared five continents of people only "almost human" because of spiritual beliefs that differed from their own.

"Animals don't have souls and can't go to heaven," my Catholic teachers told me. It was a teaching that made me long for a different version of the afterlife, a place with green vistas where animals and "almost humans" embraced their beliefs in peace. Every generation is different from the last, and I've asked my own children to look at history, and to speak when they remember the atrocities of the past. There were too many times in my life when I despaired of human love because we lived in a house that was silent. God's love is all that remains for a child living in a community filled with pain, which is a terrifying thought when one considers my sisters and I were taken to Catholic Mass, where those in control depicted God as an old white man.

The Holy Spirit was mine, I decided early on, because I could relate to its impermanent form: a swooping white dove, a jumping tongue of fire, a wind shaping the sand dunes in the desert. Unlike Dad, who thought we had to rise to be equal, I believed Christians should come down to earth and join the rest of us in our humble humanity.

I am haunted by my family's pain. Dad is haunted by the death of his childhood friends. Grandma Esther was haunted by ghosts who waited near the canal when she went to haul water or cried near the mission at dusk. Here is the last thing you need to know to understand my childhood: desert mirages remind us of unseen worlds. Shifting sands expose our impermanence. The very sunset holds the blood of our ancestors, and when the wind blows, we hear them mourn.

The day after Rocco died we played house outside while watching for our neighbor. We set up alongside the carport, fought for real estate, drew squares in the dirt to mark our homes. If we'd been playing inside, we would have stretched blankets over chairs and used books to hold the corners of our fiefdom in place. Outside, everything required more imagination. We called each other "Mary."

"Mary, can I borrow some flour?"

"Sure, Mary, but why don't you go to the store?"

"Jeez, Mary, didn't you hear the price of beer?"

We stopped and tried to convince each other to take a different name. "Why don't you be Sara?"

"You be Sara. I'm Mary."

Standing near Rocco's grave, our youngest sister snapped. "We can't all be Marys!"

She went inside and came out with our father's belt, pulled from his dirty work jeans. She swung, trying to catch our legs with the buckle. We ran around the back of our house.

She ran behind us, hitching up her shorts with one hand while striking with the other. The buckle hit the stucco of the house with a loud clap. It cracked our legs, stinging bone. We screamed, but no one came outside.

We took turns, and the whipping made us laugh. To have the courage to injure each other, to face a whipping from someone our size instead of someone bigger, to dodge and weave instead of worming to the bottom of the pile where the belt might miss, was a salve. Acceptance lessens pain because it lessens fear. There's something about being prepared.

"Poor Rocco," my sisters and I repeated when we were done hurting each other with the belt. Our faces had streaks of dirt running from the corners of our eyes to our chins. We looked at our neighbor's front door, hoping he'd appear from down the dark hall. But even with it slightly ajar, all we could see was black.

Imagine great smoking stacks, and a small town's blackened horizon. See the Navajo, Apache, Pueblo, and Yuma Indian men winding up the metal staircase to the top of the generating station, where they stand on a platform twelve stories high and look out over the desert plateau. They bow their heads and greet the sunrise together, saying a prayer in Navajo, before heading down to clean fly ash and weld. We are halfway between Shiprock and Farmington at the Four Corners Power Plant on the Navajo reservation.

After Dad met Mom, and he resolved to stay out of trouble, he hit a period of depression. He had no high school diploma, and no job prospects. Few Native people made a living wage in the 1960s— even model citizens who had never been in trouble with the law. Dad vowed never to return to prison but didn't know what to do, until one day his father came and told him about a new government program, one that would replace the boarding school attempts at assimilation.

The Indian Relocation Act, or Public Law 959, involved vocational training. Part of the government's Termination Policy, the law aimed to get young people in Native America to move to big cities and learn a trade. A medical license or law degree may have been elusive, but the government would train Natives to take the dirty jobs no one else wanted.

Many Natives who signed up for the training became welders, machinists, millworkers, and mechanics, while others dropped out before graduating. They missed their homeland, but when they tried to go back to their reservations many found that they couldn't return because the Termination Policy had taken away their tribal statuses. In this way, the program created the greatest migration of Natives in history. Ninety percent of Natives lived on their home reservations in the 1950s, while today it's only twenty. Many ended up homeless on city streets.

Relocation offices were set up in Los Angeles, Salt Lake City, and Denver. Phoenix, Saint Louis, Minneapolis, Cleveland, and Chicago followed. The Bureau of Indian Affairs was in charge of the new arrivals. A woman in high heels took Mom and Dad to JCPenney in Phoenix. She spoke slowly, with exaggerated enunciation.

She said, "This is where we come to buy things like u-ten-sils and tow-els."

When they got back to the car, my parents looked at each other and laughed.

Even with my father's training in Phoenix, my parents moved back to Yuma after welding school because no jobs were available in the city. They stayed there for six years after I was born because Dad refused to move away from his homeland for less than a living wage, and in the beginning no one would hire him. Dad worked a series of odd jobs in my earliest childhood, most of them part-time.

Uncle Gene was one of those men who never followed through with the training he received in the Indian Relocation Program, and he made fun of my father for giving in to the man. Uncle Gene was uncompromising, while Dad would do anything to provide for his family. Uncle Gene continued to fight with his fists, while Dad mutated the old physical hubris into an emotional strength. If Dad had spent his boyhood pounding his chest, solitary had given him the ability to remain quiet in the face of difficulty; and keeping one's head down—being polite to the man when you are secretly seething with anger—is not an easy practice.

James Baldwin wrote, "It demands great spiritual resilience not to hate the hater whose foot is on your neck, and an even greater miracle of perception and charity not to teach your child to hate." Dad had larger ambitions for us. He wanted us to grow up, build useful lives, and eschew the poor-me narrative he saw in his friends, whose attitudes resulted in their deaths. We were supposed to grit our teeth and be tough, even when the pain was legitimate. To discuss historic wrongs was risky. People might say we were using those reflections as an excuse for failure.

Gene regarded Dad as a Native version of Uncle Tom, though their rivalry wasn't something I fully understood until after my uncle died of alcoholism, and my dad's boss put him on a company plane for Phoenix so he would get back to the reservation in time for the funeral. Returning home after the tribal burial rites, Dad was so despondent about his brother's death, he drank too much and fell asleep at the gate, missing his flight. It was only after the funeral that Dad began to talk, and I learned to regret the way I valorized my uncle Gene.

I was a dumb kid who wanted her dad to go fight the neighbor with a dead dog, in part because I couldn't make the distinction between physical toughness and emotional resiliency, and in part because I didn't know how hurt my father was by his brother Gene. My uncle never forgave my father for taking a job at a coal-fired power plant, especially given what happened to their mother.

The canyons of the American Southwest contain Hopi healing plants alongside toxic waste. It's a place where uranium miners and high-pressure welders wait for cancer to claim them. I am talking about environmental illnesses resulting from the coal mines, power plants, uranium mines, and the first atomic bomb explosion at New Mexico's Trinity Site.

Dad's mom grew up in the village of Paguate in Laguna Pueblo, a town that sits ten miles south of the Jackpile Mine, one of the largest open-pit uranium sites in the world. In the years after Dad's training as a welder, she contracted a rare form of cancer that attacked her sinus cavity, but she refused chemotherapy or surgery. She wore bandages over the sides of her nose as the cancer ate her cheeks, and died without blaming history or the poison that bled into mountain runoff and gathered at the bottom of wells in Paguate.

Dad worked with many Navajo and Hopi men whose children were born with birth defects and whose parents died of cancer. They told him stories about playing on uranium pilings in the desert, never knowing that the small mounds were dangerous. Mom was three years old when the bomb was exploded thirty-six miles from her hometown in Socorro, yet no one in her family knew what the bright light, loud blast, and rattling windows meant. No one knew the nearby Jornada del Muerto Desert was the testing ground for nearly every missile in the Cold War arsenal—the Viking, Hermes, Nike, and others—or that rhesus monkeys were repeatedly launching into space there, most of them dying when their parachutes failed on the return. Radioactive debris fell from the sky, killing livestock and poisoning crops. That afternoon it rained, but no one warned the people of Socorro not to drink from their cisterns.

Observing Oppenheimer after the blast, physicist Isidor Rabi said, "I will never forget the way he stepped out of the car. His walk was like *High Noon*." I close my eyes and imagine the beauty of those arroyos, the red canyons lighting up in the blast. I think of my grandmother suffering, an unwitting victim of the warrior's arena. I remember my uncle Gene's rage and understand all men are seduced by violence, only some have tools that are bigger.

Dad was funneled into an environmentally destructive job due to a government assimilation program, and it pulled us out of poverty. Arizona Public Service had Native American hiring preferences that were part of a contract with the Navajo Nation because the plant was built on their reservation. He ran crews that burned coal in turbines and polluted the sky to make electricity, supplying energy to our televisions and computers. He took the paycheck and brought it home, and I judged him for it for many years. I almost died, I was so depressed, and it was the canyons and arroyos that saved my life. I hiked every day, attempting to reconnect with the sacred, all the while resenting my father because I felt he had ruined the best part of our family legacy.

How can parents decide between being arrested and sending their kids to Indian boarding schools? How can a father decide between his values and a better life for his children? I wish I had been aware, as a teenager, of the suffering my father endured in order to push me ahead. He sacrificed his life for mine, yet I spent many years judging him for his decisions.

My shame about my father's job, my judgment about his choices, and my desire to turn him into something he wasn't was all bound up in an impulse to give him the life he should have had, the life I felt he deserved. In my mind, I envisioned a green-grass utopia, and wanted to put him in it. I wanted nothing more than to turn him into the crying Indian in the public service announcement designed to discourage littering. Injustice is when someone privileged like me, someone who has reaped the benefits of electricity and national security, turns around and vilifies a poor indigenous man for taking the only job he had available to him.

I have never seen a Hopi hedge fund manager or Navajo bank owner, and I wonder how I'd feel if I did. In the meantime, I pound my desk and tremble as I tell the story of my family's moral dilemma. I tremble because I fear what environmentalists—our tribal allies and the people I most admire—will think about my father. Will they, too, feel he should have refused the job? What does it mean to save the planet? If we kill anything won't it be ourselves?

∎

Macho

FROM *The Paris Review*

A man in long shorts tossed a tiny dog
into the leaves piled at the edge
of people's yards, the dog
the same brown as the leaves.
Too small to bark
it squeaked as it was tossed.

I was seeing someone and we passed it
on our way downtown. A street where boys
stuck dollar bills over coils of shit
then watched who came along
and picked them up. Then they jeered
from the window. They were in college
living together. Girls lived together too
and it was warm enough you could
still see them tanning on their roof
or in the kiddie pools they dragged
to strips of grass along the sidewalk.

The dog's name was Macho.
Each time we walked, I hoped
to see it. He found my hope
annoying, then pathetic.
I think you wish you were that dog.

No, I *want* it; I don't want to *be* it.
I think you want to be it.

We were in love
or in some other thing love served
as cover for. It required constant testing,
trying to humiliate while seeming
innocent, uninvested. Back then
I didn't understand that everybody
did these things, choking or pissing
on each other, having the girl
impersonate a child being molested.
You got somewhere and after
you were where you started.
We drove across the river

to a discount grocer where the baggers
wore black aprons over buttoned shirts
and pushed your cart out
to your car for you, even if you
asked them not to, it was mandatory.
Next door, the gas station sold souvenirs
of itself: lighters and what looked like earring boxes
packed with thumb-size gummy pizzas.

Sun touched the river.
Complicated trees leaned out
at angles to the water.
On the radio, a man who made
a movie was explaining no one
got it: it isn't funny. The frozen
chicken triggers something
for the boy, his realization.

Around us stretched the aisles of the fields
then prairie, prairie grasses

over whose incessant restlessness the roads
and towns were pieced. And far out
moving slow across the earth
black carriages of Mennonites
drawn by horses.

My job was teaching acting at a middle school.
The skinniest of the Sams was most talented.
Asked to play an animal, the other children
jumped or squawked, but Sam's face hardened
to a twitching glare, his paws examining
the rug before they crossed it.

On the porch, coffee cans
preserved summer rain, cigarette butts
gone tender, floating. You could smoke
and look out at the uncut lawn
down to the snapped stakes of tomato plants
he'd smashed when he was angry.
It had started with us laughing

lying in the grass, him saying
let me cut off a piece of your scarf
to remember today by. No
it started from my only
feeling I was myself
when I resisted things.
I turned away. I felt
his scissors in my hair. Late fall

the town put on its festival.
Three generations wandering
in jerseys, carrying foam fingers.

He was house-sitting
and along the walls, some books I knew

wore bindings I'd never seen.
They belonged together. They were all dark red
with notches down their spines.

If you debased yourself before a man
debased you then you'd have
a little peace. It was a choice then. It was
running ahead of the others and standing
on the bank where you could see
yourself how things went—the ragged
progress of the lichen, gnats, a swimming beach,
the concrete becoming gravel.
I thought that way for years.

DAVID DRURY

■

The Lake and the Onion

FROM *Zyzzyva*

THERE ONCE WAS A LAKE who fell in love with an onion. This is merely what we 100 percent know. The evidence is spread across the night sky as far as the eye can see, so long as that eye is resting comfortably inside one of our more powerful telescopes. Substantive data is still being collected from the farthest reaches of space and stared at for a very long time in an upturned palm.

The lake was small for a lake. The onion was large for an onion. One gusty autumn day, as the lake reflected warbled images of passing clouds back to themselves, and regarded the way the leaves came off the trees in red and gold drifts, three not-animals came into the clearing. The lake had only recently heard about not-animals, and opinions were mixed. Two young men ran along the tree line throwing and catching an onion back and forth. A young woman gave chase. She both laughed and did not laugh. When she stopped chasing the young men and let her shoulders fall, she did not laugh. The young woman had been preparing soup on a strict timeline. The timeline was dictated to her by her mother, who lived in fear of what the man of the house was capable of, should the mother ever fail to please him. The daughter's soup-help was nearly as vital as her inherited duty to the same set of fears. Handsome young men running off with onions was not her idea of a good time. As she ran after them, however, she noticed the way her hair fell heartbeatingly and pretty against her chest, and for a moment she pondered how much her mood might improve if the chase became a pleasing and emotionally reciprocated time, which it did not.

How much of this the lake knew, we are not certain—but that it did happen, we are. Very are.

The lake had seen animals fight over food before, but always for the privilege of, well, eating it—immediately, ravenously, and in plain sight of the not-winner. But this new survival theater boasted a different sort of quality. When the young woman stopped chasing, the men stopped eluding, as if the chase was more appetizing than the onion.

The lake regarded all of this with fascination. The wind stopped to see what the lake was looking at. The leaves stopped to see what was keeping the wind. The young man, who held the onion, cocked his arm as if he might throw it against a tree. He looked to the young woman. The wind gasped, the leaves were a little rattled. The young woman only sighed without expression. This was not the reaction the young man was hoping for, so he shrugged and hurled the onion against the tree.

While the woman's plight stirred a sadness in the lake, the onion had taken much deeper root in the lake's heart. The lake could hardly believe that entanglements of pride had the power to render nourishment inconsequential in favor of battles of will. The onion was about to speak someone else's parting shot against the side of a tree with a thump, a spray of pulpy mash and slick slivers, and a pattering of concentric shrapnel onto the grass. Un-nested layers of demise. A bulb whose light was had been put out.

The lake could not bear to see it. Love welled from the cool of the lake's murky depths, and it desired to absorb the onion's fate. You might say it filed an unofficial appeal to the laws of nature. We do it all the time, you and I, in matters of sickness and death and lottery tickets and tummy ouches and rain clouds approaching picnics. Nature plows on ahead anyway. But as to the lake and the onion, this wasn't the last of it. The appeal was taken up by a higher court. This is only what the body of evidence totally suggests. Nature was overruled. What force this was, we do not know. When we ran the numbers through spellcheck and presented them to our finest sketch artist, he snapped all his pencils and took his estranged daughter to lunch. But the image he doodled on a napkin while at lunch seemed to depict what we would describe as a compassionate lawlessness hailing from the realms of over-nature. Don't even ask.

The bottom line is this—the lake, in that moment, was allowed to stand in for the onion. When the onion hit the tree, the lake hiccupped at its center as if punched by a fist-sized meteorite. Ripples moved to the shore, lapped at the edge, and radiated back to center. The clouds witnessed this display of solidarity and considered it nothing less than miraculous. The wind, the trees, the leaves, the rocks, they all saw it. And they saw it not only in the goings-on of the lake. It was a one-for-one switch. The onion did not burst. All who witnessed it marveled. The onion bounced off the tree like a ball and rolled unscathed into the grass. The daughter swept it into her skirts and skipped off to make soup.

The lake was beside itself with joy. The onion had been spared, at least long enough to be chopped for soup, which is a fine legacy for an onion and not a sad thing at all, certainly in comparison to being crushed against a tree. Nevertheless, the onion did not have opportunity in its short life to thank the lake or return the favor.

For the rest of the day, ripples of water continued to travel back from the shore to the center of the lake, where a mosquito-sized funnel had formed on the surface and wound straight to the bottom. By morning the lake was smaller. The next day it was even smaller. It continued to shrink until it had drained entirely. The lake bed dried, cracked, peeled, and turned to dust. The trees moved a whisper closer to the water's edge and grew thirsty looking out over the parched and dying lake. The mountains moved closer to see what the trees were up to. It was all starting. The lake just knew it. A billion-year slow collapse of all matter into a newly perforated black hole. A black hole born—not at the edge of some remote galaxy—but here and now at the center of a leaky and disgraced former lake.

Epochs and ages passed. The trees inched closer, the mountains inched closer, and the lake bed remained only a skeleton of its former self. Try as it might, the lake could not hold water. In the quiet of the night, the barren lake regarded the moon and thought only of the onion. We speculate it was the moon that the lake was looking at. Possibly several moons. Or a hole in the ozone illuminated by photons or volcanic gases. Or a reflection of the sunlight by something else in the night sky, or some combination of the above. We know two things for sure: the lake was looking up, and the lake experienced acute longing in only the places where all the water had been.

On occasion, a cloudburst or snowmelt would fill the lake, temporarily reminding any who saw it of the lake's former glory. The water always drained away a few days later. A certain man observed this pattern. He tried to dam up the lake. When that didn't work, he had a different idea. He dragged a boat to the center of the lake bed. He built a long dock to where the boat sat in the dust. He connected the two together with a length of rope. He built a house under the trees and waited. When the next big series of rainstorms rolled through and the lake filled with water, the man invited his brother's family to see his beautiful home by the lake. He then conned his brother into buying the lakefront property from him at an exorbitant price and disappeared the next morning.

The lake drained away yet again, and the invited brother and his family knew they had been cheated. The man watched his children play inside the boat moored there in the dry lake bed. When he couldn't take it anymore, he cursed at the children and dragged the boat to the house, where he broke it into firewood.

It would be months before the lake filled again. The rarest of storm surges broke over the land, battering the trees and flooding rivers and filling the lake. When the sun finally came out, the family acted on the scarce opportunity to picnic at the edge of the lake. The children kicked lake water at a swarm of mosquitos. The father paced at the lake's edge, still angry at having been sold a mirage that now taunted him with its doomed beauty. The mother sat at a wooden table up on the bluff chopping vegetables for soup.

One of the sons gathered rocks and carried them to the end of the dock to see what he could create. He hoisted the biggest rock above his head and shotput it out over the water to see how big a splash he could make. The man saw this and had an idea. While his brother, the cheat, was nowhere to be found, the man could at least take out his anger on the lake. Yes. He would fill it in with rocks and dirt and felled trees and level it off and build a tower or a temple or a grand vacation home on the spot, restoring his prospects at becoming a wealthy and respected man. Not one to miss out on free labor, he kicked at the ground to loosen more stones for his children. What the man did not see was that when his son heaved the rock from the end of the dock into the water, the water swallowed it whole without a splash of any kind. No splash or ripple at all. The child puzzled over this and went for another rock.

The mother on the bluff had been holding an onion to be chopped for soup, when it pulsed in her hand. Absent a second thought, she squeezed back as if it were a ball or a child's hand. Instead of yielding, it expanded. The woman opened her hand, and the onion burst its skin. She gasped and dropped it onto the table, expecting a feasting insect or rodent to hatch. But the onion did not move as if shaken. There was no munch or thump. It expanded slowly. It widened to the point of pulling apart. The onion drifted up into the air and bloomed in layers, radiating outward in all directions. The family gathered and watched the orb emanate above them, hanging in waves on the breeze. The layers peeled away from one another along the circumference of the onion's spires, subdividing again, and then again, and each split looked less like a rift or a divorce and more like the completion of a particularly long kiss. This kept happening until the peels were a series of sheer transparent films approaching invisibility, ever moving outward. The family was frozen in terror, or unspeakably delighted, or two dissimilar halves of a combination of both. The tears in their eyes may have been due to a large onion opening before them. We're almost certain they had no idea they were witnessing the birth of our universe. They had their own to worry about. The son at the end of the dock was the last to notice, still dropping rocks and marveling at the water which did not budge.

Similarities between this more recent lake-onion episode and the ancient one that happened eons earlier have accumulated. We must consider the possibility of a connection between the two, and so we have. Very have.

As to what the connection might be, we cannot say. Procedural guidelines dictate that we log all evidence related to the lake-onion events in the metal filing cabinet at the end of the hall marked *Universe, Origin of the,* but off the record, we keep a second copy in a file folder marked *Universe, Initiations and Reciprocations of the,* just in case. We scrawl prose poems and make graphite landscape drawings on the outside of this second folder because we cannot help ourselves, and we keep the folder hidden behind a framed picture of a boat at sea that hangs in the lobby directly above the water cooler. The contents of this second folder are discussed there in hushed, fervent tones whenever the current TV season has begun to lag.

We kill time at the water cooler arguing whether a lake is the same lake if it has all new water, or if *new water a new lake makes*. We get thirsty and debate whether onions have an oral tradition. We speculate why the little plastic cups keep running out and whether or not it is possible for a root vegetable to believe in reincarnation. We drink from the cooler using pencil cups and bare hands and promise the secretary we will lock up. We eat all the candy out of the secretary's dish, which she refills each day without complaint, and we ask aloud what the opposite of a grudge might be. We pick dry leaves off the plant next to the cooler and ruminate on what kind of fingerprints it might be that souls are capable of leaving on soulless nature. We lie on the floor and wonder what happens when love comes in direct contact with matter, and share which daytime soaps are our very favorite, and which ones we watch anyway. We lower our voices to match the lights and breathe one another's air and write into the carpet with our fingers, *What is all this magic?* One of us brings in blankets from the trunk of a car and asks what could anyone have known in any comprehensive way before metal filing cabinets? A knee touches a knee. A hand grazes a hand. One of us references the ancients who worshipped onions, seeing eternal life in its spheres. Most of those people were either drowned or destroyed by drought, we admit, presumably along with all of their onions.

We nod off, dismantling time to reach the otherwise unreachable outermost edge of dreams, only to recede light-years back to consciousness a few moments later. When these long silences begin to permanently threaten our wakeful state, a new consideration snaps us awake and rallies us to hang on till dawn. Someone recounts that when archaeologists unearthed the otherwise mummified Egyptian King Ramesses IV from his grave, they found onions in his eye sockets and a heart drained to dust.

CONTRIBUTORS' NOTES

*THE BEST AMERICAN NONREQUIRED
READING* COMMITTEE

NOTABLE NONREQUIRED READING
OF 2018

ABOUT 826 NATIONAL

ABOUT SCHOLARMATCH

CONTRIBUTORS' NOTES

Latifa Ayad is a Libyan American writer who was born and raised in Sarasota, Florida. She is a MacDowell Fellow, and the 2017 winner of the Master's Review/PEN America Flash Fiction Prize and the Indiana Review 1/2K Prize. Her work has been published in *Prairie Schooner, North American Review, Crab Orchard Review,* and others. She currently resides in Columbus, Ohio, where she is at work on her first novel.

Renée Branum currently lives in Cincinnati, where she is pursuing a PhD in fiction. She holds MFAs from the University of Montana (in creative nonfiction) and the Iowa Writers' Workshop (in fiction). Renée's fiction has appeared in *Blackbird, The Georgia Review, Tampa Review, Narrative Magazine,* and *Alaska Quarterly Review.*

Sylvia Chan is a poet from Hayward, California. Formerly a jazz pianist in the San Francisco East Bay, she teaches in the writing program at the University of Arizona and serves as nonfiction editor for *Entropy* and court advocate for foster kids in Pima County. Her debut poetry collection is *We Remain Traditional* (Center for Literary Publishing, 2018).

Andrea Long Chu is an essayist and critic living in Brooklyn. Her writing has been published in *n+1, Boston Review, New York, Bookforum, The Chronicle of Higher Education,* the *New York Times,* and elsewhere. Her work has been translated into several languages. Her first book, *Females* (Verso, 2019), is out now.

Keith Donnell Jr. received his MFA in creative writing from San Francisco State University and his MA in English from the University of Southern California. His work has appeared in journals, including *Redivider, New American Writing, Lumina,* and *Puerto del Sol*'s Black Voices Series. He was the 2017–2018 editor in chief of *Fourteen Hills: The SFSU Review.*

David Drury lives in Seattle. He has been kicked out of so many casinos he briefly earned the distinction "Most Notorious Card Counter in America." He earned a master's degree in Christian studies from Regent College, University of British Columbia. He also appeared in a rock-and-roll feature film set in Tokyo, which several people have seen and which made Dave Matthews cry. His fiction can be found at daviddruryauthor.com.

Angela Garbes is the author of *Like a Mother: A Feminist Journey Through the Science and Culture of Pregnancy,* which was named a Best Book of 2018 by NPR. Her writing has appeared in the *New York Times* and *New York Magazine*'s The Cut, and was featured on NPR's *Fresh Air.* She lives in Seattle with her husband and daughters and was a staff writer at the city's newsweekly *The Stranger.*

Kate Gaskin is the author of *Forever War* (YesYes Books, 2020), which won the Pamet River Prize. Her poems have recently appeared in *Pleiades, 32 Poems, Passages North,* and *Blackbird,* among others. She is a recipient of a Tennessee Williams Scholarship to the Sewanee Writers' Conference, as well as the winner of *The Pinch*'s 2017 Literary Award in poetry. She lives in Omaha, Nebraska.

Devin Gordon is contributing writer for a number of publications, including the *New York Times Magazine, ESPN The Magazine, GQ, The Atlantic,* and *The Guardian.* He is working on a book about the Mets and the fine art of being terrible, due out in summer 2020 (HarperCollins). Gordon lives in New York City with his wife, two kids, and their dog.

Garth Greenwell is the author of *What Belongs to You* (Farrar, Straus and Giroux, 2016), which won the British Book Award for Debut of the Year, was long-listed for the National Book Award, and was a finalist for six other awards. A new book of fiction, *Cleanness,* is forthcoming from FSG in early 2020. His fiction has appeared in *The New Yorker, The Paris Review, A Public Space,* and *VICE.* He lives in Iowa City.

Mikko Harvey is the author of *Unstable Neighbourhood Rabbit* (House of Anansi, 2018). He received a BA from Vassar College and an MFA from Ohio State University, and he currently lives in Ithaca, New York.

In September 2018, friends of Dr. Christine Blasey Ford's **Holton Arms Class of 1984** leapt to her defense. Samantha Semerad Guerry and Virginia White wrote and spearheaded the class letter to attest to Dr. Ford's character and to urge Congress to give serious consideration to her testimony before the Senate Judiciary Committee. Ms. Guerry also served as the class spokeswoman in major national and international media to protect and amplify not only Dr. Ford's story but also the voices of women across the country as they collectively broke their silence about sexual violence and trauma.

Matt Hongoltz-Hetling is a Vermont-based writer whose nationally recognized long-form journalism has appeared in *Popular Science, Foreign Policy, USA Today,* and the Weather Channel, among others. He is a recipient of the George Polk Award, a Pulitzer Prize finalist, and a Maine Journalist of the Year. His investigative work led to national reforms of the federal Section 8 housing program. His first book, *Bearing Arms,* is due out in 2020.

Matt Huynh is a Sydney-born, New York–based visual artist and storyteller. His bold brush-and-ink paintings are informed by calligraphic Eastern sumi-e ink traditions, the mechanical reproduction of popular Western comic books, and their limitations. Huynh's work has been exhibited by MoMA, the Smithsonian, the Sydney Opera House, the Brooklyn Museum, the Brooklyn Academy of Music, and the New-York Historical Society.

Charles Johnson is a novelist, essayist, literary scholar, philosopher, cartoonist, screenwriter, and professor emeritus at the University of Washington in Seattle, as well as a MacArthur fellow. His fiction includes *Night Hawks*, *Dr. King's Refrigerator*, *Dreamer*, *Faith and the Good Thing*, and *Middle Passage*, for which he won the National Book Award. In 2002 he received the Arts and Letters Award in Literature from the American Academy of Arts and Letters. He lives in Seattle.

Britteney Black Rose Kapri is a teaching artist, writer, performance poet, and playwright from Chicago. Currently she is a Teaching Artist Fellow at Young Chicago Authors and is a staff member and writer for *Black Nerd Problems*. She has been published in *Poetry*, *Vinyl*, *Day One*, *Seven Scribes*, *The Offing*, and *Kinfolks Quarterly*, and is a 2015 Rona Jaffe Writers' Award recipient. Her debut book, *Black Queer Hoe*, was released by Haymarket Books in September 2018.

Robin Coste Lewis, the winner of the National Book Award for *Voyage of the Sable Venus*, is the poet laureate of Los Angeles. She is writer-in-residence at the University of Southern California, a Cave Canem fellow, and a fellow of the Los Angeles Institute for the Humanities, as well as the recipient of a 2019 Academy of American Poets Laureate Fellowship and a 2019 Guggenheim Fellowship.

Viet Thanh Nguyen's novel *The Sympathizer* is a *New York Times* bestseller and won the Pulitzer Prize for fiction. His other books are *Nothing Ever Dies: Vietnam and the Memory of War* and *Race and Resistance: Literature and Politics in Asian America*. He is a University Professor, the Aerol Arnold Chair of English, and a professor of English, American studies and ethnicity, and comparative literature at the University of Southern California. His current book is the best-selling short story collection *The Refugees*. Most recently he has been the recipient of fellowships from the Guggenheim and MacArthur Foundations, and le Prix du meilleur livre étranger (Best Foreign Book in

France), for *The Sympathizer.* He is a contributing opinion writer for the *New York Times* and the editor of *The Displaced: Refugee Writers on Refugee Lives.*

Uche Okonkwo is a Nigerian writer and an MFA candidate in fiction at Virginia Tech. Her work has been published in *One Story, Ploughshares, Lagos Noir, Per Contra,* and *Ellipsis.*

Maddy Raskulinecz lives in San Francisco. Her fiction has appeared in *Zyzzyva, Guernica, Joyland, Diagram,* and elsewhere, and has been included in Wigleaf's Top 50 Very Short Fictions. She holds an MFA from Johns Hopkins University.

Emily Rinkema lives and teaches in Vermont, where she got her master's degree from the Bread Loaf School of English. Her short fiction has appeared in *Syntax, Phoebe, The Newer York, SmokeLong Quarterly, Sixfold,* and *The Sun.* When not working or writing, she can be found on the patio or in front of the fire with her husband, Bill, her dogs, Stella and Frankie, and Jack Reacher the cat. She can be contacted at emilyrinkema@gmail.com.

Margaret Ross is the author of *A Timeshare* (Omnidawn, 2015). Her poetry has been recognized by scholarships and fellowships from the Iowa Writers' Workshop, the Fulbright Program, the Bread Loaf Writers' Conference, the Vermont Studio Center, and Yaddo, and has appeared in *The New Republic, The New Yorker,* and *Poem-a-Day.* A former Stegner Fellow, she is currently a Jones Lecturer at Stanford.

Nathaniel Russell was born and raised in Indiana and spent several years in the San Francisco Bay Area making posters, record covers, and woodcuts. He returned to his home city of Indianapolis and now spends his time creating drawings, fake fliers, sculptures, cut-outs, and music. Russell's work is regularly shown all over the world in both traditional galleries and informal spaces. His illustration and commercial work can be seen on album covers, on skateboards, in the *New York Times,* and in independent publications both local and international.

Patricia Sammon was born and raised in Canada and earned degrees from Cornell University and Queen's University in Ontario. She now lives in the United States. Her short stories have won a Nelson Algren Award, a Hackney Literary Award, and a prize from the Asheville Writers' Workshop. Her stories have been anthologized in *Ordinary and Sacred as Blood: Alabama Women Speak* and *Alabama Bound*. They have been published in literary journals such as *december, Narrative, New Millennium Writers,* and *Mid-American Review*. She has just completed a collection of four novellas set in northwest Australia.

Deborah Taffa (Yuma/Laguna Pueblo/Shoshone Paiute) received her MFA in nonfiction from the University of Iowa in 2013. She teaches CNF at Webster University in Saint Louis, and is an Ellen Meloy Desert Writers' Award recipient. Her stories have appeared in *A Public Space, Salon, The Rumpus, Brevity, HuffPost,* and other places. Visit her website at www.deborahtaffa.com.

Jane Wong's poems can be found in *Best American Poetry 2015, The American Poetry Review, AGNI, Poetry,* and others. A Kundiman fellow, she is the recipient of a Pushcart Prize and fellowships from the US Fulbright Program, the Fine Arts Work Center, Hedgebrook, and others. She is the author of *Overpour* (Action Books, 2016) and *How to Not Be Afraid of Everything* (Alice James Books, forthcoming). She is an assistant professor at Western Washington University.

THE BEST AMERICAN
NONREQUIRED READING
COMMITTEE

 Hayden Bixler enjoys reading fiction, judging things, and casting spells. They've graduated from Independence High School and are now attending Agnes Scott College in Atlanta. They hope this collection makes you as confused, angry, happy, and inspired as it did them.

Max Chu is a senior at RASFSotA and has big dreams for the CD industry. He's invested a lot of time and money into collecting compact discs because they're about to blow up in popularity. How does he know that? You could say that Max Chu has his finger on what's hot and what's not. It's a gift of his.

 Hannah W. Duane is a senior in the Creative Writing department at the Ruth Asawa School of the Arts. She enjoys writing, reading, rock climbing, and a nice cup of green tea. Or really, that's what she says she likes, but she's sixteen, so how on earth can she be expected to know? Anyway, she hopes you read this book because reading is perhaps the best thing one can do with one's time.

.

Olivia Jacob is a freshman at UC Berkeley. She plans to study creative writing, psychology, and philosophy in college to pick apart the secrets of human motivation. This fascination drove many of her choices for *BANR*'s 2019 collection, as she and her teammates tried to find pieces that held a "quintessentially 2019" quality. She will miss everyone dearly and is grateful for her opportunity to contribute to the program.

Colette Johnson is in her junior year at Ruth Asawa San Francisco School of the Arts. She is in the Creative Writing department. When she's not writing or reading, she spends her time listening to music and discovering different makeup looks.

 Althea Kriney is a freshman at McGill University in Montreal. She has been in *BANR* for three years. She will miss the basement *BANR* was held in, but only because of the people, as the basement itself was very humid.

Juliana Lamm-Pérez is a junior at Lick-Wilmerding and has two younger sisters that have names also starting with *Juli* and ending in *-a*. She speaks Spanish fluently (*es chapina*), plays volleyball, drums, is in the school dance program, and wears winged eyeliner every day (how? she doesn't know). Her friends make fun of her fake laugh, which goes "HA ha HA hA," which she uses for things that aren't funny enough to be real-laughed at.

 Mimoh Lee is a junior at Lick-Wilmerding High School this fall. She loves cooking and baking, hanging out with friends, reading, listening to music, and playing with her dog Nessie. She plays volleyball and lacrosse and has been doing tae kwon do for eight years. Her biggest pet peeves are when the pockets in jeans stick out, and celery.

Xuan Ly is a junior at Ruth Asawa School of the Arts. While she was writing this bio, she was sitting in a black fishnet hammock, swinging over the ocean on her family's seafood farm in Vietnam, thinking about her dog and how excited she is for you to read this year's collection!

Huckleberry Shelf is a freshman at Columbia College Chicago, studying poetry. This was his second and final year at *BANR*. He hopes that the *BANR* committee next year will construct a paper model of him and burn him in effigy, honoring forever his contributions to the history and culture of the greater *BANR*sphere—or at least he hopes they will miss him a little.

Annette Vergara-Tucker is a freshman at UC Santa Cruz. They hope that you take the time to seriously reflect on the writing that the committee selected for this year's *Best American Nonrequired Reading* anthology. The pieces the committee encountered this year were incredibly reflective, moving, amusing, and entertaining, and they look forward to the book's publication. Annette will sincerely miss *BANR*, after being a member for four years, and loves the program and students deeply!

Very special thanks to Dave Eggers, Nicole Angeloro, Mark Robinson, and Molly Egan. Thanks also to Daniel Gumbiner, Clara Sankey, Sheila Heti, Sarah Vowell, Rachel Kushner, Adam Johnson, Daniel Handler, Dasha Bulatova, Mandy Workman, Annie Roach, Madeline Wright, Chad Buffington, Natalie Cantrell, Meg Schoerke, Catherine Fung, Rose Ludwig, sam sax, Tongo Eisen-Martin, Leah Tumerman, Jessica Calvanico, Rosie, Ezra and Amos, Laura Brief, Daniel Cesca, Doug Keller, Kaitlin Steele, Lauren Broder, Maggie Andrews, Tierra Alston-Johnson, Caroline Moon, Shida Zimani, Anna Griffin, Cecilia Juan, Oakailey Okai, Kona Lai, Arfi Oktavianti, Eric Cromie, Sunra Thompson, Claire Boyle, Caroline Kangas, Emily Ballaine, Diana Adamson, Marisela Garcia, Veronica Ponce-Navarrete, Juliana Sloane, Vanessa Baker, Nicholas Watson, Deborah Kang, Jenny Vu, Lisa Lopez, Monica Mendez, Marilyn Alvarez, Nirvana Felix, Kate Bueler, Jonathon Ho, Leigh Ann Coleman, Alma Zaragoza-Petty, Francisco Prado, Timothy Huynh, Kimberly Arteaga, Sam Lozano, Hannah Bardo, Leo Harrington, Paola Gonzalez, Thamara Torres, and Bianelle Vasquez.

NOTABLE
NONREQUIRED READING
OF 2018

DANIEL BORZUTZKY
The Block of Ice Is Ours, *West Branch*

TRACI BRIMHALL
Murder Ballad That Wants to be a Country Song, *Mississippi Review*

JERICHO BROWN
Duplex (I Begin with Love), *The American Poetry Review*

LISA CHEN
My Last White Boyfriend, *Epiphany*

SIDIK FOFANA
Ms. Battles, *The Sewanee Review*

JENNY GEORGE
The Sleeping Pig, *Poetry*

NAN GOLDIN
Abuse of Power, *Artforum*

NAOMI GORDON-LOEBL
My Grandmother's Survival Strategies, *Hazlitt*

SPENCER HALL
Tiger, *SB Nation*

KIM HYESOON AND LAUREN ALBIN
Cultural Revolution in My Dream, *The Southeast Review*

ABOUT 826 NATIONAL

Proceeds from this book benefit youth literacy.

826 is the largest youth writing network in the country. 826 National amplifies the impact of our national network of youth writing and publishing centers, and the words of young authors. We serve as an international proof point for writing as a tool for young people to ignite and channel their creativity, explore identity, advocate for themselves and their community, and achieve academic and professional success.

As of spring 2019, the 826 Network is in eight major US cities and serves nearly 75,000 students ages 6–18 each year through our local writing centers and online via 826 Digital. In addition, there are fifty 826-inspired organizations across the globe.

Each 826 Network chapter offers five core programs: After-School Tutoring, Field Trips, Workshops, Publishing, and In-School programs—all free of charge—for students, classes, and schools. Thanks to the support of more than 4,000 volunteers, each program offers innovative and dynamic project-based learning opportunities, building on students' classroom experience and strengthening their ability to express ideas effectively, creatively, confidently, and in their own voice.

Every chapter also has an imaginative storefront that reimagines tutoring as anything but traditional; provides a gateway for meeting families, teachers, and volunteers; and connects students with community members. And of course, sells Canned Laughter and Robot Toupées.

826 National is the hub of the 826 Network: facilitating collaboration and alignment among our chapters, and bringing the 826 Network model and approach to new communities. Learn more about our movement for writing and creativity at 826National.org.

826 VALENCIA

826Valencia.org
Retail stores: The Pirate Supply Store, King Carl's Emporium, and Woodland Creature Outfitters, Ltd.
Serves: San Francisco Unified School District
Satellites: Everett Middle School, Mission High School, and Buena Vista Horace Mann K–8

826NYC

826NYC.org
Retail store: Brooklyn Superhero Supply Co.
Serves: New York City Public Schools
Satellites: Brooklyn Public Library, Williamsburg Branch, and MS 7/Global Tech Prep

826LA

826LA.org
Retail stores: The Echo Park Time Travel Mart and The Mar Vista Time Travel Mart
Serves: Los Angeles Unified School District
Satellite: Manual Arts Senior High School and Roosevelt High School

826CHI

826Chi.org
Retail store: Wicker Park Secret Agent Supply Co.
Serves: Chicago Public School District

826MICHIGAN

826Michigan.org
Retail stores: Liberty Street Robot Supply and Repair Shop and The Detroit Robot Factory
Serves: Detroit Public Schools Community District, Ann Arbor Public Schools, and Ypsilanti Community School District
Satellites: Ypsilanti District Library and Detroit Public Library

826 BOSTON

826Boston.org
Retail store: The Greater Boston Bigfoot Research Institute
Serves: Boston Public and Greater Boston Area School Districts
Satellites: John D. O'Bryant School of Mathematics & Science, Jeremiah E. Burke High School, Boston Teachers Union School, Boston International Newcomers Academy, and Rafael Hernandez K–8 School

826DC

826DC.org
Retail store: Tivoli's Astounding Magic
Supply Co.
Serves: D.C. Public Schools and D.C.
Public Charter Schools

826 New Orleans

826NewOrleans.org
Retail store: The New Orleans Haunting Supply Co.
Serves: Orleans Parish Public Schools

ABOUT SCHOLARMATCH

Founded in 2010 by author Dave Eggers, ScholarMatch began as a crowdfunding platform for college scholarships, and has now grown into a full-service college access organization that supports low-income and first-generation students through every point of their college journeys. We serve students at our San Francisco and Los Angeles College Centers and nationwide through our Virtual Destination College program, and the ScholarMatcher—a groundbreaking college search tool optimized for the needs of low-income students. From local website to nationally reaching nonprofit, today ScholarMatch is a nimble, data-driven organization that is constantly refining programs based on what works for the 2,000+ students served annually. Our services are free for students and available for contract by community-based organizations, corporations, and foundations.

To support a student's college journey or to learn more,
visit scholarmatch.org.

THE BEST AMERICAN SERIES®

FIRST, BEST, AND BEST-SELLING

The Best American Comics

The Best American Essays

The Best American Food Writing

The Best American Mystery Stories

The Best American Nonrequired Reading

The Best American Science and Nature Writing

The Best American Science Fiction and Fantasy

The Best American Short Stories

The Best American Sports Writing

The Best American Travel Writing

Available in print and e-book wherever books are sold.
Visit our website: hmhbooks.com/series/best-american